the
cost
of all
things

the
cost
of all
things

MAGGIE LEHRMAN

BALZER + BRAY

An Imprint of HarperCollins*Publishers*

Balzer + Bray is an imprint of HarperCollins Publishers.

The Cost of All Things
Copyright © 2015 by Maggie Lehrman
All rights reserved. Printed in the United States of America. No part of this
book may be used or reproduced in any manner whatsoever without written
permission except in the case of brief quotations embodied in critical articles
and reviews. For information address HarperCollins Children's Books, a divi-
sion of HarperCollins Publishers, 195 Broadway, New York, NY 10007.
www.epicreads.com

Library of Congress Control Number: 2014952613
ISBN 978-0-06-232074-2

Typography by Jenna Stempel
15 16 17 18 19   PC/RRDH   10 9 8 7 6 5 4 3 2 1
❖
First Edition

FOR KYLE

PART I

the
hekamists

1

ARI

FIVE DAYS AFTER

There's a hekamist who lives in the run-down cluster of houses behind the high school. Everyone knows that. Lots of people have gotten spells from her over the years—study cheats and beauty touch-ups and good luck auras. Not me. The only spell I've ever taken, nearly ten years ago, was made for me by a hekamist in Boston. I remember her sterile-looking office and the slice of dry toast she put on a plate in front of me. I remember crying so hard I could barely swallow the toast.

But it worked and I stopped crying and here I am.

This hekamist works out of her kitchen. The curtains are cheap and there are water stains on the ceiling, but it's neat. The hekamist herself wears a tattered housecoat. She offers me a cup of tea and I say yes, even though I know you're never supposed to drink or eat anything from strangers—let alone from a hekamist. But it seems rude not to.

My left wrist aches. Inside, under the muscle and bone. An

old pain. My side effect. I clutch the wrist with my other hand under the table.

"Love spells don't work, you know," the hekamist says, dunking what looks like regular Lipton tea bags into two brightly colored mugs. "Whoever it is, they'll kiss you, they'll say the words, they'll believe it. But you won't. Love needs struggle." She smiles at me, a distracted smile, as if she's not sure for a second who I am or why I'm in her kitchen, and I focus on the gap between her two front teeth so as not to look in her eye and think of Win and love and struggle. "Of course I'll sell it to you. But that's my disclaimer."

"I'm not here for a love spell," I say.

She hands me one of the mugs of tea and raises her eyebrows. "Oh, I've assumed. Silly me, silly me. Tell me, then. A prom makeover? Calculus for the AP test?"

I'm glad for the heat of the mug in my hands; it distracts me from the pain in my wrist and keeps me from shivering all over. I could change my mind—say anything. Tell her I want luck or confidence. Beg for a little help with the SATs. Ask for a gift for Jess or Diana, something temporary and fun. But I've made it this far—I'm so close to finishing this. Just a little while longer and I'll never have to feel this way again.

As if the walls are closing in on me, even when I'm outside. As if the air is thinner than it used to be, as if every gasp brings less and less oxygen into my lungs. I want to cry, but if I start, I'm afraid of what will happen. I'm afraid of what I'll become.

Diana always teased me for not wanting to talk about my

feelings. True, but that never meant I didn't have any. Only meant I didn't want to let them out all at once, let them take me over. And right now, I can't hold on any longer.

Just like nine years ago, I need this.

I take a deep breath and will the tears back. "I want you to make me forget my boyfriend."

The hekamist sips her tea. Looks at me. I can't bring myself to lift my mug to my mouth.

"Permanently," I say. "None of this temporary crap."

"Permanent is more expensive. Let's say . . . five thousand dollars." I nod. Perfect. "Well, if you have the money, I can do that. Of course. Can brew it right now, in fact—you'll take it before bedtime, be emptied out in no time—forever."

"Thank you." The relief is huge, a wave that almost knocks me down. Not to have to think of Win.

No more picking me up for school in his truck. No more looking into my eyes at Homecoming, telling me he loves me. No more seeing him in the front row of my performances, watching me, glowing only for me. No more kisses and promises and plans. No more love.

No more last night on the beach. No more words in anger. No more waking up to the call from his mother. No more long walk home from the beach with sand and seaweed in my hair, stomach churning, eyes too pinched and dry to cry. All the pain of the past five days—gone.

The hekamist's hand taps the table for my attention. "But there's a cost."

"I told you I can pay," I say. The money's stuffed into the pocket of my jacket, still in the folded manila envelope I found it in. I can feel it against my ribs. Exactly five thousand dollars. I found it in the very back of my closet yesterday, in a half-crushed shoebox, while I was looking for something to wear that didn't remind me of Win. I hadn't known it was there before, and I'm not sure it actually belongs to me, but I didn't know who else could've put it there and I couldn't help feeling that finding the money was a sign, confirmation that getting this spell is what I'm supposed to do.

"I don't mean money. The spell asks its own payment. A beauty spell might kill a few brain cells. For something like this?" She considers me, and I try to look like this is new information. It's not. I got the whole side effects speech the first time around; the pain in my wrist is my proof. "Most people experience aches and pains after a memory spell, at the very least. Might affect muscle or nerve or something else. Can't predict it exactly."

It'll be worth the money, worth the collateral damage, not to have to feel this crushing weight anymore. I imagine it like falling asleep and waking up in someone else's body. Blank. Empty. Happy. Free.

"Oh!" the hekamist says, knocking on her head with a knuckle. "I'm supposed to ask, silly me, silly me. Have you ever had any other spellwork done in the past?"

"No."

"Because multiple spells get messy. Muddled. Mixed up. Side effects aren't doubled, they're increased *ex-po-nen-tial-ly*." She squints at me, her small eyes disappearing into the folds of her face. "Silly, so silly. You look familiar."

"I promise I've never had any other spells." I say it quickly so I don't have time to be caught in the lie. I'm a horrible liar; if she presses me, I'll crack. I resist the urge to grab my wrist again and massage the pain. It's been acting up all week, as if in warning: *This is what happens when you take spells.* Instead I stare down at my feet. Inside the sneakers they're red and sore. I've lost or am in the process of losing another big toenail. Lost toenails: a dancer's pride.

If she knew the truth, she'd refuse me for my own good, to avoid those compound side effects. But I can deal with more side effects like my wrist—that's what I deal with every day in ballet. Pain. Struggle.

Physical pain and *physical* struggle, though. What's a few busted muscles compared to the pain of losing Win?

If my body has to pay the price, so be it.

"All right, then," the hekamist says.

She stands and moves to the small kitchen, opening and shutting cupboards and rummaging through drawers. She dumps ingredients into a dented pot on the stove. "How about some chicken noodle soup?"

As she works, I pull out the worn envelope of bills and place it on the table in front of me, then surreptitiously rub my aching wrist. She glances over at the envelope and nods.

"You're a junior?" she asks, standing over the pot. When the soup spits and sparks, she lifts the pot over the counter—and it rests there in midair. Or so it seems from where I'm sitting.

"Yes," I say. "Well, technically a senior, I guess. School just got out."

"I have a daughter. She's a little older than you."

"Oh."

"She's special, my daughter. I know all parents think that, but it's true."

And just when I think I can't feel any worse, I get one of those unexpected pangs for my mother. It's an old pain, too, and normally I can go weeks without it flaring up—the pain in my wrist is much more persistent—but it happens. A photo in a gift catalog. A kid crying on the beach. Families coming in to the Sweet Shoppe together. And now I'm jealous of a hekamist's daughter.

As I take a deep breath and push the feeling down, the light in the apartment dims. Cold air presses in from the cracks in the walls and floor. My wrist pulses with a heartbeat. The hekamist, at the stovetop with her back to me, pulls up her sleeve and makes a quick motion with a stone held in her other hand. I can't tell what's happening with the pot of soup; she's in the way.

"You seem determined. That's good. Know your mind, know yourself. But young people don't always think things through, and no one talks about what hekame does. Not anymore. You think it's dangerous, now. If it's illegal to become a hekamist it must be bad, right? Shameful. Silly, so silly." It's almost pitch-black in the apartment except for a glow from the pot behind the hekamist. She watches it. "It's not dangerous the way you think. But memory spells can be awkward, especially when you run into this boyfriend again. Walking down the street, he tries to say hi, you don't know him, he's confused or angry—or some such and so forth."

"That's not a problem," I say. I breathe and sip my tea. Tastes like Lipton—needs milk. In the dark and cold while my salvation's being brewed, it's easy to say the hardest thing in the world. "He's dead."

2

KAY

FIVE MONTHS BEFORE

When most people think of Cape Cod, they think of beaches and boardwalks, sand and sun, families and friends eating ice cream and playing volleyball. And for four or five months every year, that's exactly what it is. Tourists fill the towns and hotels and restaurants and beaches, the sun shines and waves crash, and we have a reason for existing.

But it's not like that at all in the middle of January. The hotels and rentals empty out. It's cold. The beach isn't a beach, it's just the edge of the land, and the ocean's always there, hemming us in. Cape Cod's an island, you know. Two bridges let us on and off, but for the most part we're trapped, shut up in a narrowing strip of land that no one should've found, let alone settled. Windy, plain, brown and yellow and gray, the sky matching the ground.

In the gloom and early dark of January, Diana and Ari and I were celebrating. I'd stolen a bottle of Grey Goose from my sister Mina's secret stash, and we toasted each other and shivered in the wind. The road was covered in half-melted snow and dead leaves. We slipped and slid over them in our sneakers, laughing and holding each other up.

"To New York!" Diana said to Ari.

"To horse camp!" Ari shouted back, even though they were standing right next to each other.

"To summer!" Diana's voice rose to match Ari's.

"To freedom!"

"Yay!" I said. I couldn't think of anything to toast to, but if I didn't say anything, I wouldn't be a part of the celebration.

And, actually, I wasn't technically celebrating anything of my own. But I was happy to be out with Diana and Ari, and happy for them. They were leaving right after school ended for their dream summers. Their happiness should have been enough for me to celebrate after the past few years.

"You'll be the queen of those stuck-up horse chicks," Ari said. "Maybe find a nice stable boy to seduce."

Diana blushed and covered her eyes with her hand. "More like, I'll spend a lot of time with my horse and halfway through the summer discover that none of the humans know my name."

"Their loss."

Diana pointed the bottle at Ari. "You're the one who's going to be the queen, anyway. Take those other girls out."

"Ballet assassin. That's me." She grabbed the bottle from Diana, planted her foot, and spun in a circle, ending balanced on the planted foot, the other shooting straight up behind her like a bow string. She took a drink and didn't wobble once.

"What if I dyed my hair?" Diana held out a strand of her thick, long hair and squinted in the low light. "Something bright."

I started to agree, but Ari interrupted me.

"Oh, don't," Ari said. She lowered her foot and passed me the bottle. "You're perfect the way you are."

"I guess," Diana said, and let go of her hair.

"Where's Win?" I asked. Ari spent most of her weekend nights with her boyfriend, Win Tillman, which was why Diana had started calling me back in September.

"He's home sick. Markos is having a party but I wanted to celebrate."

"We couldn't celebrate with Markos?" Diana said, attempting to sound casual.

"But it's more fun just us."

Diana didn't argue. She had a crush on Markos Waters, Win's best friend, but Ari always said he wasn't boyfriend material. Ari hung out with him and Win all the time when she wasn't with us, so I guess she would know.

I felt a pause descending. A dreaded pause, where someone might say "It's time to go home," or "I've had enough to drink." I didn't want the night to be over. I'd only been friends with Diana and Ari for four months, since Diana and I sat together in English and started hanging out on nights when Ari was with Win. Ari and Diana had been inseparable for years, whispering in class and peeling out of the parking lot in each other's cars, and I'd wondered what it would be like to be a part of a friendship like that. Someone you chose, instead of being born with, like me and my sister, Mina.

I'd made friends with Diana first, but soon I was invited out with Ari, too, and we became a threesome. Four months of friendship. Six months since my beauty spell, which gave me the confidence to start talking to Diana in the first place. And two years since Mina got better and left me behind. I could remember each of the important dates exactly.

I didn't want the night to end, so I rushed to fill the silence.

"Look, the hekamist's house," I said, pointing down the road.

Diana and Ari turned to look at the house. It seemed normal from the outside, if a bit run-down. Back when we were in elementary school someone made up a story that there was a force field around the house that would zap you or curse you if you got too close; only years later did anyone stop to think that wasn't how hekame worked at all. You had to eat something to be spelled. So they changed the dare to eating the hekamist's grass from the front lawn. When I'd gone there to get my beauty spell six months ago, I could still see bald patches of the lawn, as if new generations of kids were still daring each other to get close.

"What's it like inside?" Diana asked.

"Diana!" Ari said, as if Diana had just said something offensive.

"It's okay," I said. "Everyone knows I got a spell. Lots of people get spells, actually, you just can't always see the results."

Ari rubbed her wrist, and I remembered, too late, about her

parents and the fire and her old spell. Diana stepped closer to Ari as if to comfort her, but Ari shrank away. I'd never seen Ari hug or touch anyone except Win.

"The spell was in a microwave burrito," I said. Stupid. The silence stretched open and I stepped into it blindly. "I thought that was so weird. Have you ever heard of anything so weird? Ari, what was your spell in—no, never mind, that's not what I wanted to—um—I think it's so crazy all the stuff people get spelled for, because I only wanted a little, uh, you know." I gestured at my face and twisted the ends of my always-smooth hair. "The hekamist was so nice about it, actually. Didn't try to flatter me and tell me I didn't need it. I appreciated that. When you're ugly you're ugly, you know?"

Sometimes when I'm talking I wish I'd gotten more spells than beauty. Wit, for example. Ari spoke so fast I couldn't always follow her. Then when I'd try to keep up, I ended up saying nonsense.

"You weren't ugly," Diana said.

"Oh, yeah, well, you have to say that." I laughed, and the sound was whipped away by wind almost immediately.

"Hey," Ari said. Her expression turned fierce, and even though she's half a foot shorter than me, I shrank back. "Don't be like that. You're great. We're all great, okay?"

Diana giggled. "I'm so awesome I can hardly stand it."

"Yes! Diana gets it." Ari turned to me, her face set. "The thing is, Kay, I'm awesome and I'm not friends with people who aren't awesome, ergo, et cetera. Can you be on board with that?"

I didn't really have any idea what she was talking about, but it sounded wonderful, whatever it was—it sounded like a promise—so I nodded and said, "Yes."

We kept walking, three friends, out late celebrating on our miserable little island.

And I could picture the next few months so clearly, I nearly burst with it. I had friends who liked me and who'd be there for me and who'd defend me—even against myself.

We had almost turned the corner away from the hekamist's house when the full picture of the future came into focus. We would be best friends, and summer would come, and they would leave me. Diana for horse camp. Ari for the Manhattan Ballet.

Meanwhile, it would be summertime in Cape Cod. Happy people spilling out of the hotels and rentals and beaches and shops.

Only I'd be alone.

I stopped walking.

They stopped a step or two later. Turned and faced me. Ari's small, sharp, dramatic face and Diana's smooth skin and large eyes and long, thick, dark blond hair. They were naturally beautiful; they would never quite understand what it was like to not be. But I loved them for not understanding, for insisting that their worldview was the right one, despite my years of evidence to the contrary.

"You okay, Kay?" Ari asked, and elbowed Diana at her own joke.

"Fine," I said. "Fine. Actually, I'm awesome. I know that now."

Reassured, they kept walking. I looked back at the hekamist's house and made a decision.

When it was light, I would come back. I would knock on the door and not be afraid. I would take the cash from my mother's wallet and ask for exactly what I needed.

And I did. Four days later, I gave Ari and Diana each a cookie baked for friendship and got to keep my best friends.

Once they'd taken the spell, they couldn't leave me. Within the week, Diana's horse camp closed because of bedbugs and Ari's aunt decided they wouldn't move to New York until the beginning of August, right before Ari's apprenticeship started.

I didn't want to change who they were—didn't want to force them to feel things they didn't feel. The spell wasn't about making something out of nothing and inventing a whole relationship. Instead, I could be me and they could be them, only the spell would nudge them to me at least once every three days, and they wouldn't be able to go more than fifty miles away, and luck and chance would bend them to me like flowers growing toward the sun. The hekamist called it a hook.

They would be loyal. They would be constant. They wouldn't leave me to go traveling the world. They *couldn't* leave me—the spell kept them near.

My spells worked better than I could've ever imagined. I had Diana and Ari and a better face and I was happy. As long as their lives went a little bit badly, we were together.

3

MARKOS

THE DAY BEFORE

I first noticed her the way you notice hot girls: out of the corner of your eye, a flash of dark hair and eyes, an urge to turn your head and stare. It was only when I followed that urge and looked closer that I recognized her. The hekamist's daughter.

The old hekamist came around my family's hardware store regularly and sometimes this girl came with, trailing behind her, staring suspiciously at everyone. She always wore dark black eyeliner and a long black coat with lots of buttons that swung around her hips, and she had short, messy black hair.

From my position at first base I watched her walking behind the bleachers. She was hot, but who had the time and energy to go after a hekamist's daughter? You'd have to be looking over your shoulder and guarding your food every second. Besides, there were a hundred other non-hekamist-daughters enrolled in school whose hotness wasn't as . . . complicated. So I can tell you absolutely that wasn't why I approached her. My reasons were purely altruistic. Well, mostly.

Win hightailed out after practice, barely waving when I called out "Tomorrow night!" As his best friend, I had his Saturday nights on lock, even when he was lame and didn't want to come, or was brooding when he did.

He'd been brooding a lot recently, and I knew, as his best friend, it was my job to cheer him up. Ari'd been trying, too, and usually with our powers combined we could pull him out of any funk. He'd always been prone to falling into dark periods, ever since we were kids, so I knew the secret to making him better: You couldn't ask him to be happy. You had to *do* something.

Fortuitously, I had almost a thousand dollars burning a hole in my pocket. If I didn't offload the cash no doubt my mother would discover it and kill me. So watching Win with his head down, silent, tires of his pickup squealing on his way out of the lot, I knew exactly how I wanted to spend it.

The hekamist's daughter looked like she might be leaving, too, so I jogged her way. The rest of the guys stayed away. They knew better than to interrupt me when I was talking solo with a girl.

"What's up," I said.

She raised an eyebrow at me.

"I'm Markos. You are?"

"I'm wondering what you want." She didn't say it angry, but I got the picture. She was a woman of business.

"I was hoping you could help me out."

"Oh, I doubt it. You seem fine on your own," she said. She turned and started walking across the baseball field. My house was in the other direction, but I followed her anyway.

"But you're the hekamist's daughter."

"So?"

"So I want to place an order."

I put a hand on her arm and she winced as if it stung and pulled out of my grip. Then she turned and faced me. Her hotness was of the variety that was slightly scary, like she might turn into a dragon and fire-breathe all over you, but in a sexy way. We were past the baseball field, past the soccer field, and a few steps into the scrubby no-man's-land between school and a shitty low-lying part of town filled with cheap clapboard houses. It reminded me of the places where Win's lived his entire life. Dead lawns. Peeling paint. Windows installed crooked. There's always a broken trike by the back door and a tangled garden hose in the driveway.

"I want to have a little party tomorrow night," I said. "Me and my best friend and his girlfriend."

"Sounds like a ton of fun."

"I want to make this a special party." I pulled out the money, and the hekamist's daughter's eyes showed their whites. "I bet your mom could help me make this extremely special."

She chewed on the side of her bottom lip, rubbing her sore arm with the opposite hand. "Did you have something specific in mind?"

I told her all about my idea, and she nodded absently, eyes on the cash.

"So you'll let her know?"

Her eyes snapped back to mine and narrowed. "You're Markos Waters, right? Waters Hardware? The one with all the brothers?"

"That's me."

"Noticed the family resemblance."

That would be our black hair, blue eyes, and roman noses. Stand all four of us together and we look like time-lapse photography. "Thank you."

She smiled and tilted her head. "It wasn't a compliment."

I smiled at her, because the conversation had gotten off track, and she might turn into a dragon any second. I enjoyed good banter as much as the next guy, but I got the sense she maybe wasn't flirting and instead actually didn't like me, which was weird. I was pretty great. Everyone knew that. "You can be kind of a bitch, you know."

"Hang on, I've got to go write that one in my tear-stained diary."

"What were you doing at practice, anyway, if not soliciting new customers?"

"None of your business," she said, and took the money out of my hand. "But I'm a hekamist myself. I'll do the spell for you."

"Oh shit," I said. "Okay."

She didn't look the way hekamists were supposed to look. Not at all old like the crones you see arguing for hekamists' rights on TV, or the villainous or misunderstood hekamists in movies; not decrepit and twisted and cackling, or willowy and braless and high on nature. There weren't supposed to be any young hekamists anymore at all. Twenty years ago a bunch of them tried to take over the government of France, and now supermarkets and restaurants are constantly under inspection, and it's illegal to join a coven pretty much everywhere, and so the ones who are left are all going crazy and dying out.

So this girl's whole life was illegal.

She counted the bills slowly and didn't look up. "You're not going to report me, are you?" she asked, trying to keep her voice casual.

"Oh definitely. This is a sting. I've got my brother on a wire—he's a cop—and he's *dying* to bust the underage hekamist trying to turn the high school baseball team into her sex slaves."

"Seriously."

"Seriously, I would never do that. I'm not a puritan; I don't care what you do. This is business."

The hekamist folded the money in half and put it in one of her jacket pockets. Her fire-breathing eyes softened. "Do you know anything about hekame?"

"No." I grinned. "Are you going to teach me?"

"You wish."

"So I take it we have a deal?"

She nodded, and I saluted her and backed away. "Pleasure doing business with you."

"Echo," she said. "That's my name."

"Echo. See you tomorrow."

I knew she would do what I asked, and not only because of the money. She struck me as someone who did what she said and said what she meant.

Also, back then, I assumed a lot of shit. I thought the world would bend to what I needed it to be. If I thought of something, I did it. If I wanted something, I took it. If reality didn't quite line up to what I had in my head, then reality was the problem, not me, and eventually reality would cave to my demands, just like the hekamist's daughter had.

I didn't understand. I'd been nothing but lucky the whole time. The world doesn't bend for anyone, not even Markos Waters.

The next night, Win was dead.

PART II

side
effects

4

WIN

My favorite memory of Ari is from a dance—no surprise. Not one of her performances, which were beautiful and complicated like moving sculpture, but the Homecoming dance junior year. We'd been going out for a few months, and I knew I liked her—a lot—but Homecoming changed everything.

It didn't start out great. The suit my mother had found at Goodwill and the homemade corsage my sister, Kara, had made for Ari from a neighbor's rosebush—they made me feel like an imposter, like a con man who'd lied his way into someone else's life. I blamed that for the black cloud that followed me into the gym, even though the truth was I'd been under the cloud for days—maybe weeks.

(Maybe even my whole life. For as long as I could remember there'd been a weight attached to me. Some days it barely registered on the scale; others it felt as heavy as sandbags. This started out as a sandbag day.)

It didn't help that dating Ari felt like the biggest act of fakery of all. She was so beautiful and talented and strong and blah blah blah. Those were the things that had drawn me to her, but now that we were together, her beauty and talent and strength seemed to keep me at arm's length. I was average in every way. I played shortstop (decently) and the trumpet (badly). I had a sister and a mother who I loved, plus good grades and loyal friends. Ari was exceptional. She was one of the best ballet dancers in the country. She had overcome a tragic past. She was vivid, the part of the painting the artist spent all day on before hurriedly sketching me into a corner.

On the night of Homecoming, once we arrived at the gym, Ari found her friends and went off to dance. Markos and I stood in a corner trading Markos's flask back and forth.

"Hottest girl in the grade?" Markos asked.

"Ari."

"Come on. For real."

"I'm for real. What are you saying about my girlfriend?"

He rolled his eyes. "Fine. I'll rephrase. Hottest girl who I could hook up with?"

"Serena Simonsen."

"You came up with that quick! You sure you don't want to go for her yourself?"

"Dude, come on. You know I wouldn't."

He saluted with the flask. "Always such a good boy."

Across the room I spotted Ari dancing, and I could tell she was really trying to let loose—stop counting the beats, stop spotting her turns. She wanted to fit in with the rest of us normals.

The fact that I knew her well enough to know what she was thinking hit me with a pang right between my ribs, and I felt sorry for Markos that he thought being a "good boy" was a bad thing.

"How about Kay Charpal?" I said, since she was dancing right next to Ari.

Markos shook his head. "Too Frankenspelled."

"Half the girls here have had a spell touch-up. Who cares?"

"Most of them looked fine before. You remember Kay's old face . . ." He twisted his own into a sour expression.

"You are *such* an ass."

"I'm honest. Not my fault if people can't handle the truth."

"I'd say Diana, but then Ari would kill you."

"Plus I require a bare minimum of a personality." He laughed and checked his watch.

"Oh no," I said.

"What?" His eyes opened wide, as if that might make him look innocent.

"Please tell me you didn't plan something."

Markos grinned. "I've got a legacy to uphold."

Markos's older brothers had been telling us for years about their Homecoming pranks. Brian brought a goat in a tuxedo as his "date," Dev rigged the basketball hoop with a laser light projector that spelled out insults onto one of the walls, and Cal replaced all of the DJ's music with the Jackson 5's "ABC."

"Didn't they do theirs senior year?"

Markos tapped the side of his nose. "The admin will be

watching me like a hawk senior year. This is all about the element of surprise."

He peered into the crowd intently, and I watched the dancing, trying to see what he saw. Everyone seemed normal and happy to me. They all belonged exactly where they were. When I turned back to Markos, he'd gone. I thought about trying to find him but figured it would ruin the surprise, so I took a deep breath and elbowed my way into the crowd to join Ari. She shouted "Win!" and tucked her arm into mine, still dancing. I shuffled back and forth, trying not to step on her.

She had on a strapless blue dress, longer in the back than the front. I'd seen her bare, slightly freckly shoulders before—in her performances—and maybe that's why I pictured her being lifted up overhead, arching her back and soaring. I couldn't do that for her, so I shuffled.

When a slow song came on, she turned to face me, putting her hands on my shoulders. I placed mine on her waist and swayed back and forth. The blue material of her dress was warm from her body but so shiny I thought my hands might slide off. I was afraid to hold her too tight—not that I thought I'd hurt her, because I knew she was way stronger than me, but because it might give away how much I wanted to hold her, and she'd have to pull back, and it would become clear that she didn't want me as much as I wanted her. Our dancing—our relationship—balanced on a seesaw. If I put my full weight into it, I'd go crashing down and she'd fly away.

"Feel the music in your core," Ari said in a European

accent—her "ballet master" voice. "What does the music say to you?"

I listened. "It says, 'I am a boy-band ballad with nonsensical lyrics.'"

Ari laughed. "How dare you. I'm thinking of getting these lyrics tattooed on my butt."

"'Waking this spire for you'?"

"It's 'quaking desire for you,' actually."

"Well, of course when you say it, it's poetry."

She smiled at me, a welcome kick in the ribs. Before I could chicken out I leaned in and gave her a kiss. She was still smiling when I pulled back, and maybe her cheeks were redder than before.

"You're kind of the best, Win Tillman," she said.

That was it—I was going to say something that would make it obvious how much I liked her, and the seesaw would come crashing down. I could feel words coming up my chest and I didn't know how to stop them, or if I wanted to.

Something wet and sudsy dripped from the ceiling into my eyes. I let go of Ari to wipe it away, and that's when the shouting started. When my eyes were clear, I could see Ari staring up toward the dark gym ceiling, laughing. Big soapy drips plopped from the ceiling vents. Around us, girls tried to shield their updos, and guys slipped in their formal shoes.

"I love it, but I don't get it," Ari said. "Where's Markos?"

I grabbed her hand and we slip-n-slided to the doors to the gym. People were mostly streaming out to the parking lot, so we turned in the other direction, heading deeper into the dark school. At a fork in the hallway we paused until we heard voices.

Down the hall to the right, Markos had his back against a locker, his arms crossed over his chest. A cop stood in front of him.

". . . lucky it was me and not someone else assigned to the school. This is so unbelievably stupid, Markos," the cop was saying, and I knew before we got close enough to see that it was Markos's oldest brother, Brian. I hurried the last thirty feet to them, Ari close at my heels. Brian turned to us. "Win, get back to the dance."

"What's the problem?" I asked.

"Markos put bubble machines in the heating vents."

"I don't know what you're talking about," Markos said.

"Really? So if I check inventory at the store there won't be a bunch of supplies missing?"

"Good luck with that." Markos's family's hardware store was notoriously disorganized; Markos probably banked on that fact. Brian knew it, too, and his frown deepened.

"I should take you in, Markos. Might teach you a lesson."

"Come on, Brian! What about all the pranks you and Dev and Cal did?"

Brian glared. "That's different. You flooded the gym."

"Flooded? It's only a few bubbles."

"They're not bubbles after they go through the heating vent, dumbass. They're just soap."

"You're such a hypocrite."

"And you're such a fuckup. That's thousands of dollars of damage and no one can even tell what it's supposed to be. You can't even plan a simple prank right."

Markos flinched. I stepped toward him out of instinct—no one was allowed to hurt my best friend—but before I could reach him, Ari ducked in between Markos and his brother. "It wasn't Markos," she said. "He's been with us all night."

Brian rolled his eyes. "I found him out here, not in with you."

"He *just* left, I swear. There's no way he'd have time to set all this up," she insisted. "And it doesn't make sense, Brian—I mean Officer Waters. You guys always did your pranks senior year, right? So why would Markos do one now?"

Brian took a second to absorb this piece of logic, then turned to Markos. "Is this true?" Markos didn't look any of us in the eye, but he nodded. "What were you doing out here, then?"

Markos cleared his throat and looked up and down the hall. For the briefest second, when he caught my eye, he winked. "Meeting a girl. You probably scared her away. Thanks a lot, by the way."

Brian made a disgusted noise and turned to Ari. "So you're going to vouch for him."

Ari planted her feet and looked at him levelly. "Markos didn't do it, Officer."

Brian turned to me. So did Markos and Ari. It was my turn to decide what to do.

But for me and Markos, it's never really a decision. I always have his back and he has mine. "Ari's telling the truth."

Brian stared at us for a moment, then pivoted on his heel and stomped down the hall.

When he was out of sight, Markos grinned. "That was fun."

Ari punched him in the shoulder. "You idiot. I just lied to a cop."

"He wanted to believe you. That way I'm not such a failure." Markos saluted and stood up from leaning on the locker, straightening his suit jacket. "Have a fantastic rest of your evening, lovebirds."

"Where are you going?" I asked.

"Oh, I never lie to my family."

From behind us I heard a giggle—Serena Simonsen waved from the doorway of a dark classroom, and Markos waved back. Ari rolled her eyes, and as Markos passed me, he put a hand on my shoulder and leaned in. "She's all right. You can keep her around," he muttered into my ear, as if it was his decision (or even mine) whether or not Ari stayed with me.

I grabbed his arm before he could walk away. "She might not agree." *She might not really want me. Average me. Imposter me.*

"Are you kidding me? She's all in. Get your head out of your ass and look at her."

Ari and I watched Markos and Serena disappear into the empty classroom, then we headed back the way we came. As we walked I did what Markos said and I looked at her. Not the idea of her. Not the Ari who wore toe shoes and floated onstage. Not the one whose parents died when she was little. The girl in front of me. Leaning toward me. Looking right back at me.

As soon as we stepped back into the gym, our arms were around each other. Soapy water still sputtered from the vents in the ceiling. Ari's dress was so slippery and the floor so slick I had to hold her as tight as I wanted to or I'd lose her and we'd fall. My hands met at the small of her back. She held me just as tight—her hands linked at the back of my neck, twisted in my hair, her cheek pressed close against my collarbone—and I could feel her heart beating through the fabric of my secondhand suit.

Anyone upset by their ruined clothes and hair had long since left, but a fair number of us had stayed. Someone had cut the lights, probably afraid of electrocution, so it was dark in the gym except for the glow of people's cell phones flashing off the sparkle of dresses. It smelled like a laundromat, and since the DJ had long since given up, we could hear people laughing and splashing and attempting to dance to a small portable speaker someone had plugged into their phone. It was only a matter of time before Brian or some other authority figure came by and kicked us out, so we seized the moment.

Ari relaxed into me. All effort left her. We melted together.

"You saved Markos's ass," I said to her.

"Brian's too harsh on him."

"I didn't even think you liked him. Markos, I mean."

She sighed deeper into my arms. Her hair was wet and flattened, half her makeup had run down her face and was now being rubbed onto me, and her dress had gone shapeless and bedraggled. But she was the most beautiful I'd ever seen her when she raised her head just enough to whisper in my ear.

"Not as much as I like you."

Her soapy skin so close to mine. Her arms holding me and holding me up. She shook slightly, maybe a shiver. She wasn't stone and marble; she wasn't perfect and remote. She was here, in front of me. Choosing me.

"I love you," I said.

She looked at me, eyes bright. She wasn't surprised, I noted with relief. "I love you, too."

We swayed back and forth. Dancing. In the dark and wet, the two of us together.

It's my favorite memory of Ari out of a thousand memories. It's the one I keep on hand, the talisman. That was the girl I loved.

5

ARI

Everyone kept telling me how much I loved Win. Aunt Jess, Diana. Even myself: there was the note I found under my pillow. Sometimes I thought I would start feeling it. As if one day I'd wake up and be sad again. As if grief was a virus and my vaccine was only temporary.

The note. At least I'd thought to write the note.

I woke up Friday morning—the first Friday in June, just after school let out—with my wrist pounding, partially the old side effect and partially because I'd slept with my arm under my pillow, a piece of paper clutched in my hand. I read the note again and again. It had been torn out of a bound journal and had a ragged edge. I recognized the handwriting—mine—and if I focused very hard I could remember writing the words. But it was a strange type of memory, more like watching a movie than recalling something from the inside. I could remember moving my pen across the page, but I couldn't remember what I was thinking as I was doing it.

You had a boyfriend. Win Tillman. You loved him. For over a year. He died. It's too hard. If this spell works, you won't remember him.

Win. Win Tillman. Win, Win, Win . . .

I could not put a face to the name.

I remembered, in that same movie-watching way, going to the hekamist's house behind the school and paying for a spell from the money I'd found in my closet. I could see myself doing it. I looked so sad. But again, the memory wasn't something I'd experienced. The only thing that felt true and real was the moment when she'd told me about her daughter, and I'd thought of my mom. That exchange bloomed into three dimensions.

I couldn't remember anyone named Win. As far as I could recall, I'd never had a boyfriend at all. I'd made out with my pas de deux partner at the Summer Institute last year, but that was perfunctory, nothing serious.

I must've been so sad. I remembered wanting to cry and feeling like I might break in two. But I didn't remember why.

I wasn't sad anymore. Just confused.

So I called Diana. She answered right away, her voice strangely low and serious. "How are you doing?"

"Um. Fine."

"You want me to come over?"

"No, that's okay."

"Funeral's tomorrow."

"Oh? Oh yeah. Of course."

"Do you know what you're going to say?"

"I . . . uh . . ."

Diana didn't seem to mind that I couldn't find any words. "Every day I wake up and I still can't believe he's gone. I just . . . I can't believe it. I mean, we don't have to talk about it if you don't want to. In fact, let's not. I'm sorry I brought it up. But I don't want you to think I'm ignoring it. Because I'm thinking about it. God. I can't even . . . I can't believe it."

I looked at the note and then out the window, flexing my wrist absently. I obviously hadn't told Diana about the spell. Should I? The note didn't say. The way my head felt—full of starts and stops, black holes and fuzzy edges—I couldn't seem to make a decision. Diana and I did everything together, told each other everything. Didn't we?

Outside, the sun was bright and the grass green. A beautiful day. I had ballet class in half an hour, and I wanted to go. At least in class, I wouldn't have to talk.

I could tell Diana what I'd done later.

"Neither can I," I said.

"Kay's been calling nonstop. Wants to bake you casseroles."

"Nice of her."

"Yeah. If I want to come over, she'll probably have to drive." Diana's car had been breaking down a lot, which meant begging a ride from Kay.

"Maybe don't come over."

"God, Ari. I don't know what to do."

"Yeah. Me neither."

"You don't have to do anything. I mean you can do what you want."

"I want to go to class," I said.

There was a pause on the other end of the line. "You should take it easy for a while. Not push yourself."

"Ballet is all I really want right now."

It was Friday. The last time I remembered dancing was over a week ago. I could recall the combination we were working on, the music, every step. I remembered how my body felt. I felt like . . . one muscle. My arm and my ankle and my hip and my eyelid—all one, strung together taut and ready.

Everything would be okay if I could only get to dance.

I said goodbye to Diana and threw on my dance clothes as fast as I could. Something felt strange right away. Nothing I could point my finger at, but an allover oddness. I figured I was sore, but nothing actually hurt, apart from the pain in my wrist.

A feeling unfurled in my stomach. Something worse than nervousness, but maybe not quite panic. Not yet. I held my sore wrist close to my chest as if to protect it.

Aunt Jess seemed startled when I stumbled down the stairs, twisting my hair into a bun.

"You're going?" she said.

Her eyes were red. I touched the skin around my eyes: puffy, tender. I'd been crying, too.

She wore the same work pants and plaid button-down

short-sleeved shirt as always, but for the first time, she looked old to me. She was only fifteen years older than me, but her sadness brought out the lines in her face, and I could swear she had more gray hairs than the last time I'd looked. Someday soon someone at her coffee shop would call her a "tough old broad" and they'd be right.

"I thought we could talk," she said. "Spend some time together. I took off work."

"That's nice of you. Thank you."

"Of course I'd take off work." She seemed offended that I thanked her.

It was clear I had not told Jess I was getting the spell, either. She thought I was grieving, still, like her. I had to tell her.

My legs started shaking.

Later.

Dance first. Dance, and then I would come clean.

"I really want to dance," I said. "It's . . . all I want to do."

Jess stared at me with her no-shit-taking stare that usually came with flexed biceps to show off her tattoos, and then she softened, deflated, and nodded. "Come right back afterward."

"I will."

I hugged her, and she clutched me tightly. In our miniature family of two, we weren't much for hugging. But it wasn't only my lack of experience making me feel awkward. That feeling I'd had in my room—the strangeness, the not-rightness—ran down my arms like goose bumps.

"I love you," she said.

"I love you, too," I said, and hurried for the door. "See you soon."

The worried feeling in my stomach only grew.

The other dancers stared at me when I stepped into the changing room.

"I'msosorryforyourloss," one of them said, then the rest all mumbled something similar. Then they looked down at their pink shoes and tried not to catch my eye.

Rowena, a former prima ballerina at the Royal Ballet and my teacher for the past nine years, hugged me when I came in (just as awkward and just as well-meaning as Jess's), but she didn't seem surprised to see me. Perhaps going to dance was the right thing to do after all. I belonged here, in this wood-floor practice room, with its three walls of mirrors and one of windows. The ancient piano player noodled gently in the corner as always, and as always the room smelled like sweat and talcum.

I closed my eyes and tried to concentrate on dance, on getting my body ready to move. But my mind wouldn't settle. I could think of nothing in particular: my thoughts cast about in a large white room, nothing to land on, nowhere to rest. I tried checking in with my muscles and joints, but could only feel the insistent, pulsing pain in my wrist. Usually I could ignore that—I'd had years of practice—but this time I couldn't quite block it out.

By the time we started warming up, my breathing had gotten shallow. I didn't know what it was, yet, but something was wrong.

The piano music. There. That was vivid in my head; the same

chords, same melodies, same movements as always. It existed complete in my mind, elegant, precise.

I began to move.

First position. Second. Fourth. To the front. To the right. To the back. And then the left side.

I kept my eyes closed and concentrated on the steps.

I needed to relax. To get into the steps.

In the middle of a plié, I felt a pressure on my bad wrist—Rowena's hand—and I opened my eyes.

"Watch the mirror, please," Rowena said.

I nodded, keeping my face stoic, even though that was a request she made when someone was screwing up so badly they'd lost all perspective on their body.

In the mirror, I watched myself go through the warm-up again. It took several measures to sink in, since I was so used to seeing myself the way I usually moved. The smooth mental image needed time to be wiped away and replaced with what I saw: a jumble of elbows, jerky knees, awkward arms, wrists off-kilter. The harder I tried to force my body in line, the worse it got. Actually, as far as my brain could tell, I *was* doing it beautifully. But somewhere in between my mind and my body, the signals sputtered out and were lost.

When the warm-up ended, I couldn't move. The other girls scurried around me for the next part of class. I looked at myself in the mirror.

No. That wasn't me. It couldn't be. I was out of practice. It would come back. I had to push through.

We cleared the barre and lined up to cross the floor for a simple combination. Rowena made small gestures with her hands and called out what she wanted ("Tombé, pirouette, relevé and extend, pas de bourrée, and balancé, balancé . . ."), and I counted off, waiting for my turn.

As soon as I started across the floor, I knew I was not simply out of practice.

I knew why it had felt odd to get dressed for dance.

I knew that I had done something terrible.

In my head, I could see the steps, could feel the way they would work together. With eyes closed, it felt almost like it always had.

But with my eyes open and a wall of mirrors right in front of me, I could see what my body actually looked like.

Stiff. Jerky. No smoothness, no graceful transitions. Angles all wrong. Arms over-rotating. Legs pigeon-toed. If it hadn't been so terrifying, it would've been funny, like a scene in a movie where a romantic heroine who bluffed that she could dance was being proved grotesquely wrong.

I focused and tried harder. But the me in the mirror looked as out of joint as before. I could not make corrections when I had no way to calibrate them; I could not fix what already felt like perfection.

When I pushed even harder, ignoring the signals my body was giving me and relying purely on the mirror, I managed to hit myself in the face with a hand, and I lost my balance, falling right in the middle of the floor.

The smack of the floor on my hip—*that* I felt. The humiliation—those synapses were working fine.

The piano stopped. The other girls looked down at me, still lying on the floor, their faces full of pity and also disgust. Who *falls* in the middle of a simple combination?

Not me. I was going to be in the Manhattan Ballet junior corps. I was going to get out of here and make everyone proud.

I didn't trust myself to stand. Rowena appeared next to me. She took hold of my elbow and hoisted me to my feet, making it look as much as possible like she was only offering support. But without her I'd have stayed on the ground flailing like a turtle on its back.

In the hall, she didn't let go, even when I sat on the changing bench. Her fingers were daggers in my skin. "I'm okay," I said. She still didn't let go. "I'm *fine.*"

Cautiously, she released my arm. "You should take as long as you need, Ariadne."

"I don't want to take any time."

Rowena shook her head. "Sometimes the body knows what the mind does not."

That sounded like one of those solemn dancerisms that could explain anything from a stiff hip to a nervous breakdown, but still I wondered if she was right. The pulse of my bad wrist felt like it was spreading through my whole body, and I could barely feel anything else. Not even shame.

"This is the thing you can never plan for," she said. "One of life's tragedies."

"Yes, but . . . New York."

"When are you leaving?"

"August first."

"Two months. Plenty of time to prepare."

"Jess and I—we've been planning for years. It's my chance. I *have* to be ready."

"Then you will," she said simply. "And I have to go back to class. Stay, and we'll talk more?"

I nodded, but as soon as she left the changing room I pushed myself to my feet and ran, awkwardly, out the door.

My body didn't feel like one muscle anymore, and it didn't feel like twenty muscles. It felt like thousands. The parts of me that weren't working weren't out of practice—they were out of my control completely.

I had traded in my ability to dance for some stupid boy. A boy I probably would've broken up with anyway when I moved away to New York. That boy somehow was worth nine years of effort, practicing five hours a day, auditions and competitions and pain, everything I always thought I would be, the only thing I've ever been any good at. In order to forget my past, I'd obliterated my future.

The me of yesterday had been a selfish, foolish bitch.

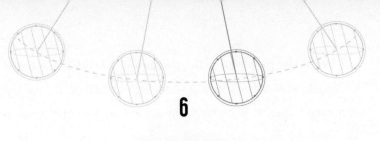

6

MARKOS

My brothers got me to the church for Win's funeral. They sat me in a pew. They surrounded me like linebackers. Like goddamn secret service in black suits. I didn't remember my dad's funeral, but I could see all of them remembering it, comparing it, sharing sad, knowing glances. Their shared tragedy. The thing that bonded them together. Their stupid club I could never join. Fuck them. This was my friend. This was Win's day, not Dad's. This was my torture, not theirs.

I looked straight up at the ceiling. Wood beams. Sunlight. A white banner tucked into a corner. I looked at my feet. Black shoes. Black laces. Gray carpet. I looked at my hands. Cut up. Splintered. Bleeding around the half dozen Band-Aids my mom had stuck on them before I snapped at her to stop. I'd ripped down the rotting treehouse in the backyard the night before. My hands closed into fists, over nothing.

Up at the front of the room there was a white casket. I didn't have to look to know it was there.

I heard the pastor clear his throat and I knew if I listened to a single word this man said—this self-important dick who'd never even talked to Win, who only knew him from the pictures that lined the aisles and looked up at the bottom of our chins from Xeroxed programs on every lap—I would start screaming and never stop.

I pushed past Cal, who didn't try to stop me, and my mom, who made a lunge for my arm but missed. I ran away from the coffin into the entryway, but there were more people coming in, streams and streams of them, and outside it was sunny and summery and unbearable, a beautiful June weekend, the first weekend of the summer, what a stunning fucking miracle, so I turned before I reached the outer door and stepped into a closet filled with bunting and banners. In the dark, I leaned into the fabric until I could only see black, and I talked to myself.

—Coward.

—I'm not afraid.

—Then why hide?

—I don't want to be a part of this phony bullshit.

—You're hiding. You don't want anyone to see you. Boo-hoo, poor Markos. You think they haven't noticed that you've left?

—I don't care what they think.

—Even your brothers? They're out there. They're wondering what the hell's wrong with you.

—They don't care about Win.

—But you do. Stop being a coward and get out there.

—Why?

—It's up to you. You have to.

—Why me?

—Because you're a Waters. Suck it up.

I took a couple more breaths into the fabric and was about to head back out when the door opened. I lunged for the handle to close it and practically ran face-first into Ari Madrigal.

"Hi," I said.

She stared at me. Her eyes were red-rimmed. But her sadness didn't make me angry like the rest of the crowd's did. She had earned it. She, like me, had loved Win well enough to be entitled to this pain.

"What are you doing in here?" she asked.

I shrugged. "Why did you open the door?"

"To get away for a minute."

"Yeah."

She glanced from side to side and let go of the door. "Sorry to bother you," she said.

"Wait!" I grabbed her arm. She looked at my hand, and I let go. "Are you—will you be at the house later?"

"Yeah, probably."

"We should talk," I said.

Her eyes grew big and she swallowed. Almost like she was afraid.

Coward.

"I don't think that's a good idea," she said.

"Why not?"

"I . . . want to be alone."

I remembered a flash of the night Win died, the sand and rain and sky, how happy and how awful it was. Then I lurched forward, extended my arms, and hugged her.

She didn't hug back. Her entire body tensed. When I leaned back to see her face even her teeth were clenched.

"Sorry," I said, and let go.

She backed away, shuffled into the church with the last of the stragglers. The pastor had begun his bland speech but I couldn't hear the words from out in the entryway.

Ari wasn't someone I would've ever chosen to be friends with. She came with Win. At first she seemed like any other girl, but you spend enough time with someone, and they surprise you—they do something unexpected or unusual that gives them three dimensions. Ari had made me laugh, and that made her real.

She was probably my closest friend now. Not my best friend—not the way Win was my best friend. Just that she was the only person who knew me for real.

She went out there and sat and listened. She knew Win. If she could do it, so could I.

I took a step into the church.

Black jackets.

Bowed heads.

White coffin.

Win's sister Kara sitting in the front row breathing little-kid breaths, trying to keep it together.

I took a step back out into the entry. Then another step, and another, until I was running out to my mom's car in the parking lot. I didn't have the keys, so I sat on the ground with my back against a wheel and tried to breathe.

Coward.

I wasn't as strong as Ari. Win always said she was tough, that she could handle anything, and I guess he was right. I couldn't do it. Not even for my best friend.

7

KAY

I sat in the row behind my best friends near the front of the church. Ari stared blankly as people hugged her over and over, and Diana cried too hard to talk to anyone. I kept close and waited for someone to need me.

I had liked Win. He was quiet and sweet and would nod to me in the hall or ask how things were going. When we all hung out in a group, which was rarely, he included me in conversation. Nothing huge, but it meant something.

Plus there was the fact that I wouldn't have friends at all if it weren't for him. If Ari hadn't been busy with Win, Diana never would've been lonely enough to call me. I'd always been grateful for that.

In the past week, his death had loomed over me, the idea that he was gone forever and never coming back, the great big black wings of fear bearing down on me. I hadn't felt that clutching in my heart since before my sister Mina left for her world tour, and I didn't miss it. This was what was supposed to happen to Mina for so many years when she was sick: the huge dark bird would scoop her up in his talons and she'd disappear. I'd pictured sitting at Mina's funeral many times; I'd pictured it so well that when I sat behind Diana and Ari in the church for Win's, I felt I'd been there before.

But in actuality this was the first funeral I'd ever attended. Mina got better and went away. She was back for the summer now, but I could no longer stand the sight of her.

In the row in front of me, Diana put her arm around Ari's shoulder, and I felt a stab of jealousy. I reached out to rest my hand on top of Diana's, but Ari shook off Diana's arm and I let my hand drop back into my lap. Ari didn't look at Diana, but Diana watched her intently through her tears, looking for some clue as to what she should do and how she could help. I watched them both, wondering the same thing.

The pastor talked, there were long, horrible silences, and then Ari made it to the top of the steps to the podium before turning back around and sitting down without saying anything. She tripped on the way down the steps, and the entire church gasped. Ari, whose feet did exactly every impossible thing she wanted them to do, nearly fell. She stumbled back to her seat, her hair over her face.

An uncle talked, or maybe a neighbor—I was starting to lose track. Pockets of crying kept erupting from the back and the sides of the church. The coffin sat up on the stage, a shiny white brick. I felt the dark wings flapping closer. I wished the coffin had been open so I could be sure who was in it.

I couldn't think about death or that great giant bird would get too near, so I thought of what I wished I could tell Ari and Diana instead, what the weakest, softest, most useless part of me felt. Stuff I'd never told them, because you don't talk about depressing stuff like your sister's near-death experiences, hanging out in the hospital every day after school, watching her waste away. No one would want a bummer like that around. And I wanted them to want me around, not only put up with me because my spell made them. The spell, at least, gave me the opportunity. I had to take advantage of it.

But still, I was full of weakness.

When Mina first got sick, four years ago, we went to a hekamist. Well, first we went to the doctor, had all the tests done, cried, got a second opinion, went back to the first doctor, had more tests, started chemo—and then we went to the hekamist. Back then Mina insisted I come with her when she had big appointments. "Katelyn's old enough. She deserves to be there," she said, but I could tell in her eyes—because we were that close—that she was afraid to go alone.

So I went with them the day they had the appointment. It wasn't the townie hekamist who lived in the neighborhood behind the high school; this one had been highly recommended by the best of the best—my dad wouldn't go to anything less. She had a real office next to a hospital in Boston. Money had never been a consideration for my parents. Or perhaps it was the only consideration—the only thing they knew to do when tragedy struck was to spend.

We'd heard that hekamists couldn't cure people, but we'd also heard the rumors: that you had to find the right hekamist. That covens gave their members an extended lifespan. That hekamists stopped curing people in retaliation for the government making joining covens illegal twenty years ago. And Mina was sick—possibly dying, we didn't know—so we had to try.

"None of that's true," the hekamist said. Her face was so full of lines her eyes almost disappeared. She wore a white lab coat and spoke in a dry, lecturing tone. "A hekamist operates like a spiritual accountant. We rearrange three areas—traditionally, the body, mind, and soul; or the physical, mental, and the aura, as I prefer. Say your budget has plenty of smarts but not much in the beauty department." I could have sworn that everyone in the room looked at me, except Mina. "We rearrange the way that resources are allocated so that some of the brain's stockpile is converted to beauty. When someone is as sick as Mina is—and I'm so sorry, my dear—the cost to her mental abilities could be catastrophic."

"She'd live, though?" my mom asked. Mina had inherited our mother's sleek black hair, dark smooth skin, and elegant nose, though not her tasteful fashion sense and obsessive gardening habit. I'd inherited my dad's sallow, acne-prone skin and small eyes, and I didn't know what else, since he spent most of his time in Boston earning us a lot of money so my mother could garden in peace.

The hekamist shook her head. "She'd be a vegetable."

Mina sighed and my parents started to argue between

themselves in whispers. "If there was even a chance, the doctor would've told us," I said to Mina.

"And lose all his future business?" she answered, running her hand over her newly bald head. She hadn't yet found a hat that didn't itch like hell. She whispered so the hekamist wouldn't hear us. "I hate this place."

"What do you mean? It's fine."

"Don't you feel weird? This is where people go when they're desperate." The hekamist was watching us, and Mina smiled at her as she lowered her voice even more. "They can't live with themselves."

"Tons of people get spells."

"People do extreme things when they hate themselves."

"I hate cancer," I said. "You hate cancer, right?"

"That's like hating snow or the color red."

She didn't explain what she meant by that, but I've had a lot of time to think about it, and I think she meant cancer was simply a thing, like snow, and there was no point hating it because it didn't care about you. Hating it wouldn't change it, it only meant you were holding on to hate. At the time, I couldn't think of anything to say back to her, and then we were getting up and thanking the hekamist for her time and fleeing to our car in the lot across the street.

I thought of that conversation when I went for my beauty spell three years later. Mina hadn't said much when I told her I was doing it. Not surprising, with half the world between us. Her email response was only a line long—"No time here. Good luck. Love you."—like she was sending a telegraph and paying by the word, instead of dealing with spotty internet cafés in Uttar Pradesh. She could've written more, but she didn't care. She'd left me.

And I thought of it again when I got the friendship binding spell. While I waited for the hekamist to make the spell, in a small living room totally unlike the antiseptic office of the faux-doctor we'd gone to for Mina, I remembered what Mina had said: Everyone who sat in this chair was desperate, and they hated themselves.

I thought about it, and as much as I wanted to disagree with Mina, it was true. I was desperate, and I hated myself. Everything she said about spelltakers was true.

The hekamist unwrapped a new box of cookies and shook out a handful onto the counter. "We call this kind of spell a hook," she said, fiddling with the cookies and a jagged stone. "You eat one, and you give one to each of your friends, and they won't be able to leave you."

"How long will it last?"

"Good question. Good, good, good. How much can you pay?"

"I've got four thousand dollars." I'd taken out the daily max from my savings account and emptied my mother's wallet for four days in a row. Mom hadn't even noticed. The tall stack of crisp bills sat in the middle of the table, incongruous in the dingy house.

The hekamist stopped moving and turned to look at me. "That's enough to make it permanent."

"Sounds good to me," I said.

"People grow up. People change. Are you sure?"

"Sure I'm sure." I pushed the stack of bills so that the money fanned out over the table. "I won't be alone."

The hekamist didn't say anything else and turned back to the counter. Eventually she presented me with a plate of four cookies. I poked at them. "There's an extra one," I said.

She looked down at the plate, as if trying to focus and count moving objects. "Ah . . . I see. Well, keep it. You never know."

"My beauty spell affected my brain," I said (and I had the D in chem to prove it), "but this hook—what department does that steal from?"

She hesitated a second, and I thought she might not tell me, or she might lie. She already had my money—what did she care? But when she answered, it sounded like the truth.

"Hooks are about location and control. It'll keep your loved ones near you, using luck and coincidence and chance. They'll see you every three days; they'll go no farther than fifty miles away, no matter what. You might find that other parts of your life . . . dislocate."

"What does that mean?"

"The hook stays hooked. Other things unhook."

"What things? What do you mean unhook?"

The hekamist shrugged. She wouldn't—or couldn't—explain any more.

I tried not to worry about it and instead thought of all I'd given Mina—years of my life, my every thought or hope or wish—and how when she'd recovered she'd immediately left me behind. The cancer hadn't taken her like I'd always thought it would, but she surgically removed herself from my life anyway. And she was my sister, who said she loved me. If she could do that, anyone could.

I ate my cookie in two bites.

People who went to hekamists were desperate. I couldn't argue with that, Mina. But it's easy not to hate yourself when you're beautiful and when you have friends. It wasn't my fault I hated myself. I needed to be fixed before I could be lovable—like Mina's chemo. I didn't see a difference between chemo and the cookie. Chemo did even more messed-up things to your body than hekame. So did Mina hate herself when she went in for treatment? No. She hated cancer, I know she did. And I hated my face and my loneliness.

Luckily for both of us, there was a cure.

8

ARI

At the funeral, it wasn't difficult to look stricken and severe, and to feel like I'd lost something important. No one could tell I was mourning dance and not Win.

If they could've peered behind my red eyes and grimace, they would've seen me leaping and spinning in unison with the corps, elegantly romantic in a pas de deux, shimmering like a mirage in a solo. They would've seen me replay over and over the fall I'd taken in class, humiliating, inexplicable. They would've seen me catalog each of my muscles one by one, knowing I couldn't control any of them the way I needed to.

But they couldn't see inside my mind, and so I let them believe that I was sad about Win. I faked it.

I had thought I would tell Diana and Jess the truth about the spell, but then I'd gone to class and fallen. When I got home, Jess looked up from her book and asked me how it went.

"Fine," I said. In the past, class had sometimes been painful or joyous or exhausting or boring, but at its core, it had never been anything other than "fine."

My mouth didn't know how to form the words to explain how not fine I really was.

"I'm glad," Jess said. She took a deep breath as if steeling herself. "Do you have class Wednesday afternoon?"

"I have class in the morning and the Sweet Shoppe in the afternoon. Why?"

"I made an appointment for you with a therapist."

"No," I said.

"You're going through something tough."

"No, no—dance will help me. You shouldn't be spending money on something like that anyway. We need it for New York."

Jess worried the fraying fabric on the back of the couch. "Maybe we should think about whether it's the right time to move."

"Of course it's the right time. August first. The date's set. The Manhattan Ballet chose me. They invited me." My voice shook, too loud, and I couldn't stop talking. "They might not want me in another year—I'll be too old. I've learned everything I can from Rowena, and I need to get professional training now so that I don't develop bad habits, and you know they cast most of the company from the junior corps, so I could get a real job there in a year. I don't want to wait. I can't sit here rotting away for another year. Jess, please. We have to go. We have to."

During my speech I stepped closer to where Jess was sitting on our old velvet couch. A lamp stood a foot or two away, hardly close enough for me to reach, if I'd even thought about it at all, but of course I didn't and I banged one gesticulating arm on it then tripped on the edge of the carpet. Jess stood up and put her arms around me, catching me out of my stumble. I stiffened and twisted out of her grip.

"We'll move, Ari. We'll do whatever you need to do." She half smiled. "But you still have to go to therapy."

"I won't have anything to say."

"I'm sure you'll think of something. Talk about dance if you don't want to talk about Win."

"The therapist won't understand."

"So explain it. It's not good to let these things fester."

The truth faded further away with each breath. How could I open my mouth now and say, "I've done something terrible," tell her about Win and the side effects, after arguing so hard for New York? Jess loved me, and she would understand, but she'd pity me, too. She and Diana and everyone else. They'd know I wasn't strong enough to handle the sadness. They'd know I cared more about some boy than I did about dancing, which was impossible. I didn't know who I was without dancing. I didn't know how to live without it, because I'd never had to live without it.

And I wouldn't. This couldn't be the end—this couldn't be forever. I would dance again. I *had* to dance again. I was moving to New York August first, and that was the most important thing—more important than a stranger named Win, anyway.

"Fine," I said to Jess. Fine, I would go to the therapist. Fine, I would pretend.

I would let them believe that I remembered this Win Tillman. It would make them feel better, not disrupting what they already believed to be true, and I wouldn't have to explain the inexplicable. And I'd figure out how to dance again.

I got serious about dance soon after my parents died. Jess moved into town from San Francisco to take care of me, breaking up with her girlfriend to do it. I'd only met Jess a couple of times before that, so she was practically a stranger, mourning her older sister and brother-in-law and crying over her busted relationship.

Out in public, everywhere I went I was reminded that I was different from everyone else. They all had parents. I had none. It was bad enough when someone at recess casually mentioned their mom or dad. Worse was when someone had obviously been told about me, and so carefully avoided saying *mom* or *dad* or even *fire*, which eventually meant carefully avoiding me.

Jess didn't avoid me, but she didn't know what to do with me, either. She took me to the hekamist for the trauma erasing spell, so I wouldn't have nightmares about seeing the house collapse with my parents in it, and then she left me alone as I crept through our new house, trying not to jump at every creak of the floorboards. I listened to a lot of music to cover any weird sounds, on the iPod I had somehow saved from the old house—the one possession not lost in the fire. I slept with the window open even in winter, in case I had to jump out in the middle of the night. I checked the burglar alarm three or four times a night.

Jess didn't know what kids were like and she didn't know

what I was like before; she didn't know this wasn't normal. (Plus she never noticed I checked the burglar alarm at all. She could sleep through anything—which made me even more anxious.) She probably would've caught on eventually, or I would've started acting out even more. But instead, I threw myself into dance.

I'd been taking the beginner classes casually for a couple of years, like everyone else. But that year, class became something else. For an hour at a time, I didn't have to listen for strange noises. It didn't matter who I was or what had happened to me. I could make myself move beautifully. Even early on, I could tell that I had control in a way the other girls didn't.

When I told Jess I wanted to start going to dance every day, she didn't blink. She nodded and added it to the giant calendar she had taped on the kitchen wall. She picked me up from school, drove me to dance, and picked me up again when it was over, and she never complained. And we became a family.

So dance saved me. Not only because Jess and I were forced to interact for that hour a day we spent in the car, but also because dance itself—when you do it with your whole heart and being, and when your training sinks into your bones—is transporting. I was lifted out of my body and into the music. It became the thing I poured myself into, the container for my messy, wobbly, bursting-at-the-seams emotions. I let myself flow into ballet, and it remade me into someone who was strong, capable, and free.

I remembered that. I flew.

Without dance, I was back again to nothing, a shadow creeping through the house, different and alone. For weeks after the funeral, I watched videos of famous prima ballerinas on the internet, or Aunt Jess's sneaky shots of my performances at competitions or shows.

I knew how it felt to make those movements, familiar as a favorite song, but as I watched I also felt a creeping hot anger that started in the back of my neck and spread up to my cheeks and down through my arms and back.

The worst part was, I didn't have anyone to be mad at. I'd done this to myself. Old Ari—the Ari that was—had taken away the only thing that made any sense to me. The only thing I was good at. The only thing I loved.

I pored over glimpses of her. After my performances were over, Aunt Jess kept the camera running when I came out to meet her in the lobby. So I got to see someone who looked exactly like me do things I had no memory of doing. Because there, in the lobby, was Win.

He was the first person I'd hug when I arrived on the scene, and we'd keep holding hands as I accepted congratulations from Jess and my friends. He was cute in a somewhat rumpled way, light brown hair curling slightly into his gray eyes, shirts wrinkled, shoes scuffed.

But he was a stranger. I'd never seen him talk or move in real life, at least not that I remembered. In the videos he seemed almost shy, though maybe it was the context—he hung back, smiled a lot, but let me interact with my audience.

"Ari, who are you wearing! Turn and smile for the camera, darling!" Jess riffed and zoomed in the camera close to my face;

I swatted her away and leaned on Win's arm to give him a kiss.

"Guys, deceptively youthful parental authority, standing right in front of you."

The old Ari ignored Jess and casually went en pointe in her sneakers to whisper in Win's ear, and I replayed the moment a dozen times hoping to make out what I was saying, but I could never quite tell.

"—authority, standing right in front of you." Lean, kiss, toes, whisper.

"—rity, standing right in front of you." Kiss, toes, whisper.

"—standing right in front of you." Toes, whisper.

"—right in front of you." Whisper.

It was private forever between those two—both of them gone. I couldn't be nostalgic, though, or sad or wistful. How could I miss a precious moment with someone who, as far as I knew, I'd never met?

Mostly I watched for some clue—a *hint*—to what on earth made that girl punish me like this, taking away dance and leaving me with nothing.

And maybe somewhere in there, there would be a hint to how I could get it back.

9

WIN

One more thing about Ari. Just one more.

When she was invited to join the Manhattan Ballet junior corps, January of our junior year, she couldn't stop crying.

No one else knows this. Not Diana, not Kay, not her aunt Jess. I didn't tell Markos or Kara or my mom.

We sat in her bedroom while her aunt was at work. She had curled into a ball in the corner of her twin bed, back against the wall. I sat in place of the pillow, her head in my lap.

"Wh-wh-wh-what is hap-hap-happening to me?" she asked, taking these desperate, heaving little gasps of breath in between almost every word.

"You're sad," I said.

"N-n-n-n-n," she said, meaning no. "I'm g-going to b-b-be a—a—a *prima ballerina*."

"I know."

"I'm g-g-g-going to l-l-live in *New York* and take classes w-w-with *legends* and—and—and—"

"I know."

"I never cr-cr-cry."

"I know you don't. You're Ari Madrigal."

She broke down into another sob, and I stroked her hair away from her face. Soft hair, damp from her tears. Her skin was hot and each breath rattled her whole body.

"If I were you," I said, just loud enough for her to hear, "I'd be scared. Scared to leave home, scared to be around strangers. Scared to mess up. Or scared to *not* mess up."

She hiccupped, still crying, but I could tell she was listening.

"But luckily I'm not you. You are. You've got no reason to be scared. They picked you because they saw how talented you are. How passionate. They'll be lucky to have you."

"But I'm sc-sc-scared, too."

I sighed, and the breath ruffled the dry hairs around her neck. "Good."

She stopped crying out of surprise. "Good?"

"We have something in common."

She lifted her head and swiveled so that she was sitting curled in my lap, legs tucked over one of my knees, head right above my collarbone. I could rub her back now, and I did.

"You probably think I'm an idiot," she said, with only minimal gasps.

"I will never think you're an idiot."

"Never?"

"Never."

"What if I move away and you forget me?"

"Never."

"What if I go to New York and root for the Yankees?"

"Not even then."

She snuggled closer, chin nuzzling my neck. "So you'll never leave me."

"Never."

"You're mine, then."

I bent my head so I could kiss her. Salty, warm. "Always."

10

ARI

"We *always* go to the bonfire." Diana opened my closet doors and rooted around violently. "Always. No arguments—we're picking up Kay in ten minutes."

I swiveled in my desk chair, wishing Diana would leave so I could go back to watching my dance videos. It had been a month since I took the memory spell, the weeks passing at a crawl, as if I were stuck in a picture, expression fixed. I still couldn't dance. August first—our move-out date, settled months ago—was less than a month away. Jess had started collecting boxes, which she piled behind the doors of every room.

But Diana wanted to go to the bonfire. The Fourth of July existed solely for the tourists, so the Waters clan claimed the third for a beach bonfire for their friends. I remembered most of the bonfire from two years ago, but last year's bonfire memory was Swiss cheese. I hadn't even considered going until Diana burst into my room.

"I know it's only been a month since Win . . ." Diana paused, then rushed through to her next thought. "It's only been a month but it would mean a lot to me if you went. I mean, not just me, but everybody. To see you out there—it means that we'll survive this, you know?" She abandoned my closet and sat on my bed and curled her arms over her knees. "And I think not only for us, but for you—you haven't been anywhere in weeks, Ari."

"I go to work. And to class." Not true; I hadn't been to class since I fell, the day after the spell. Lies, lies, lies.

"And then you come right home. You sit with me and Kay for forty-five minutes, maybe an hour, and then the look on your face when you can kick us out . . . You're relieved." Diana shook her head. "I miss you."

"I'm sorry."

"Don't be sorry. You're going through stuff. But I don't want you to think you're alone." She shrugged, self-conscious. "You've always got me."

"I know."

"And Kay, too."

"Right. Kay."

Diana jumped up and dug around for a couple of shirts, which she tossed at me. "Try these on."

I hugged the shirts to my chest. "I don't know if I can go, Diana."

"I'm pretending I didn't just hear that. La la la la." She plugged her ears until her eyes fell on my wrist, red from all the times I'd pinched it. Then she dropped her hands and looked serious. "Ari, are you—is everything okay?"

I was fine in the way she was asking about, and miserable in ways I couldn't tell her.

"Let's have a movie night instead," I said. "We haven't had a movie night in weeks."

Diana shook her head, half smiling. "We haven't had a movie night in over a year."

"We haven't?" I shook off my confusion and tried to look sad. "Oh, right, sorry, of course. Win . . ."

"You guys always did homework on Sundays."

"Right. Well, let's bring movie night back."

Diana bit her lip. "But I want to go to the bonfire."

"Come on, Diana. Why do you care so much?"

"Why don't you care at all?" Diana shot back.

Because I didn't remember enough to care. The bonfire belonged to Old Ari. I wanted to be left alone.

But I couldn't say that to Diana, and normally, I wouldn't have to. She'd never argued with me like that before. The Diana I remembered usually did what I wanted to do, back when I actually wanted to do anything. When we became friends in fourth grade, she didn't call me until we'd been hanging out at each other's houses every day for six months. She cried easily and hated conflict—normally I'd have to push her to express an opinion so I knew I wasn't steamrolling her. She wasn't the type to take charge.

This Diana seemed different. More forceful. And then

there was her hair, which she'd dyed bright red a week or two after the funeral. I didn't understand what had happened. The hair was weird enough—she hadn't even consulted me before doing it, and something that big should've been worthy of discussion. I wanted to ask her why she'd done it, but I was afraid it was something I should know already, and admitting I didn't would mean admitting everything else I couldn't remember.

"Your hair," I said. "I keep forgetting and then being surprised again."

Diana twisted a red strand around her finger and pulled it forward to look at it. "You know what's funny? I got used to it right away. Like my hair had always been red underneath the mousy blond."

"It looks good."

"Stop trying to change the subject. Why don't you want to go?"

"I'm . . . nervous about seeing everyone," I said.

"Come on, it's the Waters bonfire, and everyone loves you," she said, elbowing me gently. "Plus, you have to humor me— Markos will be there."

"Oh, Diana," I said, groaning.

"What?" she asked. "Can't a girl dream?"

"Markos is great, but he treats girls so bad."

Diana laughed. "You just said he was great! How can he be great and also bad?"

"Context."

"Don't worry, he'll probably ignore me like he has hundreds of times before. But you should come and be my moral support anyway, don't you think?"

I no longer remembered how or why I became friends with Markos, but I knew we were in each other's corner. He was fun and less of an asshole than he seemed—but I wasn't dating him. Diana was too sweet and sheltered; if they got together he'd hurt her without even realizing it. She needed someone serious and kind like she was. "Isn't there literally anyone else on the planet you could have a crush on?"

"No, I'm stuck with Markos forever. Does this mean you'll come?"

I glanced at my wall, where there was a picture of me and Win with our arms around each other. He was wearing a baseball uniform, and I had on the cap. She seemed happy—I mean *I* did. If I went to the bonfire, it would mean a whole night of pretending to be that girl, avoiding pointed questions or boozy reminiscences, hoping no one noticed my awkward walk or lack of memory. It wouldn't bring me any closer to dancing again.

But it was either that or another night of videos and self-recriminations and questions without answers. Another night of Diana changing. In my memory, we were the same as always. But in hers, we hadn't had a movie night in a year. She didn't feel the need to get my opinion on her hair. She'd brought in Kay to pick up my slack.

I only had a few more weeks left until I moved to New

York—maybe I could go and pretend to be someone I wasn't, just for her sake.

"All right," I said.

Diana squealed and hugged me and dressed me and I left the safety of my room for a life I didn't remember.

11

KAY

Diana picked me up for the bonfire. Ari was already in the front seat of Diana's mother's Impala. I'd seen them like clockwork the past couple of months, just as the hekamist promised back in January. At least every three days, no matter what, I'd get a call or Diana would need a ride or I'd run into one of them at the grocery store. Sometimes I'd think there was no way the spell could come through, and this would be the day it fell apart, but always, without fail, it worked.

I helped it out as much as I could. I was available at all hours and on all days. I went by Ari's work and Diana's house and sent texts and emails, making it easy for them to respond, to invite me in. Without the spell, maybe they would've let my calls and emails linger. Maybe they wouldn't call back at all.

This way, they always called back. Even if they didn't always have something to say.

I'd been looking forward to the bonfire. I'd never been before. For years I didn't even know it existed, and then when

Mina left and I started paying attention, I was afraid to go by myself. Maybe showing up out of nowhere would be against the rules. It would be much better going with Ari and Diana, who were bonfire experts. Up until the day of the party I didn't know if they would want to go, but I should've known better than to doubt the spell.

For a while I thought that Ari losing Win might help us. Not in a horrible way—I wasn't glad that he died or anything like that. I wouldn't wish that on anyone. But I had thought that maybe his death would soften Ari, make her rethink her priorities and relationships, and make us closer friends. It would certainly give her more time for us.

That hadn't happened. If anything, she'd gotten harder since Win's death. Colder. Sometimes I felt like she wasn't even there behind her eyes, and the Ari we saw was a placeholder.

"Thanks for the ride," I said. They didn't respond. "Ari, your shirt's really cute."

Ari shook herself, as if waking up from a nap. "Thanks."

"So do you guys know where to go? Is it always in the same place? Where does everybody park?"

"You've really never been before?" Diana asked. "Were you living under a rock?"

I couldn't tell from her tone if she was teasing in a nice way or a mean way. I turned to Ari to check, but she was staring out the window, gone again.

"I guess I was. Ha." I fiddled with the seatbelt across my chest, which had twisted my shirt almost all the way around my body. Diana and Ari, as usual, looked gorgeous. "I like your hair, Di."

Diana half turned in her seat—I thought to accept the compliment. "Diana," she said.

"Sorry," I said. "I like your hair, *Diana*."

Diana kept driving and Ari looked out the window. This was the time when I would say something charming or thoughtful or witty and they would laugh, and we would be a trio. There had to be charmed words, somewhere, to make that happen. The spell had given me the opportunity to be in the car with these girls. Now all I had to do was take it and make it real.

When we pulled into the beach parking lot, Ari lingered in the car after Diana cut the engine.

"Sure about this?" she asked.

Diana nodded. "Go ahead. We'll meet you down there."

Ari took a deep breath and started to make her way carefully down the beach. Diana sighed, leaned back in her seat, and watched her.

"She seems . . . out of it," I said.

"Yeah," Diana said. "I thought this would be good for her but now I'm not so sure."

"She'll be all right. You're doing everything you can."

Diana ran a hand through her hair, recently dyed bright red. "I'm going to give her some space for a little while tonight. I don't want to push too hard. Maybe you should, too."

"Okay."

"And maybe some space from me, too."

"Oh . . . sure."

"We don't always have to do everything together."

"Of course not."

My face must have looked stricken, because Diana focused in on me in the rearview mirror. "You're going to be fine. It's just a party."

"I know," I said, and laughed. Just a party. As if I even knew what that meant.

Diana got out of the car, waiting for me to exit before locking it, but not waiting for me to catch up as she walked down the beach toward the fire.

"I'll find you later," I said to her back, her long red hair swinging behind her. I hated how my voice sounded, so desperate, pathetic. I hated that Diana's hair swung naturally and mine was a spell meant to imitate hers. I even hated Ari a little bit for holding back from us so determinedly. But those were also the things I loved about Diana and Ari. Diana's naturalness. She was unaffected. Ari's stubbornness. She had guts. The spell let them be themselves—that was what was so great about it. Nonintrusive. Harmless, really.

Diana melted into the crowd, and I stood alone on the edge. I should've been used to it—it was, after all, my entire life before Diana and Ari—but I was meant to be with people. Alone, I disappeared.

I got a half-foam beer from the keg, poured by one of Markos Waters's older brothers, and watched Diana and Ari from the sidelines. Diana walked off with Markos. A punk girl in a black coat watched Ari. Mina was there, too, wearing a thrift-store men's shirt as a dress, talking to some people from her grade.

When she saw me, she made her way to me through the crowd.

"Hey, Katelyn, what's—"

"What are you doing here?"

Mina laughed. "I'm here for the bonfire. Just like you."

"You're not staying, though, are you?"

"Why not?"

"Because this is my party."

She looked around. "It looks like everyone's party."

"You know what I mean."

"Actually, I don't. What's going on, Katelyn?"

"My name is Kay."

"Oh, well, nice to meet you, Kay. Have you seen my sister? She used to be such a nice girl. . . . I wonder where she could've gone. . . ."

"Har har. Please, Mina. Just leave me alone."

I could see her throat constrict in her too-thin neck. "Why?"

"Because for one night I don't want to be Mina Charpal's little sister. Okay?"

I couldn't see her eyes in the dark. Firelight flashed off her piercings as she nodded. "Fair enough."

She threw her plastic cup onto the ground and turned away. I expected her to drift into conversation with someone, but she waved goodbye to a couple of people and then started walking up the dune and toward the parking lot.

Well, I'd asked her to leave me alone. This was good.

Mina walking away. I should've been used to it.

As I watched her go, a guy stumbled and bumped into me and I dropped my cup. He apologized quickly, then looked into my face. I had to stop myself from wincing, because sometimes I forget I'm beautiful now.

"I'm Cal!" he practically shouted. "Cal Waters. Are you in Markos's class?"

"Yeah. I'm Kay."

"Have we met? I feel like I would have remembered you."

I looked up at Cal. He was handsome. He was a Waters. That meant something.

"I'm Kay," I said, stupidly, again.

"Oh-*Kay*," he said, laughed, and flicked a silver lighter to light a cigarette. "Can't believe I wouldn't remember someone who looked like you."

He was drunk. Diana and Ari would warn me away, probably—Ari would make fun of him to his face and Diana would whisper jokes in my ear.

But Diana and Ari weren't there. Maybe I needed to make some new friends.

I smiled my now-flawless smile and touched Cal's arm like I'd seen other girls do.

"You can remember me now," I said.

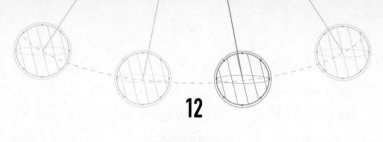

12

MARKOS

Win died and everyone around me got simultaneous lobotomies. No, that wasn't right. What happened was this: Win died and I became the only person in this entire town whose congenital lobotomy spontaneously reversed itself. I could see everything they couldn't. Win dying opened my eyes.

Or maybe that's not exactly it, either. It sounds like some hippie shit. Here's what probably happened: Win died and I was the only person who cared enough to know what the hell that meant.

Win was dead. See, I could say it right out loud. Dead. I no longer had a best friend and never would again. You couldn't be best friends except with someone who knew you forever, since before you could remember.

My mother talked loudly and fed me. My brothers punched my arm and stared into the middle distance. Even Ari—we didn't avoid each other, but we didn't hang out or talk, either, not since the funeral when she made it clear she wasn't interested in commiseration. Fine. Good. She had the right idea. It hurt to look at her, anyway.

Here was what it meant, Win's death: It meant that the world was unfair. The wrong guys came out on top. Nothing anyone did mattered because eventually we all came to the same end. What was the point of loving or being loved or any of that shit when death was so absolutely permanent?

I hung out by the keg at the bonfire and watched them all laughing, everyone I knew, everyone Win and I used to call friends. If you'd asked them, they would've said they were sad about Win. But it sure didn't seem that way from where I was standing.

My brothers kept the party going, Brian turning a blind eye to the underage drinking, Dev starting games of tackle football in the dark, Cal smiling and glad-handing from group to group. They had a crowd of people around them at all times. They made everyone laugh. For them it seemed effortless to be a Waters, to be the guys who threw the party, who knew everyone, who had no worries.

Brian came up to me first, stepping away from a trio of girls. If he saw the look I was giving him—a very special get-the-fuck-away-from-me glare—he pretended like he didn't. "Little bro," he said, swinging a heavy arm around my neck. "In my professional opinion, it does not look like you're having the time of your life."

"Maybe I'm not."

He went on as if he didn't hear me. "In my professional opinion," he repeated, "you're sulking."

"What profession are you talking about? Law enforcement?"

"Being an older brother is my profession."

I ducked out of his arm. "Can I talk to your manager, then?"

He frowned, which clearly pained him—Waters boys didn't frown at parties. "I know you're upset. But you'll be fine if you just relax, okay? And if you're not up for it, you can always go home. Skip the party this year. I'll drive you, just let me know."

Kicked out of my own party by my brothers. No way.

I turned my back on Brian and saw Diana North, Ari's best friend, staring into the fire. She had dyed her hair a blinding red and was wearing an open shirt over a neon green bikini top. She'd always been vaguely off-limits because of Ari. And she used to be mousy and quiet, shy in a boring way, doing whatever Ari told her to do; it had never seemed worth pissing off Ari to flirt with her. Now I looked at Diana's red hair and bikini and thought about Win and how pointless and impossible everything was and I thought: fuck it. There was no point in spending time with someone I actually liked. They would only disappoint me. I could talk to Diana North and not care if it ended or began.

That was probably awful. Ari would've told me I was being a pig and dragged Diana away. But Ari wasn't around. Besides, why did I have to listen to Ari? Win was dead. She was no longer my annoying conscience.

I left Brian talking to a group of girls that had materialized around him and walked over to Diana. She pretended not to notice. "You look different," I said. That's one of those things that is true but noncommittal. I didn't like to have my words thrown back at me—"you're beautiful" could be turned into some nuclear-level shit.

Diana ran a hand through her newly red hair, worrying the ends of it. She smelled good—shampoo and suntan lotion, even though it was dark out.

"I dyed it," she said. "I've wanted to for ages but I never did—afraid, I guess, though it sounds dumb to be afraid of a hair color. I thought if I dyed my hair I wouldn't know who I was anymore, but the exact opposite happened. I feel . . ." She looked up at me, as if she'd forgotten who she was talking to, or as if she'd heard her words coming out of someone else's mouth. "Um. Well. You look exactly the same."

That was blatantly not true, I mean not only on a physical level, because I had lost ten pounds in the last month, but on a deeper level, too. My insides were a mess, like the wrapped present you shake so hard it breaks the toy inside, so there's nothing but shards of plastic rolling around. Even this July third beach bonfire, which I had been going to since I was seven, when Brian threw the first one, felt different.

"Let's take a walk," I said, which in bonfire-speak means make out, at a minimum. Diana froze.

"Come on," I said, grabbing her hand.

We walked down the beach, not talking, passing couples making out lying in the sand or standing ankle-deep in the waves. The ones in the waves were always the ones deeply in love. Soulmates splashing each other and carrying their shoes.

I spotted Ari talking to my brother Cal. She didn't see me and Diana. Something seemed off about her, and I realized she wasn't standing up straight. She slouched. I don't think I'd ever seen her like that. Some automatic gut response made me wonder what was wrong with her, until I remembered what was wrong with us both.

But she didn't want to talk. Okay. I should be more like Ari. I should be able to handle this on my own.

"I think everyone misses Win," Diana said. I pointed to the frolicking couples and she shook her head. "I think they do, inside. In their way."

"I miss him," I said.

"Of course you do."

"Just because I'm not sobbing my guts out doesn't mean I don't miss him."

"You don't have to—"

"Wait," I said.

I stopped walking, dug my heels into the sand. Diana stopped walking, too, and looked up into my face. I had the urge to be mean to her. Like, really mean. Her hopefulness and sensitivity were there, right in front of me, and if I wanted I could stomp her down until she understood what the rest of the lobotomized horde didn't: this was all pointless.

Maybe that was why I brought her out here after so many years of ignoring her. Maybe I could tell that it was within my power to make her feel as shitty as I felt all the time. It would be so fucking easy. As easy as kissing her would be. She had no defenses at all. I could be a bastard—laugh at her, as I'm pretty sure I've laughed at her before—or a dream come true, giving her a romantic memory to treasure forever. Well, not forever, since there's no such thing. Till the end.

I sank onto the sand and Diana sat next to me. If she came any closer I would have had to choose—bastard or dreamboat—but she didn't. She looked out at the dark ocean and waited.

I breathed in through my nose. My heart was beating like I'd run up the dune. I told myself to calm down, but the panic only got worse. The ground tilted like I was going to be thrown off the planet.

"We'll be seniors soon," I said. It was by far the stupidest thing I'd said all day, and if any of my brothers had heard it they would've laughed so hard they hurt themselves, but of course Diana didn't make fun of me for it. She seemed to almost understand my need for stupid chatter, because she didn't say Win's name again.

We talked. About her hair and her cat and her babysitting job, things she cared about. About my brothers and the bonfire and the ocean, things I could see right in front of me. Every time she shifted in the sand my heart drilled again, but I never had to choose which person to be. I was not responsible for anything or anyone. I just was.

13

ARI

The bonfire roared in the middle of the crowd. It was a warm night, and the closer I came to the fire the hotter it got. Diana had put me in my jean jacket and I was sweating, but I didn't take it off; I wrapped it tighter around my shoulders for protection. I may not have a memory of the day my parents died, but I still avoid fire.

Most people steered away from me. I tried to exude tortured brooding. I don't know what I would've done if a big group had surrounded me, offering their reminiscences and sympathy, like they had at the funeral. I couldn't take more lying. I wasn't capable of it, and if I kept trying, someone was bound to find out the truth.

She might've thought of this. Old Ari, that is. She knew there would be a bonfire. Yet another thing she didn't bother taking into consideration.

I hated her.

I dug the toe of my sneaker into the sand and watched Diana

make her way to the keg. I'd come to the party for her sake, but it didn't look like she needed me at all. Maybe it would've been better if I'd stayed home and practiced dancing after all.

"Ari?" said a voice by my shoulder. I saw dark hair and a blinding smile and for a second I thought it was Markos, and my shoulders tensed, ready to start lying.

But it was Markos's next-oldest brother, Cal, in front of me. "Hi, Cal," I said, and tried to tell my shoulders to relax. They wouldn't.

"It's been forever," he said. He had an unlit cigarette dangling from his mouth and was playing with a metal Zippo lighter with one hand, flipping it open and closed, lighting it with a flick of his wrist. The other hand held a beer. "How are you?"

"I'm . . . fine."

"Come on. Spill."

I attempted to smile up at him. Cal was the nicest Waters brother. Brian was a know-it-all cop, Dev turned the family charm into sleaze, and Markos—well, he's Markos. Cal was good-looking like the others, sure, but he was too uncoordinated to do well in sports, and his agreeable nature probably meant he'd have been bad at them anyway. He'd gone through a wild couple of years after his dad died, but that seemed to have gotten the rebellion out of his system.

But just because he was the least of four evils didn't mean he was someone I wanted to get confessional with. "Dead boyfriend exemption. I'm allowed to submit half-truths to invasive questions."

He laughed, and the cigarette fell out of his mouth. "That's funny. I forgot you were funny."

"Well . . . thanks."

"And if you ever need anyone, let me know."

I swallowed down a lump in my throat despite myself. "Thanks."

He reached out the hand holding the closed lighter, hesitated, and then rested it on my own, which was clenched around the opposite elbow. My bad wrist throbbed, but I couldn't move to stretch it out. I didn't know what to do.

I was not a hugger. But since having my memory ripped from me, I'd been hugged, kissed, squeezed, petted, pinched, smothered, and any number of other space invasions.

This was what people did when they wanted to express comfort. They touched. I couldn't twist away. I couldn't snap and tell them to leave me alone. Their gestures were supposed to make me—the sufferer—feel better. But since I wasn't suffering—or, at least, not suffering the way they thought I was—I endured their pokes and prods because it made *them* feel better.

I held my breath, tried to ignore the pain in my wrist, and waited for Cal to remove his hand. His skin was warm but the lighter was cold metal. I was on three-Mississippi when a girl stood next to him and stared at him until he dropped his hand. I didn't recognize her.

"Bye," she said to him, shooing him away.

Cal looked like he might say something, then seemed to change his mind. He waved at me with his plastic cup, but he waved too hard and dropped it, then lunged for it and missed. He shrugged and went off in search of another one.

The girl turned to me. She had short black hair and was wearing a long, elaborately buckled coat and lace-up boots despite the warm night. "Ari Madrigal," she said. Her face twisted into a scowl. I hoped her scowl was default and not specific to me.

"That was a little rude," I said.

She shrugged. "I need to talk to you. He doesn't."

"Sounds . . . dramatic."

I looked around for Diana. I didn't see her by the keg, and the light of the bonfire only extended so far. Maybe she'd gone down to the water. Or maybe she would arrive any second and rescue me. Cal Waters had found Kay. He lit a cigarette for her and leaned in like they shared a secret. Kay and Cal—that would be an unexpected pairing. I tried to remember if Kay had ever had a boyfriend before, but the girl in front of me snapped her fingers in my face.

"I will never understand what Win saw in you," she said.

So the scowl wasn't a default. "Excuse me. Do I know you?"

"Probably not, but I know you."

I looked at her more closely. I didn't recognize her—at least, not her face. Something about her seemed familiar, though. Her expression was fierce, but I remembered . . . lightness. Buoyancy.

Weird.

"You owe me five thousand dollars," she said, unblinking.

I stared at her right back. "What?"

"Win's mother never found it—I've been watching. She

would've spent it by now, but she's got nothing. He had to have left it with you. But he owed it to me. So pay up."

My hands had started to shake. Five thousand dollars. That's how much my spell to erase Win had cost. I remembered finding an envelope thick with bills at the very back of my closet in a shoebox, and I remembered laying it on the hekamist's kitchen table. Close-up details, snippets of a movie I'd seen and mostly forgotten. I'd told myself it was my money, my windfall—left by my parents, maybe, like guardian angels. Meant for me.

But maybe it had been Win's money. I had no way of knowing.

"Listen, uh . . ."

"My name is Echo," she snapped. "We've met. But of course you wouldn't remember."

"Echo," I said. "I don't know what you're talking about. I don't have any money of Win's."

"You do, though. Or at least you did before you spent it. I didn't make the connection until I was sure it wasn't with Win's mom, but it's so obvious now. You're going to pay me what I'm owed or I'm going to tell everyone that you erased Win with a spell."

I stopped breathing.

How did she know?

When my lungs filled with air again, I managed a feeble protest. "I didn't erase Win."

She breathed out through her nose, frustrated. "Don't even try to play that game because you'll lose. Pay me my money or everyone finds out."

If this girl really knew what I'd done, she could tell everyone. And they'd all know I'd lied to them. They'd find out I couldn't dance, and that I'd wasted everything for this boy they all still loved.

"I told you," I said, trying to sound sure of myself. "I don't have any money, and I didn't do that. Didn't erase him."

She took a step back. Licked her chapped lips. "All right then. Prove it. When I met you the first time, what were we doing?"

"I don't have to answer—"

"It's a simple question, not a trick. Answer me."

I tried to turn away but couldn't pivot in the sand. In a flash, Echo was there, blocking me.

"Go ahead. Take a guess. When did we meet?"

Nothing. There was nothing to remember. You couldn't focus in and piece things together when there was nothing there to piece. "We were on the beach," I hazarded. "We were hanging out near here."

"Lucky guess. Doing what?"

"Hanging out. Just . . . hanging out."

Her hand rose to touch her mouth; she swallowed. "Nice try."

"You must not have made a big impression."

"I need that money, Ari."

"You can't prove—"

"I'm not the one who has to prove anything." She gestured at the bonfire. "Want me to call over some people, see if your memory works then?"

Wood snapped in the bonfire. One of Markos's brothers tossed on fresh fuel. If I had seen Diana out there maybe I would've thought of a way out of this. Figured a way to convince Echo I was whole, normal, unblackmailable. Maybe if Diana had been with me I wouldn't have given up so easily.

Only Echo was right, of course. I didn't remember Win.

"I'm sorry," I said.

"You're—what?"

"I don't have any more money. It all went to the spell."

She seemed shaken for a moment, hands grasping together. "No."

"I'm sorry I can't—"

"Stop saying that!" Her uncertainty vanished, replaced by the now-familiar glower. "You can get the money. Put some effort into it. If Win came up with the money, you can too." She nodded, as if this made perfect practical sense. "I'll give you two weeks, Ari. Five thousand dollars."

I nodded back, because there was nothing else I could do, and Echo stepped away. As she got farther away, the party noises seemed to get louder around me, people having fun, going on with their ordinary lives.

Mine had just gotten complicated. More than I could pretend away.

I needed to get out of here. Out of this bonfire. Off of this island. Whatever I was feeling—guilt and fear and confusion and worry, plus the ever-present regret of getting the stupid spell in the first place—it was bigger than this bonfire, bigger than Cape Cod.

Diana could help. I'd tell her the truth and we'd figure out a way through it together. I couldn't be blackmailed if I told people the truth myself.

I tried not to trip in the sand as I ran in search of my best friend.

14

MARKOS

I would've stayed with Diana, talking, avoiding my brothers, but Ari came and found us—found Diana, that is. She wasn't looking for me. She said hello and pulled Diana away, and I knew I had no right to complain, so I stayed sitting in the sand.

"Let's get out of here," Ari said, linking her arm with Diana's. "Let's drive to Boston and get tattoos."

"Really?" Diana said.

"No, tattoos are too expensive. Let's go to New York and dance in the Lincoln Center fountain."

Diana laughed as if something heavy had been lifted from her shoulders. She glanced at me for a second—with regret, maybe, or disappointment—but she was already following Ari up the dune.

I didn't watch her go.

What was there to regret? All we'd done was talk.

I watched the crowd as if it were alive, expanding and contracting like a heart. Then I heard a scream. Before I knew I was doing it, I was standing and running to her.

Diana had tripped and fallen and bashed one side of her face on a cooler so badly it formed an immediate bruise, visible even in the dim light of the bonfire.

She started crying. Ari stood next to her, just looking, stricken.

Somehow my arm wrapped around Diana's shoulder, all tangled up in her long hair, as I kneeled next to her in the sand. I comforted her.

"It'll be okay. Shhh, it's not so bad. That dumbass needs to move his shit, I'm going to kill him. Shhh, shhh. It's okay."

I kneeled next to her, touching her but only to comfort and not because I wanted something, and maybe that meant I was the fakest faker out of all the fakers at this party, in this town, in the world: I was pretending to be someone who gave a shit.

15

WIN

I never thought I'd need to go to a hekamist. I'd heard of people getting spells for looks or luck or brains, but if you ask for those things, you must believe you don't have any to begin with. I wasn't ugly or dumb or unlucky at all. I was Win Tillman. Varsity shortstop. Boyfriend of the prettiest girl in school. Good grades. Good skin. Good all around. Other people went to hekamists. Not me.

I mean, Ari had her spell, of course, but she didn't choose to get it, and she was so young and it was such a long time ago that it wasn't the same. (For the record, I would've gotten a spell to erase the sight of my house burning down with my parents inside, too. It's not something anyone needs in their brain.)

On one side, there were the spelltakers: kind of silly, kind of sad. On the other side, there was me.

But then it started changing. The world, or the way I understood it.

The day after Ari broke down in her bedroom after getting

into the Manhattan Ballet, I had a panic attack and couldn't go to school. I thought I was dying. I thought I'd absorbed Ari's misery—Ari, who after that one day, never shed another tear. I was pretty sure my heart was exploding, but I figured my panic would go away as fast as hers did. Faster, because it was only borrowed.

Then I had another panic attack in band when I couldn't hit the note. Then, over the next couple of weeks, I had panic attacks in my car, in the shower, and on the floor of my bedroom. The floor of my bedroom, the floor of my bedroom, the floor of my bedroom again and again and again. I got to know the bedroom floor very well. Just the feel of the scratchy wall-to-wall carpeting could make me start to lose my breath.

I couldn't sleep.

Three days in a row, I stayed in bed until two or three p.m. and my mom called me in sick, but I wasn't sick, I was crying. I cried so much I got dehydrated and fainted. My mom took me to the walk-in clinic, but when I was there I felt fine and looked like myself.

I'd always been prone to sad periods, days of introspection, thinking about things so hard they disassembled and broke into pieces. Markos would call me morose, but he could always cheer me up. This was different.

Nothing was wrong. I was wrong.

I looked up pills online. Sometimes when you're young the pills have the opposite effect—they make you sadder, more likely to kill yourself. I also heard they make you fat, and I was scared to not be me both inside and out. So I didn't tell my mom how bad it got.

I told Ari. Of course I told Ari; we told each other everything. But I probably didn't tell her completely. I never said, "I think about killing myself." I said, "I think about dying," which is totally different because everyone thinks about death sometimes, but not everyone imagines going through with it, picking a belt and beam or a razor and tub.

Not that I thought about that every day. No. Most days I was pretty much fine. I was best with Markos. Pretending was easiest with Markos because I've known him forever, and everything's a show with him anyway. *The Markos Waters Hour.* All I had to do was show up and recite my lines.

It was hard everywhere else. So hard. It hurt to breathe sometimes. My mom took me to an allergist that she couldn't afford because it was out-of-network, but it wasn't allergies or the environment or gluten. It was all in me. My mind wouldn't cooperate. Wouldn't recognize all that was wonderful about being Win Tillman.

In the fall of junior year, this girl Katelyn had come back from summer break beautiful, and looking at her successful spellwork after my panic attacks came on, I started to consider it. Going to a hekamist, that is. I'd barely made it through a week where I thought I was literally drowning and this girl Katelyn—Ari and Diana called her Kay when they started spending time together—tossed her newly shiny hair at me and seemed fine. I asked Ari what she thought about it.

"I guess if it makes her happy," Ari said.

"Everyone should do it if it gives you that rack," Markos said, but I know how to speak Markos, and that actually meant *she's desperate.*

But I was desperate, too.

There weren't that many hekamists left—they were dying off. It had been illegal to join a coven for twenty years. There were probably only ten thousand left in the United States and only the one in Cape Cod, an old lady who'd been there forever. So I was surprised when I went to the hekamist's and the only person in the house was my age.

The girl said her name was Echo, and I liked her right away. Not liked her in a romantic way—those days I couldn't even make it happen with Ari, who I loved—but she seemed kind. On her kitchen table there was a half-eaten apple next to an array of playing cards; I'd interrupted a game of solitaire. There was something normal about that, I thought. Something human.

I sat opposite the solitaire spread. Echo sat across from me. I wasn't very good at noticing my surroundings, but I could tell this place was run-down and barely big enough for one person, let alone a family. The couch separated the kitchen from the living room, sitting crooked in the open space. I remembered that because it seemed like you'd always be tripping over it. I knew about small spaces and furniture that didn't quite fit. I knew about the cheap construction and old carpet that never smelled quite right. Those things made me feel at home.

"Where's the hekamist?" I said in order to stop thinking about anything else.

"Out," she said.

"Oh."

A pause, seconds dripping like a leaky faucet.

"So you'd like a spell." With her fingertips, Echo picked up the apple core and tossed it in the trash. "What's wrong with you?"

I could feel something crack and break in my chest; I was going to start crying again for sure. "I'm . . . sad," I said.

Ridiculous. Such a small, stupid word that in no way touched upon the truth. She should've laughed me out of her tiny apartment.

She didn't. "How sad?"

"Sad enough that I'm sitting here," I said.

That was almost a joke, but still she didn't laugh, and not laughing made me feel like I was doing the right thing, and that she was listening and hearing me in a way I hadn't been listened to or heard in a long time.

"My mother could make you something that would wipe all that away."

"Great," I said. "Great."

"Or I could make it for you." She glanced up at me. Her eyes were ringed with dark makeup that made the whites seem extra white. "And we could keep it between us."

I swallowed. She was too young to be a hekamist, which meant she was illegal. If anyone found out, she and her mom and anyone else in their coven would go to jail.

But what did that matter? I needed a spell.

"It's fine," I said.

My indifference didn't seem to make her feel better. Her frown deepened, as if I wasn't getting something. "My mom charges five thousand dollars for permanent spells." I didn't have anywhere near that much money, but I didn't think about that. "If you wanted to feel okay for a day or week or two, that would be a couple hundred since you'd have to come back every once in a while and re-up, but I won't do that to you."

"Great. Thanks," I said.

"You have five thousand dollars?" she asked, and I sort of half nodded.

"I don't have it on me, but I can get it."

"I want to practice some before I give it to you, make sure it's all right."

"Fine."

"Win, I'm going to be in your brain. You're going to have to be okay with that."

"Okay. I'm okay with it."

She frowned and pulled her long sleeves over her hands, clenching them into fists. "You don't even know me."

I looked at her and the cards laid out on the table in front of her. I looked at the couch sticking into the room, then back at Echo. Even with my dampened emotions I felt for Echo. Something in the way she held herself, or the depth in her eyes. A young hekamist. She shouldn't even exist. How did she go anywhere? Meet anyone? For a stark moment I forgot my own drowning and felt how it would be to live in this house, to live Echo's life.

It would be lonely.

"I trust you," I said.

Finally she let her face relax into an expression of pure sunshine, a strange contrast with the black leather and fierce makeup. "Great. I'm going to fix you, Win Tillman. You're going to be as good as new."

She had me describe how it felt, then, and I tried to tell her. How the world seemed dimmer than it used to be. How when Ari kissed me I didn't feel anything, or I felt only a crushing panic. She made notes and flipped through cupboards and listened, and I found myself—not happy, but relieved.

I told her about faking normal with Markos and my wariness of drugs and my fear that I wasn't strong enough to live through it all.

"You are," she said, and I believed her.

16

KAY

I woke up with sand in my mouth, head resting on my balled-up jacket, Cal Waters's legs tangled with mine. The light was gray and misty, and the waves hitting the shore sounded like someone retching. No, that *was* someone retching—fifty feet down the beach, on her hands and knees in the wet sand. The bonfire had dimmed to a couple of red embers in black.

I extracted myself from Cal and shook out my jacket. He woke up and rubbed his eyes, which only ground more sand into them. Nothing about this seemed romantic or fun anymore.

"Hey, so, goodbye," I said.

"Yeah, okay." He stood up and reached for my hand. To shake it? I clasped mine behind my back, and he dropped his, grinning cheerfully. "Nice to meet you, Kay."

"Same."

He leaned forward faster than I could step away in the sand and kissed me, but both of our mouths were flavored with rotting alcohol, and I could see—because I was too startled to close my eyes—that his eyes weren't closed, either. He was staring at me while our dry tongues and dirty mouths pressed together like pieces of raw bacon.

Definitely not romantic.

But at least he remembered my name. At least I hadn't been so bad at kissing that he couldn't bear to look at me. I waved goodbye to him, already back on the ground and half asleep again, and then made my way up the beach to the parking lot.

A year ago, when I used to hear people talking about the aftermath of some awesome party, I always pictured it brightly lit and hilarious. I never would've pictured this group of sad, tired leftovers. I needed to find Ari and Diana and tell them what happened; maybe that would make it real and exciting. Maybe they'd missed me and had stories of their own to tell.

In the parking lot I saw Diana's car where we left it. Ari was sitting in the driver's seat, staring straight ahead.

"Have fun?" she asked when I opened the passenger-side door. Diana lay curled up in the backseat, asleep.

"Yes," I said, and waited for her to ask more so I could tell her about Cal.

She turned to me, and I could see there were tears on her cheeks, and her normally tough face was quivering. "Something happened," she said.

My Cal story flew out of my head. She hadn't even cried at the funeral. "What's wrong?"

"Diana . . ."

As if Diana sensed she was entering the story, she stirred in her sleep, turning her head toward the front of the car. I gasped. The left side of her face was a solid bruise, purple and black and mottled.

"What happened?" I asked.

"She fell," Ari said.

"Oh my god."

"We were running up the dune. I had this idea. . . . We were going to go to Boston or New York . . . just drive."

"You were going to go without me?"

Ari had the grace to look guilty, although there was a little anger mixed in, too. "It was spur-of-the-moment."

"How would I have gotten home?"

"Didn't seem like you wanted to go home."

So she'd seen me with Cal. It didn't seem like such a fun story to share anymore.

"Still, I would've gone with you guys," I said. "If you're going to go somewhere you should tell me."

"I'm sorry, Kay. It was just a dumb idea. We would've called from the road."

"Calling from the road isn't good enough."

"Why?"

"Because we're friends."

Ari pushed her hair out of her face and wiped at her tears roughly. "I don't know why you're giving me a hard time. We didn't go anywhere, did we? We were heading up the dune, Diana fell, and we stayed here."

I blinked slowly, trying to keep all the muscles of my face

from jumping. They'd planned to leave. They were going to go without telling me. A hundred miles to Boston. Three hundred miles to New York.

But in the end they couldn't leave. Diana had gotten hurt and they stayed.

Unlike Diana's horse camp and Ari moving to New York, the idea to drive to New York or Boston had come on suddenly. In order to keep them here, the spell had to act fast and make sure they didn't even reach the car.

It could've been an accident, but it fit too neatly, and anyway the spell worked through accidents and coincidence. They wanted to leave, but they couldn't. My spell had done that. My spell had hurt Diana.

"Why didn't you go home?" I asked.

"Didn't want to scare Diana's parents."

"And we waited for you," Diana said.

I glanced back at her. She was touching her bruised cheek with a finger and working her jaw silently.

I couldn't believe the spell was that strong.

"Let's go home," I said.

Diana nodded, and Ari started the car.

They had tried, but they couldn't go without me. It was exactly what I'd wanted.

Yes. Exactly what I wanted.

"It'll be okay," I said to them both. "It was an accident."

Of course I didn't want Diana to get hurt, but a part of me was glad that the hekamist was so good at her job, and that the spell was working so well, and that they didn't leave me alone on the beach. It gave me this opportunity to show them who I am. Why they should care. Why we were meant to be friends after all.

17

ARI

"I'm going to be fine, you know," Diana said. We were sitting in Diana's car watching Kay walk up the steps to her house and then wave enthusiastically from behind the inset glass. "To be honest, it was kind of the best bonfire ever."

I shuddered at the thought of Echo demanding her money, and the sound of Diana's scream. "I'm glad you think so."

"Yeah. I got to talk to Markos, and you seemed . . . better."

I rubbed my temple. It felt like a long time ago, the idea that I would run off to New York and tell Diana the truth about Win and everything would be perfectly fine. It wouldn't. I couldn't tell her. What did I imagine she could do—conjure five thousand dollars from nothing?

I made nine dollars an hour selling ice cream at the Sweet Shoppe, twenty hours a week. To earn Echo's money I'd have to work for a year, nonstop, and probably much more when you factored in taxes and school and the fact that the Sweet Shoppe was closed October through April. Or I'd have to use our New

York money, which was the last of my parents' life insurance. But I couldn't use that; I needed it to live on while I danced with the junior corps.

So I had to keep Echo from telling anyone until we left for New York. Which was so obviously impossible the idea squeezed me, like trying to plié in new leather pants.

"Where was Kay all night?" Diana asked.

"Saw her with Cal Waters."

"Like . . . talking?" she asked.

"It looked more like flirting."

"Wow. Seriously?" I nodded, and Diana's eyes narrowed. "You're not going to warn her away from him like you always warn me away from Markos?"

"Cal's the nice one."

Diana gave me a withering look, which must have hurt the bruise on her face, because she winced.

"All right, if it'll make you feel better, I'll make sure she's properly cautioned about getting involved with the Waters boys."

Diana shifted in her seat and raised a hand to her face, but didn't touch the bruise; she held her hand over it like it radiated heat. I backed the car out of Kay's driveway and started for home. "Did you have an okay time, Ari?"

I'd been blackmailed and my best friend had bashed her face in.

In my mind, we ran up the dune again and again. I stumbled over and over; I couldn't find my footing. It was funny at the time. The sand slid and reshaped itself.

Was I holding on to Diana's arm when she fell? Could I have tipped her over? Did I make her as unstable and uncoordinated as I was?

Was she better off without me?

I managed to smile at Diana, though it didn't feel right. My smiles had become as clumsy as the rest of me. I pushed harder, and the effort hurt my cheeks, my teeth, and the very back of my neck. "Sure. Very memorable."

Diana dropped me off and promised to call later. I went to my room and did my exercises like usual, which is to say, I did them terribly.

The only way I was going to get better was to push through it. This was my plan: keep practicing until I could re-teach myself grace.

After that first attempt at ballet the Friday after I'd taken the spell, I had tried to get the side effects reversed. It seemed obvious. Whip up another spell and make it go back to the way it was. Whoever this dead boy was, there was no way he was worth screwing up my career.

So I had gone straight from that disastrous dance class to the hekamist's house. The familiar middle-aged woman with curly gray hair and a foggy look in her eye answered the door.

"I know you," she said.

I blinked. "I was here yesterday," I said.

"Was it yesterday?" She smiled and made a gesture with her hand like she was waving away moths.

"So," I said. "About that spell . . ."

The hekamist leaned against the doorframe. Behind her I could see the crowded living room and a dingy kitchen. I knew I'd been there the day before, but it looked familiar in a distant way, as if I'd only seen photos of it in a book.

"I hope it worked," she said. "No refunds."

"The spell worked. But I can't dance anymore."

"You're a dancer? Oh. How lovely."

"It seems like I'm dancing, like my brain is telling me to move, to be graceful, but my body won't listen." I shifted on my feet. "I fell down in class."

She shrugged. "Some side effects are to be expected. I'm sure I mentioned it."

"This isn't 'some side effects.' I can't do anything I used to be able to do."

"But you've forgotten your dead boyfriend. You feel better."

"I guess. I don't remember how I felt before."

"True, true. So strange, memory spells. When they work, everyone always wonders why they got them." She looked up and down the road behind me, blinking. It occurred to me that she was going crazy. Hekamists lose it when the rest of their coven dies. I'd heard about it, but I didn't know what it looked like until then. She pressed her cheek into the door frame, covering one eye and letting the other one focus in and out slowly. "You're unhappy about your side effects. Hmm. Have you had other spells?"

I wanted to scream with frustration, but instead I gripped

my swollen left wrist and pinched the pain down. "Yes. I had one when I was eight years old. Permanent trauma removal."

"Oh. I see. You didn't say that yesterday." She kept her face smashed into the door frame, still staring at me closely. "Trauma spell. That means memory, too. Boyfriend dead. Memory gone. Two permanent memory spells. Sad, sad, sad, aren't you?"

My wrist throbbed. "My parents—died. In a fire. I saw the house burn down. Apparently I had nightmares."

"A fire. An accident?"

I gritted my teeth and squeezed my toes in my shoes. "Someone broke in. Lit fireworks in the fireplace."

Her mouth dropped open and she moved away from the door frame. "Oh."

"Listen, you have to undo this spell. Please. I'm going to New York in August to study ballet and I can't even—"

"No," she said. "Those memories are gone and there's no way to get them back."

"Fine. Whatever. I don't care about the memories. I want my body to work right. Can you fix that?"

Her mood had shifted. Instead of looking out at the street, she glanced back into her house and shrank away from me. Afraid. "A hekamist could fix you. Add another spell to counteract the side effect. You'd be as graceful as a gazelle. But then that spell comes with its own set of side effects, and then you're up to three permanent spells—very bad. Very risky. Side effects cascading."

I bit my lip. The other girls had talked about spells at the

Summer Institute last year. Rumor had it that one of the prima ballerinas at the Manhattan Ballet had gotten a spell to make her a star, and that was why she was so dull to talk to. Or there was the girl who couldn't nail a double pirouette—kept losing her balance right at the end—and then one day she came in and did fourteen in a row flawlessly. She cried every morning when she woke up because she couldn't remember where she was, but she could dance. Last I heard she was an apprentice at the San Francisco Ballet.

I'd always thought those were selfish spells—shortcuts to greatness. The prima ballerina and the pirouette girl could've practiced and maybe they would've gotten where they needed to go anyway. I couldn't even practice. I looked like a fool. The side effects bent and twisted me. I needed a spell to get me back to normal, to be *me* again.

But would I really be myself if I couldn't remember my own name?

"Not me," the hekamist said, interrupting my thoughts.

"What?"

"Not this hekamist. Silly me, silly me. No no no. I can't. I can't."

"Why not?"

She started to close the door, and I put a hand out to stop her.

She took a deep breath and seemed to gather herself together. "You are a sweet girl. I can tell. And you seemed sad the other day about your dead boyfriend. I think you made the right decision."

No one who knew me would have ever described me as sweet. And I knew I didn't make the right decision.

"No, there's no way. . . . Please. I love dance more than anything."

"*Now* you do." She pushed the door hard against my hand. "Yesterday you loved your boyfriend more. Try to think that you've done yourself a favor."

With a final shove, the door closed. I knocked on it a couple more times, but she didn't come out again.

Even if I decided to risk the compound side effects, she wouldn't do the spell, and she was the only hekamist in town. Plus there was the question of payment—no way another five thousand dollars would show up in the back of my closet. Especially since Echo told me Win had put it there.

So I had to keep practicing.

The morning after the bonfire, July fourth, I bent at the waist and reached for the floor. I used to be able to flatten my whole torso against my legs and wrap my arms around them so that my hands touched the sides of my face. Now, the tips of my fingers barely grazed the carpet. I squeezed my eyes closed and willed myself not to start crying. I had another hour to get through.

I was stuck in this uncooperative body. And Echo was going to tell the truth about Win to everyone I knew unless I figured out a way to stop her.

18

MARKOS

The day after the bonfire I woke up with a hangover beating at my head and an urge in the pit of my stomach to burn down the world. At a certain point during the bonfire, after Diana had hurt herself and then gone off with Ari to recuperate, I'd gotten drunk enough that I'd forgotten Win was gone. I remembered that feeling of security, knowing—but not dwelling on—the fact that my best friend was out there somewhere and any moment he would emerge from the crowd, dump my drink in the sand, and drive me home. But of course he didn't, so I kept drinking. More than the alcohol hangover there was the hangover from forgetting. I was paying for my lobotomized night.

I could hear my brothers gathering in the kitchen before I got out of bed. My back clenched, but I went down the stairs like usual, ready to be the usual Markos.

"You look *rough*," Dev declared as soon as he saw me.

"Yikes!" Cal echoed.

"Oh, Markos," my mom said, and hurried to pour me an orange juice.

Brian leaned back in his chair, arms crossed over his uniformed chest. "You make it hard for me not to arrest you sometimes, dude."

"Whatever." I opened the cabinet door and stared at the boxes of cereal.

"Don't 'whatever' me. If someone else at the party had called the cops on you, I would've been in big trouble."

"No one did, did they?"

Dev spoke through a mouthful of scrambled eggs. "If you're going to binge, at least be a funny drunk."

Cal cackled. "You told me I was a phony, selfish dickpocket. What's a dickpocket?"

"Like a pocket for your dick, duh," Dev said.

"What, like a pouch? Or a sock with a pocket sewn on it?"

"Boys . . ." Mom murmured from her seat by the window. She didn't care what we said, but occasionally felt the need to remind us that she could hear that we were saying it.

"Regardless," Brian said. "Maybe try to have a little self-control next time."

I slammed the cabinet door shut. No one even flinched. They all blinked at me—Brian, Dev, Cal, and Mom—as if I hadn't done anything at all.

It didn't matter what I did. I would always be the youngest, the baby, the fuckup. They didn't see me when they looked at me; they saw a Markos-shaped animatron. I could slam doors and scream and tear the place apart and they'd barely look up from their cornflakes.

"I'm going out," I said, and left before anyone could stop me.

I called Diana North. We hadn't hooked up, so I didn't have to wait a few days. I hadn't been an ass to her, which meant she actually answered the phone. She met me at the bagel place with a patio out back, and we bought bagels and sat at a table in the sun. The light was too bright and hot—it was past noon already and my head ached—but I did not suggest moving to the shade. The hurt was what I deserved for forgetting Win the night before.

She looked prim in a dress with a collar, though her long, thick hair was still a color red not found in nature and the bruise on the side of her face looked both tender and angry. She ate her bagel in tiny bites, wincing when she had to move her right cheek, and stared at me with her bloodshot eyes when she thought I wasn't looking.

"How's your face?"

She shrugged, which made her wince again. "Nothing broken."

"You could tell people you got into a fight."

She snorted. "Yeah. Very believable. Did you have a good time the rest of the night?"

"Fine," I said. I didn't mention my brothers, and I didn't say the thing about forgetting Win was dead, but I must've been thinking about Win because of what came out of my mouth next. "Usually Win would come by with coffee and donuts. On July fourth, I mean."

Diana scraped cream cheese off her bagel carefully. "Usually

Ari would sleep over. I guess we sort of did because we slept in my car. My mom's car."

"What?"

"I didn't feel like going home."

"Why not?"

Diana spoke to the bagel. "My mom kind of freaked out over my face. Knew she would."

"It's not like it was your fault."

"She's super protective. I didn't want to have to hear the whole routine: should've been more careful, should've watched where I was going, shouldn't have been running—or at a party— to begin with."

"That's crazy. Tell her to shut her face."

Diana looked up from the bagel, her good eye wide. "I could never do that."

"Why not?"

"You tell your mother to shut her face?"

I thought of my mother, who's been distracted most of my life. By the store, by one of my brothers, by a series of disasters— illnesses, injuries, money troubles. But when it was your turn to have a crisis, she would claw anyone's eyes out for you. If I came home with a bashed-in face, she'd toss me a bag of peas and demand to know who it was she should be suing for damages. "My mother doesn't think anything's our fault."

"You guys are saints, then?"

"Yup."

"My mom's okay. She's always looked after me—too much,

probably. Trying to keep me safe and happy always. Between her and Ari—sometimes it felt like they were living my life for me." She stopped talking and flushed.

I thought of my brothers with their endless reams of advice, and the expectation that I would be exactly like them. "But you don't feel that way anymore?"

"No," Diana said, seemingly surprising herself. "No, I don't. Actually—it's because of Win. Ari started spending so much time with him . . . I was on my own."

I swallowed half a bagel in three bites. "What's up with Ari anyway?"

Diana looked at me out of the corner of her eye, like I was setting a trap. "I don't know. She doesn't talk to me much anymore."

"Well, she hasn't talked to me much either."

"Really? But you were such good friends."

I shifted on my metal seat. It burned the backs of my knees. "She was Win's girlfriend."

"Come on. You were friends, too."

"Yeah, but what's the point now? We're going to sit around and share our feelings?"

Diana picked at her bagel. "It might be good for both of you to talk about all this stuff."

"Doesn't seem fucking likely. Ari having a heart-to-heart? Come on. That's one good thing about her—she's not a sappy romantic. Thank god. If she'd been needy with Win he'd have been needy right back and it would have been unbearable. He was so—" I threw the rest of my bagel down onto my plate. "He was so damn nice all the time."

Diana didn't look startled, but I felt strange—like on the beach: heart racing, breathing coming in weird gasps. I made myself inhale and hold it for five seconds before opening my mouth again.

"Do you think about what happens when you die?" I asked.

"Yes."

"Not like heaven or angels or whatever—that's stupid—but the end of everything. How nothing matters after that." *How nothing matters now*, I wanted to say, but I could tell that would bring on the weird breathing, and she wouldn't understand anyway.

"I think about how upset my parents would be," Diana started to say, "and my little cousins, and Ari. She's been through enough, with the fire, and then Win. But you know—" She stopped suddenly, looked at me like she was remembering who I was, then continued more slowly. "It doesn't make me sad to think about it. It's, like, I almost want to see it, because then I'd know what people really thought of me. If they really cared."

That should've made me angry, because of Win. Because Win didn't ask to die, and we all really did go through that torture, and it wasn't part of some selfish, self-centered fantasy. But I wasn't angry. I wasn't panicking anymore, either.

"That's messed up," I said, and smiled, and Diana drank that smile up like it was sunlight and she was a fucking flower. Even the bruise on her cheek seemed to shrink in her glow.

That was a nice feeling. I thought about the night before and how I didn't want to kiss her and it seemed stupid now. Why shouldn't I? Seeing her in the bright morning light of the bagel shop backyard, seeing how her happiness shone, I figured if that made me feel okay, there was no harm in making her more happy. We were both getting something out of it—so what if it wasn't the same thing?

We left the bagel place and started walking down the street toward the beach. There were tourists everywhere; it was the height of the season, the biggest holiday of the year on the Cape. We passed my family's hardware store and I turned away from the windows. There wasn't much chance of anyone inside seeing me through the mounds of junk on display, but I didn't want to risk making eye contact with my brothers or mother.

"Ari's afraid to go in there," Diana said, nodding at the store.

"It's a hardware store."

"Yeah, but she hates it. Says the walls crowd in on her."

"Maybe it's me."

She elbowed me jokingly. I hadn't ever thought that mousy Diana North, the one who laughed at Ari's jokes and wore polos buttoned all the way up to her neck, would be capable of joking with me.

"I'm telling you," she said. "If anyone could talk to her, you could."

"Maybe," I said, and smiled again.

The look on her face was so perfect—surprised and pleased—that I laughed, and she started turning red all around the black and blue of the bruise. "I'm not laughing at you," I said. "I'm laughing because . . ."

But I didn't know why I was laughing. Because I was alive? Was that the big joke?

Or was it funny—surprising—to remember that I scared people or made them glow or whatever? In my house I felt sometimes like a broken TV: people looked at me then turned away because I was always the same. The same mistakes, the same disappointments. Nothing I did made a dent to them.

Not like with Diana. Everything I did with her was new, everything mattered. She didn't expect me to be one way or another, and what I did affected what she did in return.

With her I could put a dent in the world.

19

WIN

Echo said she needed to practice the spell a couple times to be sure but she'd let me know when it was ready. I said I'd work on the money, and I fully intended to work on it immediately, but it's a funny thing about being depressed: it's pretty fucking hard to make and follow through with a plan.

I had no money. My mom had no money. My sister, Kara, was eleven—and she had no money. Ari had enough savings from her parents' life insurance to get her life started in New York, which was one of those almost invisible but huge differences between us, and though she might've given me the money, I couldn't ask. It was her parents' life insurance, for one thing. And she and her aunt needed that money. I couldn't take New York away from her. Nice Win, upstanding boyfriend, Good Guy, definitely couldn't do that. Asking for it would mean admitting I wasn't Nice Win Good Guy anymore. Plus, if she knew what I was doing she would blame herself, and seeing that on her face would make me feel worse.

I loved her. But it was like loving someone through six feet of bulletproof glass. She was muffled, distant.

That left Markos. Markos himself had no money, and his mom had constant problems paying suppliers for the hardware store and covering their mortgage, but at least she had the store—people came in every day and handed them cash. I didn't know how to ask him for it, though.

Knowing that the spell was on its way, I got my appetite back some, and I even managed to play a few baseball games without faking knee pain and sitting in the dugout.

It probably sounds strange that I was counting on the spell but made no attempt to figure out how to pay for it. I wasn't planning on ripping Echo off or anything. I wanted to pay my debt. It's just—I wanted to get better more. I wanted out of the hole.

It was a lot like a hole. Or more like a well, maybe: dark and claustrophobic, with the fingernail marks along the walls that the other prisoners made as they attempted their escapes. I'd look up and see a pinprick of light, but then I'd blink and the darkness would come in again; I'd start thinking about how my mom couldn't catch a break and Kara would eventually get bitter and Ari probably didn't really love me and Markos thought of me as an obligation, and I didn't even blame them for any of it, because I knew I deserved to be treated like shit. Because I'd never done anything to make the world a better place, I wasn't an upstanding moral citizen by any stretch of the imagination, and the fact that I couldn't enjoy my life like a normal person probably meant I was an evolutionary mistake that needed to be stomped out.

The world belonged to the happy people, the carefree souls. I didn't begrudge them that. I only wanted out of their way.

One of the things that had originally drawn me to Ari was that she wasn't one of the carefree souls. This was before I fell down the well for real, when I could still pretty much fake my way through a day, even the dark ones. We had been in school together forever, but I feel like I really noticed her for the first time in trig, which we both had first period sophomore year.

She sat so straight, like the line of her hair down her back. That type of posture could read snobby to some people, but I'd been going to school with her for a long time, and I knew her history. The tragedy of her parents, killed in a fire; the fact that she lived with her aunt, who had tattoos and worked in a coffee shop; and that she was a dancer, and good at it.

She'd lived through something *bad*. I didn't pity her for it; it made me respect her.

I started talking to her before and after class, and we became friends. I couldn't tell you how. The mechanics of how a person becomes friends, especially with a girl: it all takes place in gestures and moments and looks and jokes, and then before you know it you're always at a person's locker in the morning or at their house after school and plans on Friday are assumed, as are Christmas gifts and bad days and hurt feelings and last-minute rides to school. Impossible to track or re-create. We were friends for a year, and then we were together. It happened.

We were doing homework in her kitchen near the end of sophomore year, right before we started dating, when I was trying so hard to think of anything but how much I wanted to kiss her, so I asked her if she thought her spell was worth it.

"Yes," she said without hesitating. "You know how people say 'I can't imagine how awful that must have been?' Well, now I can say that, too. I can't imagine it."

For some reason I didn't want to let go of the topic, even though I could tell Ari had said pretty much all she wanted to say about it. She rubbed her wrist with her thumb, frowning, and stared at her trig book intently. "Who do you think did it?"

"A tourist."

"Why?"

"They found the remnants of fireworks in the grate. That always made me think of someone on vacation—someone here to have a good time. So what I think is that a tourist kid broke in, probably high, set off some fireworks, and it got out of control." She said it matter-of-factly, as if reading a news report.

"So not on purpose."

She shook her head slowly. "I can't imagine that someone would do this on purpose. I just . . . can't believe that."

"If you believe it was a tourist, how can you even look at them now?"

"Kind of hard to avoid them."

"They think they own everything." They did own everything, at least compared to me. They could take vacations.

My mom drove me and Kara to Rhode Island and we took

the ferry to Block Island for the day once when I was eleven. It seemed a lot like home: tourists everywhere, beaches, seafood. She bought us ice cream. I felt, even more than usual, like I was supposed to be having a good time, and I was mad at myself for not feeling it. But that day I wasn't the only one; none of our smiles stayed fixed.

Ari hadn't said anything, and I wondered if I'd gone too far. Finally she shook her head. "I can't get angry at every tourist. I wouldn't be able to function. But I can't help hating them all a little, too."

"And if they caught the guy? Would you feel better?"

"No." She exhaled so hard it fluttered the pages of her notebook. "Besides, it's been almost eight years. He's long gone by now. I doubt he even knows the house burned down. It wasn't like he did it maliciously."

I felt my heart clunk down to my gut as I realized what she was saying. She'd given up hope.

Something inside of me warmed to that bleakness. Drew closer. Sitting next to her at the table, I actually felt the room get smaller, and the two of us slide together like water pouring down a drain.

"I'm sorry," I said. "I don't know why I'm asking about all this stuff."

"It's okay," she said. She even smiled a little bit. "I'd rather you ask than never ever mention it like it was some sort of horrible secret. I'm fine now."

"Right," I said. "Of course you are."

"I have Jess and Diana and dancing—and I have you, too."
She said the last bit quickly, like she wasn't sure if she was going
too far, claiming me as hers.

She wasn't going too far. I felt good—great, even—being
in the list of things she lived for, because I felt the same way
without realizing it: she fit into a hole in my life I hadn't known
I'd had until then. That was the moment I decided I wasn't just
going to think about kissing her, but I was actually going to do it.
I didn't end up doing it for a little while longer, but the decision
could be traced back to that conversation.

"I'm fine," she said again, and elbowed me with her sharp,
precise elbow.

But I didn't believe her. She wasn't fine, and neither was I.

20

KAY

We were not okay. After the bonfire, if I didn't hear from Ari or Diana for a day, I'd start to get panicky—picturing Diana's bruise or worse. That big black shadowy bird hovered over my head daily, threatening to swoop down and carry my friends away. I had to be on constant alert so that no one would get hurt again.

Now that I knew that they'd considered leaving town without me, I became convinced that they were trying to leave all the time. I pictured worse and worse things happening to them. It wasn't enough that we spent time together. They really, really had to *want* to be around me, and not in some hypothetical future time. This moment. Before they could get any more great ideas.

But something was broken. We sat around at the ice cream shop where Ari worked or someone's basement or Ari's aunt's coffee shop and didn't talk to each other.

The thing was, I didn't think Ari and Diana were talking to each other, either. Ari stayed silent and distant, gone someplace far away behind her eyes. Diana only smiled when she thought the rest of us weren't looking, and spent the rest of the time touching her bruised face with a fingertip and wincing. No one said anything. It wasn't fun.

I kept trying, though.

"You still look beautiful," I told Diana. "And it's healing fast."

We were in Ari's basement, the least finished of all our basements, with not even a tiny high-up window to let the summer sun in. Ari lay on her back behind the sofa trying to stretch her leg over her head, and Diana looked at her face through her phone's camera. She *was* still beautiful. She had her red hair and clear skin and big eyes. She didn't respond to me, though, and didn't put down the phone.

If there was one thing I'd learned from Mina's illness, it was proper bedside manner. So I'd been taking care of Diana—bringing her magazines and candy and occasionally one-sided conversations, so she could rest and recover.

I tried to give her a couple of Tylenol and a water bottle from my bag. She waved them away. "I'm fine."

"You know, that bruise, if it had been on me, would've made me look like a zombie. But it's so obvious how pretty you are, it doesn't matter about all that."

"Okay, okay," Diana said, finally putting down the phone. "I get it."

"I was only saying—"

"And you've said it. I don't need to hear it anymore."

Ari spoke up from the floor. "Kay can tell me I'm beautiful if she really must."

"You *are* beautiful. Like, seriously."

Ari let out a single sharp *ha*. "You say that to everyone. You're devaluing your compliments."

"I mean it!" They both laughed then, more genuinely, until laughing hurt Diana's face and she went back to pressing it slowly and carefully with a finger.

"Oh, I forgot to say. I got us tickets to *Wicked* in Boston!" I said.

Neither of them responded.

"I thought because you guys mentioned wanting to go to Boston at the bonfire . . ."

"That wasn't really what we had in mind," Ari said, sitting up and cracking her back. "But thank you, Kay."

"We'll go, though, right? I mean my parents got us these tickets, and I don't think they're refundable. . . ."

Diana glanced at Ari, who shrugged. "I don't know," Diana said. "I've been busy."

"Busy with what?"

She ignored the question. "But maybe there's some guy you want to ask . . . like Cal Waters. . . ."

"To go see *Wicked*?"

Ari hugged a leg to her cheek. "I think that's Diana's way of asking if you're going to see Cal again."

"Oh." I hadn't thought of him much since the bonfire. "I don't know if that's a thing that's going to be an ongoing, you know, thing."

"That's good," Ari said. "I mean, he's old. And he's a Waters.

I love Markos but you know what they're like."

"He's only like twenty, and he seemed pretty nice."

"Yeah, exactly," Ari said. "They start nice. But they'll get you to like them and then ditch you. I don't want you getting your hopes up."

"I don't have any hopes," I said, but I could feel an inner part of me shrinking and twisting under Ari's unasked-for advice. Had I put hopes into Cal? Did he think I was pining over him? Did he brag to his brothers about hooking up with me? If I didn't want to date him, did that make me a slut?

Is that what Ari was trying to say, pretending to be concerned?

"The Waters boys make terrible boyfriends," she was saying. "I've seen it enough times to know."

"I never said I wanted him to be my boyfriend."

"Good."

We went back to not speaking. And slowly, an inner tide rising, I filled up with anger. There was no good reason why I shouldn't date Cal. Twenty wasn't that old. What was wrong with me that Ari thought I needed to be warned away? I didn't believe that because he was a Waters and I was me, there was no chance.

In fact, I knew there was a chance. In the pocket of my winter coat, there was a partially smushed chocolate chip cookie that could prove to Ari and Diana that I wasn't just some girl who Cal took advantage of. They were wrong about me; I only had to show them.

The next day, I wrapped the cookie in blue cellophane and a green ribbon and walked to Waters Hardware. Cal was manning the cash register, and I waited as a couple bought bug spray and aloe. He smiled at them even as they fumbled through endless fanny-pack pockets to find correct change. He smiled at me when he saw me. I was used to Ari and Diana and Mina, who almost never smiled nowadays. Cal's cheerfulness seemed otherworldly.

"Hey," he said. "Kay, right? What's up?"

"Nothing much," I said. "I was just around and thought I'd stop and say hi."

"Oh. Hi."

"I, uh—" I held the cookie out and stared at it, willing it to explain itself. "This is a cookie. Chocolate chip."

His smile receded. "Did you . . . make me a cookie?"

"What? No!" I pretended to laugh and tossed my hair. "It's a good luck spell. Lasts a day. My grandma sent it to me. But my hekamist said I'm not supposed to take more spells because of side effects, so it was going to go to waste, and so when I passed by, I don't know—I thought you might appreciate it. I, uh—I had a good time at the bonfire."

"Oh. Thanks," he said, and took the cookie out of my hand. I think he did it more to shut me up than because he really wanted it.

A man got into line behind me with a bunch of fishing gear. I saw Cal's smile re-affix itself as he glanced over my shoulder.

"So I guess I'll see you around," he said.

"Yeah. For sure. I'm around."

"Thanks again for the spell."

"No problem." I didn't move from my place in line. He hadn't eaten it yet; I couldn't risk him giving it to one of his brothers or a customer or anyone else. "You should eat it."

"What—now? Shouldn't I save it for a special—"

"No!" I said. "That's cheating, to take it when you know you need it. It's more fun if you take it on a random day. Like today."

"Okay." He glanced at the fisherman behind me, who sighed and shifted on his feet. Cal's smile didn't waver; he pulled the ribbon and stuffed the cookie in his mouth. "Mmm. Thanks."

I snatched the cellophane and crumbs out of his hand before they were eaten by rats and I became the Pied Piper of Cape Cod. "Great! I'll throw this away for you. Bye!"

Before I reached the door, he'd already started a conversation about fishing spots with the next customer. And for two and a half days after that, I heard nothing.

Then Ari and Diana and I went to see *Wicked* in Boston. I didn't even think about the one-hundred-plus miles we were traveling; I was too relieved that they'd agreed to come after all.

During intermission, while Ari and Diana sat silently on either side of me, I checked my phone. There was a text from Cal Waters.

Thinking of you

Shit. I'd left him behind. Too far away.

Heyyyy! What are you up to? I typed, hoping that sounded more casual than it felt.

Ditched work and took the ferry to Boston. We should hang out when I get back.

When I get back. He didn't know I was in Boston. The spell had drawn him here unconsciously.

For a second I allowed myself to forget about the hook, and felt what it was like to have a boy text you that he wanted to hang out. I warmed to it. And the words blossomed and grew.

It was only a text, I knew that. But it reminded me of the early days of becoming friends with Diana and Ari, when we were natural and fun together, rather than silent and weird and awkward. Back then, every time we hung out, it was a new adventure.

Full of possibility.

21

ARI

A week and a half after the bonfire, with less than three weeks left until we moved to New York on August first, I drove to the beach and walked to approximately the spot where Echo had found me.

I sat in the sand for the whole ninety minutes of "class," which is where Jess thought I was. I watched the tourists and the seagulls, trying to think of a way to get Echo to leave me alone, forcing myself not to turn and look at the spot where Diana fell, imagining what was going to happen to me the longer I did nothing.

1. I would never work through my side effects.
2. Echo would tell everyone I had the memory of Win erased.
3. They would be furious/disappointed/repulsed.
4. Dancing would be impossible forever.
5. I might never get out of Cape Cod.

6. If I did get out, the Manhattan Ballet would kick me out of the junior corps on the first day.

7. I'd die here, having accomplished nothing and been nowhere.

None of these were worries I could share with Dr. Pitts, the therapist that Jess made me go to. So when I sat down for our appointment, I disappointed her again. Not opening up. Not sharing. Not showing the proper sorrow. I tried to push through the session so I could go back to attempting to dance again, but I had to say something to pass the time.

"I'm not that girl anymore," I said. The vaguer and more apocalyptic, the easier it was to lie.

"What do you mean?"

Uh-oh. "I mean . . . I feel different. There's the me before Win died, and the me now."

"Different how?"

Sometimes I thought Dr. Pitts was quizzing me. That she suspected I wasn't right. "In ballet, some girls can't recover after they get their period. It's not just that they have boobs and they're taller. They get scared. Their brain won't let them jump anymore, or they start to doubt their balance."

"Did that happen to you?"

"No." I rolled my eyes. "It's a metaphor."

"How so?"

I blinked. "Well. I guess that some people react to a loss or a change or whatever by freaking out and losing themselves in grief. And then some people—like me—manage to be different but not let it change them completely." That sounded good.

"So you don't think losing people changes you?" She tapped her legal pad with her fancy silver pen. "Grief over loss—it's something only weak people succumb to?"

I shrugged.

Dr. Pitts leaned forward. She was wrapped in scarves like a mummy; I didn't even know if she was fat or thin, because she always wore them, along with huge flowing pants and boots that went up who knows how high because of all the fabric engulfing them. "Grief is not a weakness, Ari. It's not something to push down and power through. Yes, it can change you, but that's what people do—change, grow. It concerns me that you're in denial."

I felt my face flush. "I'm not in denial. I . . . miss Win."

"Really?"

"Yes, really! Maybe I'm not, like, prostrate every day, but that doesn't mean I'm not sad. What kind of therapist are you, insisting I act as sad as everyone else in the world? That's sick. I'm dealing with this in my own way."

Dr. Pitts looked satisfied for a few seconds, which was extra infuriating. "Anger is good," she said, and it made me want to upend a coffee table and storm out. If her plan was to get me angry, bravo. "Tell me about your parents."

"No," I snapped before I could control myself.

"Why not?"

"They died almost ten years ago. It's not relevant."

"You lost them. You lost Win. It makes sense to be angry."

"I'm angry at *you*, not because people keep dying!"

She nodded, as if people said they were angry with her all the time. Maybe they were.

I forced myself to lean back on the couch. In my mind, I moved smoothly, and the motion suggested I was relaxed, at home, unbothered. But I knew very well that to Dr. Pitts I probably looked as jerky and angry as I actually felt.

I thought of my new tapes. Every morning I got up, turned on the camera, put on some music, and attempted a simple sequence of steps: something from a showcase; an audition piece from the Institute; even the chorus girl choreography from last year's musical. I remembered them all perfectly. In my head, I performed them perfectly, too.

I forced myself to go through each and every motion, even though I tripped and fell, even though I knew what the camera would show. Me, making a mockery of ballet. Me, like one of those girls who lose their nerve after puberty, except a thousand times worse, since I had the nerve—I just didn't have the control.

In dance, you have to feel the music in order to express it. I used to be able to summon the love, fear, anger, joy, or whatever else the piece demanded. The music brought the feeling forward, an alchemical process in my mind transformed that feeling into steps and motion, and then when you watched me, you felt it, too.

Now, I could think that I was feeling love, fear, anger, joy, or whatever, but my brain wouldn't transform those feelings into expressions and gestures. I'd lost the connection.

Adjusting my seat on Dr. Pitts's couch, I struggled to keep my face neutral, as if I chose to flail on her couch for no reason.

It occurred to me that if I didn't find a way to stop Echo from telling, I wouldn't have to go to therapy anymore, because Echo would spill the beans and Dr. Pitts wouldn't expect me to be grief-stricken and tortured over Win anymore. That would be nice. But that would perhaps be the only nice thing.

"What's the point?" I asked. I meant what's the point of making me angry, but Dr. Pitts didn't hear it that way.

"The point is that there will always be grief, disappointments, tragedy. The point is that you have to learn to deal with them, so they don't derail your life. The point is letting go of fear. You refuse to talk about your parents. You've managed to tell me practically nothing about Win. But I drive by the spot on the road where he crashed and there are notes, signs, remembrances. What's the difference between all those people and you?"

"They didn't know him. Not really."

"But you did. I don't want you to go leave a teddy bear in the pile, but I want you to think about why all those people chose to honor Win like that. They could've left the road alone, but they didn't. They were compelled to mark the spot."

They wanted to remember him, of course. That was what she was getting at. As much as she drove me crazy, sometimes I left her office convinced. Only it wasn't stubbornness or fear keeping me from being a model patient, it was Old Ari, screwing things up yet again.

Back in my car after the session ended, I asked myself again what the point was. Unless I discovered another surprise stash of money, it was all moot. All the lying, the sneaking off to "ballet," the practiced sad face, Dr. Pitts's questions, all of it—pointless.

Old Ari stole from her dead boyfriend, and now I was the one who had to pay it back. It was my offering to Win's roadside memorial. I couldn't feel grief, so I gave the money instead.

I started the car, but instead of driving to the Sweet Shoppe, where my shift began at noon, I drove to Waters Hardware to talk to Markos Waters.

22

MARKOS

Wednesday was the first day in a long time that I didn't wake up scowling. It wasn't like there were suddenly birds tweeting and grass growing and love transforming my heart or any of that garbage. I just felt . . . better. For the first time since Win died. Like instead of being buried alive in shit, I was suspended weightless in some nicer substance. It was easier to breathe.

I'd seen Diana every day since the bonfire. I didn't even care that she probably thought I was in love with her. She never said anything weird about it. I could call her or show up at her house because it felt right and was what I wanted to do.

I still hadn't tried to get anywhere with her, though I thought about it sometimes. I considered leaning over and kissing her in the middle of a sentence, or touching under her shirt while we were watching TV. I could've done it. She never gave me any sign that she wouldn't be totally into it. But the fact that I *could* do it kept the idea banked, ready to use should I ever really need it.

It wasn't like with some girls who made you look at them

and expected you to want them and who were only listening because they thought that's what you wanted. Diana listened because she wanted to hear what I said. She let things surprise her, instead of greeting each new moment with a sneer.

In the past, I'd only ever seen her as Ari's shadow. She sat silently next to Ari at lunch, or faded away when Win and I would pick up Ari at her locker. She wasn't funny like Ari, or confident, and that made it seem like she had nothing going on. At least nothing that would be worth seeking out.

But she seemed different now. It was like she said: with Ari otherwise occupied, she had to do something. Be someone. She still wasn't particularly funny or confident, not when compared to Ari or other girls. But it turns out there are lots of other things you can be besides funny and confident. Like . . . compassionate, I guess is the social-worker word for it. Thoughtful not as in "nice" but as in *thought*-ful, full of thoughts. Nonlobotomized.

When I was around her, I didn't have to be together and cool and Waters-ish and okay. And because there was no expectation to be happy, I managed to feel better anyway.

So Wednesday I felt as good as it was possible for a nonlobotomized person to feel—not that my family noticed. They crowded around the kitchen table for breakfast like they always did, despite the fact that Brian and Dev didn't even live there anymore.

"Sweep up the woodshop today, all right, Markos?" my mom asked. She had her big accounting ledger out and was erasing something furiously. We'd all tried to convince her to computerize her accounts, but she clung to the ledger, wouldn't let any of the rest of us touch it.

"Where've you been, anyway?" Brian asked.

"Asleep in my room."

Brian rolled his eyes, and Dev flicked a Cheerio at my face. "Been doing something in his room, that's for sure."

"Oh! Markos has a girlfriend," Cal said. "I saw them walking together by Junior's Auto."

"Oooh, who is she? Hot?" Dev asked.

"Not bad. Her name's Diana North. Crazy red hair."

"Fiery," Dev said.

"She's in his year, I think," Cal said. "Friends with Ari Madrigal."

They barely paused at Ari's name, just long enough to think of Win—Win and Ari, Ari and Win—and then hurriedly covered up the thought with more talk.

"Bring her over, Markos, I want to meet her," Mom said.

"It's not like that."

Mom frowned. "What's it like, then?"

"You embarrassed of us?"

"Afraid we're going to steal her away?"

"Friendly advice," Brian said, which was practically a catchphrase for him. "Bring her over, don't bring her over, but don't get too committed going into senior year. You're going to want all your options open."

"You're too young to commit to anything, is what Brian means," Mom said, and Brian shrugged in semi-agreement.

"Still, bring her around," Dev said. "Once Markos gives her up, maybe she'll want to go out with me."

"You're not her type," I said, and Dev laughed. "Besides, we're just friends."

The whole table turned and looked at me. I shouldn't have said anything. Better for them to think I was hooking up than to wonder *What's wrong with Markos now?* I could see them gearing up to ask questions I didn't want to answer, and so I got up before they could open their mouths.

"I'm going to sweep the woodshop."

As soon as I was outside I had the urge to find Diana and complain about them. I didn't think she'd understand, and she wouldn't like that they talked about her, and anyway she was babysitting all day and I had shit to do, so the idea faded.

I had an imaginary conversation with myself instead, letting my mind wander as I walked into town.

—I hate my family.

—You don't hate them.

—I hate that they think they know me.

—Don't they?

—No! They think I'm exactly like them but younger. Like I *am* them when they were younger. Dev sometimes forgets I don't play water polo, you know? Because he did.

—They love you.

—Yeah. As long as I don't embarrass them.

—What would embarrass them?

—Not being a real Waters man.

—What does that mean?

—Not being cool. Getting too drunk at the bonfire. My failed Homecoming prank. Everything I do.

—What else?

—Diana. No. I don't know. Maybe. She's not what they're used to.

—You're not giving them enough credit.

I stopped walking. Leaned over. Put hands on my knees. Gulped air. Felt the ground tilt under my feet. A normal block, vacation rentals on all sides, no one out yet because it was too early in the morning for tourists.

In my head, for a second, I wasn't talking to myself. All I could hear was Win.

Win had loved my brothers. And they loved him, too—not that we ever talked about Win since he died. Not that we talked about anything real at all. Sometimes the three of them and Mom talked about Dad, but it was always the same carefully preserved stories, and I didn't remember any of them. Win, we ignored. If I had died instead of Win, I bet they would've been happy to share stories about me with Win all day long. But there was something about me that made them shut their mouths.

When I could move again, I stopped thinking of anything at all and ran the rest of the way to Waters Hardware. In the back of the store, there was a full woodshop with all the carpentry and other manly gadgets anyone could ever want. It's my understanding that my dad opened the hardware store so he could make himself this woodshop.

I ducked past rows and rows of junk and unlocked the shop's tiny, almost hidden door. I swept up quickly—Mom would never notice the difference—and decided to weld some leftover pipe into a bong, even though I'm not supposed to use the welder on my own. They even locked it up in a corner cage in the shop, as if I didn't know exactly where they kept the key on a hook by the woodshop door. Welding took up all my concentration, so I made five more—there's always a market for drug paraphernalia, as long as Brian didn't find it—and the hours went by, until I saw Ari Madrigal in the shop's closed-circuit camera bank.

Since the store was such a crowded, confusing labyrinth, there was a real chance someone could walk off with half the inventory without any of us noticing. But instead of cleaning it up and organizing it—because god forbid the Waters clan attempt anything that ambitious—we installed more and more cameras. They peeked around all the many corners and into each of the several dead ends. A flat-screen monitor displayed a grid with all the angles.

Ari wandered from aisle to aisle, sometimes in circles, looking around with a pathetic expression on her face. I smiled. She'd been here countless times, but she could never seem to figure it out. No way she'd find me without some help. I flipped on the intercom. "Right at the sandpaper." She jumped, stumbled, but made the right. "The door's to the left of the paint chips."

She hopped from box to box on the monitor and a few seconds later she was standing in person in the doorway to the shop. My good mood from the morning must've been stronger than I thought because I was glad to see her. It didn't hurt to look at her, to be reminded of Win, because I was already thinking of Win. Instead, it was like an old friend who I hadn't seen in ages stopping by.

Which she was, actually. Maybe Diana was right and I should've been talking to her this whole time.

Thinking of Diana, though, my stomach sank. Ari had to be there because of all the time I'd been spending with Diana. I had been repeatedly and emphatically warned away from Diana more times than I could count, and I didn't care to get into the same discussion again.

So I took my time as I switched off the welder and pushed it back into its cage, clanging the chain link door shut behind it and locking it. Then I flipped up my visor and tossed the last bong onto the floor with the others. She flinched at the sound.

I remembered what Diana said about Ari being scared to come into the store. I figured only Diana herself would make her do it.

"Ari Madrigal," I said, drawing it out. "The fuck are you doing here?"

She looked around the shop, gaze lingering on the bongs and the mess I'd made. Her ultrastraight hair, normally so razor-edged, had gotten raggedy at the ends, and she held one wrist with the other as if she was taking her own pulse. She was still pretty in that small, delicate, deceptive way, but I never understood what it was that made Win so crazy about her. One time I saw her point her foot all the way over her head, so maybe it was a ballet thing.

"Hello to you, too, Markos," she said pleasantly.

"Where've you been?"

"Oh, everywhere. I'm a social butterfly."

"Is that right?"

"Yeah, and I've taken up knitting. I'm fabricating doghouses for homeless dogs."

"Nice to see you working for the less fortunate."

"It's an important charity. They're doing such vital work in the area of knitted domesticated animal enclosures." She shifted on the balls of her feet. "I've been meaning to call."

"Bullshit."

"Well. You could've called me."

"Why? So you could recruit me to knit?" She half shrugged. I pressed on. "Or so we could cry together? I dunno, you made it pretty clear at the funeral you weren't into talking about Win, but you know, the knitting sounds great, go ahead and sign me up for six." I yawned, stretching my hands over my head. "Why are you here, Ari?"

She straightened her shoulders, which was odd because she usually didn't need to. I prepared myself. *Stay away from Diana. Stop messing with her head. What's your evil plan?* But there was nothing she could make me do. I was ready. I was reminded of my brothers giving me advice at breakfast: They thought they knew what was going on, and they gave advice to control me. But they didn't and they couldn't.

"I need to borrow five thousand dollars," she said finally.

All the air *whooshed* out of me, but the next second I was back, mental guard in place. "Ha ha," I said. "Those dogs need a lot of yarn."

"I'm not joking. I need it. I'm sorry to ask you, but I didn't know who else—"

"I'm not a bank," I said.

"I know. But you have the, uh, pipe sideline—and the store—"

"It's my mom's store. What the hell do you need five thousand dollars for?"

"I can't tell you."

"That worked for Win, but it won't work for you."

Her forehead crinkled. "What do you mean it—oh. He got it from you." She rubbed her eyes with the palms of her hands. "Shit."

Of course Ari knew about Win's borrowed cash. I'd thought I was the only one he told, but that was stupid of me. "He didn't tell you where the money came from?"

She hesitated, and then shook her head. "No."

Great. I got cut out of the story entirely. "Did he tell you what it was for?"

"No."

At least he hadn't told her that; I would've felt like a complete chump if she knew that and I didn't. "This is an amazing coincidence, isn't it? Both of you asking me for the exact same amount of money." I kicked the locker next to my workbench and the lid fell down and snapped shut. "I guess I know what you both think of me. Thought of me."

"Please, Markos. You know I wouldn't ask unless it was important."

"And what's so important?"

She wrapped a hand around the opposite elbow and bit her lip. "Win owes someone five thousand dollars."

"Yeah, and I gave him five thousand dollars. So that's done."

"She didn't get that."

"Why not?"

"Because . . . I spent it."

I exhaled all the air in my chest.

"I didn't know it was his," Ari said. "I mean, yours. I found it in my closet. He must've hidden it there."

"So return whatever you bought and give this person the money."

She shook her head. She wasn't going to say what she spent it on; I could see that. I think she thought I would be grateful that she told me anything at all.

"Fine, then," I said. "Win's debts died with him. Tell this person you went on a shopping spree and they can fuck off."

"I can't."

"Why not?"

"It's kind of a long story."

I brushed scrap metal off the table and took a step closer to her. "I should give you five thousand dollars—why? You basically already stole five thousand from me. You won't tell me what you spent it on. You won't talk to me at all. Where have you been all summer?"

She frowned, a mulish expression on her small face. "If Win asked, you would lend him the money right away. You *did* lend it to him. Bet you didn't give him the third degree, either."

"You think we're friends like me and Win were friends?"

Her stubborn expression didn't budge. "I have your back. You should have mine."

"Win was my *best* friend. There's no one else I would treat the same, and no one else I ever will. Ever. You and I haven't even hung out in weeks. You think I owe you what I owed Win? Because he loved you? No. In fact, as of right now, we're not friends. You understand?"

"Come on, Markos—"

"No. I'm serious. Why keep pretending? We don't have anything in common anymore. I'm not sure we ever did." That wasn't what I wanted to say, and probably wasn't even true, but I couldn't stop. "I don't like you. I don't like your jokes. I don't feel sorry for you because you have such a tragic past. There's nothing about you that's in any way interesting to me."

She seemed defeated, but not as completely as I'd hoped. I had hoped for a massive meltdown. I wanted her to feel on the outside as shitty as I felt inside.

"You could have just said no," she said.

"And you can show yourself out," I said, and turned my back on her. "Good luck finding the door."

Win, I'd steal for. Win, I'd die for. Ari was not Win.

She left, stumbling a little through the woodshop door. On the flat screen, I watched her turn and double back through the store, always choosing the wrong way. Lost.

And I did not help her.

23

WIN

Echo had agreed to help me, but practicing the spell took time—hers and mine. She'd tell me when to come over and I'd sit on her couch and she'd ask me more questions about how I felt and how I wanted to feel, or she'd tell me what she'd read in one of her mother's books about mental spells and what I might expect as far as side effects.

She also told me about her mother, who wasn't well. "She's forgetting things. Losing pieces of herself," Echo said. I thought she meant dementia, but it was more than that: this was what happened when hekamists outlived their covens. Echo was the only one her mother had left. A coven had to have at least three—and ideally more than seven—in order to be stable. "When she dies, I'll go totally nuts," Echo said matter-of-factly.

"Are you mad at her for making you join?"

"She didn't make me do anything. I joined when the second-to-last member of her coven got cancer. I wanted to. I couldn't let my mother fall apart." She grinned a red-lipsticked grin.

"Besides, being a hekamist has plenty of perks. If I hadn't joined, I couldn't help you."

On one of these visits, while she frowned into pots and pans and made me taste tiny crumbs of cheddar and Parmesan and Camembert and Boursin, Echo told me how she'd gotten kicked out of college and fired from her waitressing job and how apartments had filled with rats and suspicious supers had torn up leases and forced her home again.

"It's almost like my mom's given me a hook," she said, rolling her eyes.

"What's a hook?"

"Type of spell to keep me close to her. It would make sense—she's worried about me because I'm illegal. She's afraid I'll get caught and go to jail forever."

"Would you?"

"Well. Yes." She waved away the threat. "I'd go to jail, she'd go to jail. Anyone in a coven who makes a new hekamist goes to prison for life. Which is why I need to get out there and find another coven—convince them to take us on. They'll need some persuading, maybe even some cash, because it's such a risk to take on someone underage. But I have to do something to save my mother. Save me."

I leaned forward across the kitchen table, surprised to find myself interested—not a word I'd use to describe myself often those days.

"So the hook spell keeps you close to her?"

"If she gave one to me, which I don't think she did."

"Why not?"

"Hooks are for assholes," Echo scoffed. "Pinning specimens under glass. Plus hekamists don't spell each other. It's bad form."

"But she could have. . . ."

Echo shook her head. "My mother loves me, but she knows better. Sometimes bad luck is just bad luck."

I scratched my arms and wondered if I'd ever be able to think bad luck wasn't entirely my fault. If I were Echo, I'd want to believe that it was a hook keeping me from what I wanted— anything but "just the way things are sometimes."

"If it was a hook, though, you could break it," I said.

"You say it like that's even possible."

The thing about spells, Echo told me, is that you can't break them, you can only wait for them to run out (if they're temporary) or try to layer another spell over them (if they're permanent). It's slightly easier to try to correct the side effects and not the spell itself, but even that gets complicated, because you're adding another spell on top of the one you have, and once you start doubling and tripling up the side effects go totally wonky. And if you're looking to reverse the spell itself, not the side effect, you're mostly out of luck. Sometimes, if the hekamist was good enough and the moon was in the right phase and you didn't bake the wrong kind of soufflé, a hekamist could come up with the right spell with the right side effects to nudge a person nearly back in their original direction. But trying that could be dangerous. A well-made spell protects itself. It will act on the world to prevent being destroyed, according to Echo.

A week later, I came back to collect my spell.

It felt weird thinking about the cheese sandwich in my hands as having its own will, but that's what Echo had said. *It will act on the world to protect itself.* She sliced the crusts off the bread, cut it diagonally, and put it in a plastic bag for me.

"The spell's in the cheese," she said. Her face was hopeful, proud. Maybe even a little bashful underneath the slashes of makeup. "I like cheese."

I held in my hands the answer to all my problems. It looked, however, like a boring cheese sandwich.

I could've run with it right then—or gobbled it down—and then dealt with the money later. But I couldn't do that to Echo, who'd done nothing but try to help, and who had problems of her own—a sick mother and her own eventual madness. "I don't have the money," I said. "Not yet."

Her pride drained away, disappointment taking its place. She sat at the kitchen table and pushed her hair off her forehead with both hands. She looked not just sad but afraid. Not that I could blame her.

I shifted on my feet, moving the sandwich from one hand to the other. "Should I give this back?"

Echo looked up. "You are going to get the money, right? You're not going to leave me hanging?"

"Yes," I said. Because what else was I going to say?

"Take the spell, then. Feel better. Bring me the money when you have it."

"You trust me?"

She looked up at me, her black-rimmed eyes swimming. "I'm the one who made you an irreversible brain whammy. Do *you* trust *me?*"

"Hadn't thought of it that way." I looked at the sandwich. One corner had been pressed down where Echo's thumb had held the bread. "Do your spells usually work?"

Echo didn't answer.

"Echo? This—this isn't your first spell, is it?"

She wouldn't look at me. "I've cast spells before. Plenty. My mom taught me a few before she started to get too . . . lost. But no one actually took any of those."

"Is that why the spell took you so long?"

"I'm being extra cautious. I want to get it right."

I swallowed to relieve the sudden dryness in my throat. "If no one took them, you don't know if any of those practice spells even worked."

She stood up and looked me in the eye, daring me to argue. "It'll work, Win. Your pain—gone. The side effects will be physical, so you might not get to play baseball for a little while, but you also won't kill yourself, so . . ."

"How do you know I play baseball?" I wasn't trying to accuse her of anything. I didn't want to think about my brain/body connection, which freaked me out if I let myself ponder it for too long. (Was I good at baseball because I was bad at keeping myself happy?) But Echo blushed, a deep red rising from her neck to her cheeks.

"Research," she mumbled, and in that second I knew she'd

been to a game—she'd watched me without me knowing. She watched me, and she trusted me, and she blushed like a—I don't know—like a *girl*.

I decided not to think any further along that path.

She must've decided the same thing, because she stood up and dumped the cutting board and knife into the sink, then started scrubbing them furiously, her back to me.

"Eat it before you go to sleep," she said. "It'll kick in by morning."

I lifted the bag by the ziplocked edge and looked in at the sandwich. Ordinary. But it wasn't; somehow it was a permanent sandwich. "How long will it stay good?"

She turned off the faucet and faced me, blush gone, only the usual guarded curiosity in its place. "As long as it takes. The bread might get stale but the cheese won't spoil."

"Thanks," I said.

"You're not going to take it right away?"

I shrugged. She was the one who felt the need to scare me with tales of unbreakable spells. She was the one who hadn't told me until the last possible minute that she was a raw amateur. "It's my brain. I want to be sure."

She wiped her hands on a dish towel and came over to stand directly in front of me. I thought she might touch me, and goose bumps erupted all over my skin.

She didn't touch me, simply stared at me. I didn't like it, but couldn't look away. Maybe a hekamist thing. "Promise me something," she said.

"I'll get the money."

"No. Well, yes, get the money—but promise me this: if it gets to the point where it's eating this sandwich or slitting your wrists, you eat the sandwich, okay?"

There wasn't enough air in the room. My lungs burned. I could only nod.

She nodded back and sent me on my way.

24

MARKOS

Of course I gave Win the money. I would've done anything for him.

He asked me and I knew he was serious. He never asked for shit and I knew my entire life that he was poor. His mom acted like the rest of the moms and paid for dance for Kara like she could compete with the other girls of the dance world, but Win always had secondhand gear for baseball, generic cereal, houses that weren't exactly dirty but always came with some sort of ground-in smell. He moved a lot and didn't say why. Sometimes nicer places, sometimes real shitholes. I didn't question that he needed the money.

And I didn't ask for what. It was money. I had it, or at least could get it, and he didn't or couldn't. It wasn't fair, but that was the way our lives fell out. Why should I insist on knowing his personal shit because I was in the position to do him a favor? I trusted him. That was enough.

That's not to say I didn't think about it—wonder why. I knew he was worried about something. He'd ignore my texts for days, and sometimes, like at poker night or warming up before a game, he would *go*—disappear from behind his eyes, leaving a Win shell behind.

When I let myself ponder what he might need the money for, I thought it was his mom or sister—something serious. I figured when it got bad enough we'd all know, but for now they wanted to keep it quiet. I thought I was the only one he told.

And I thought that up until the day Ari came into the shop to ask for more. What a fucking chump I was.

I'd gotten hell from my mother about the money for Win, too, so it wasn't like it had been easy. Even with her ancient ledger, no way would she let that much cash slip away from the store without noticing. But I was smart. I didn't take it from the store's till or anything like that. Every four weeks Mom left a manila envelope in the store for the old hekamist to pick up. Must've been four or five inches thick, some months. I first noticed it years ago when I was watching the security monitor in the woodshop. Mom and the hekamist never talked, never even looked each other in the eye; Mom left the envelope in the power tool display, and an hour later the hekamist picked it up.

They acted like it was some big secret, black hats and espionage. Mom was probably paying to keep people coming to the store. A lot of struggling businesses did it. Or maybe it was a protection spell to keep me and Cal and Dev and Brian safe, something motherly. But it didn't matter. I knew that the envelope would appear an hour before closing on every fourth Sunday.

Win asked me for the money at the right time. When Sunday rolled around, I swiped it before the hekamist could come pick it up.

There was six thousand dollars in it, to my surprise. I didn't think spells were that expensive, but then again I'd never bought one, so what did I know. I pocketed the extra thousand for a rainy day and gave the rest to Win at school the next day.

A few days after that, Mom stormed into my room.

"Where's the money, Markos?"

I could tell from the look on her face there was no point in playing dumb or blaming one of my brothers. She practically vibrated with rage, all her gray curls quivering, and her face turned red and splotchy. But there was something else, too—something I couldn't place right away.

"It's gone," I said.

She grabbed my arm, fingernails pinching, but I didn't wince. "This is not a game. You need to give it to me now."

Then it clicked. Mom looked scared.

"What's so important? Afraid of a few more gray hairs?"

"It's not for me, you idiot. Your brother—" And she stopped.

"My brother what?"

"You have no idea what you could've done."

"Who's it for? Dev? Cal? Why? What's wrong with them?"

Her eyes snapped to my face. "Nothing's wrong with any-one," she said. "Give me the money, Markos. I'm not joking."

I crossed my arms and stared her down. "Tell me what it's for."

She blinked at me. She was considering telling me it, whatever it was. I had no clue and didn't really care. It was convenient that she didn't want to tell me, that's all. And then if she did tell me—bonus. I wouldn't turn down free information.

But she didn't tell me. Something in her expression twisted and she actually smirked at me. She went over to my dresser and pulled open the middle drawer, where I keep some of the bongs I make in the shop before distributing them to customers. I didn't know she knew about the bongs so it took a second for all that to filter through what passed for my brain.

"Uh . . ." was all I said before she pulled out a bong with a flourish.

"You don't have secrets from me, Markos, I'm your mother." She brandished the bong like a baton. "You think I don't know about this? I know it all. I know who you talk to, what you do with them. I know how much money you have in your wallet. I know who your girlfriends are, and I know their parents. I know what type of porn sites you visit."

"Mom, please—"

She pointed the bong at my head. "I know everything about you, Markos. You're my child. If you think you can keep the money hidden . . ."

"Find it, then. If you know everything about me. Show me where the money is." I kept my eyes on her and not on the pair of disgusting old sneakers in the bottom of my gym bag where I'd rolled up and shoved the extra cash. She stared at me, didn't move. Seemed to be waiting for me to give away the money's location.

"You know you're grounded," she said finally.

"Good luck with that."

Tears sprang to her eyes, out of sadness or frustration, I didn't know. "I would do anything for you boys. I have done everything, and I have no regrets." I had no idea what she was talking about, but even I am not so cold as to feel nothing when my mom cries. "You don't know how hard it is—every month—but it's worth it. You ungrateful, spoiled little shit."

"Aw, Mom—"

"Don't touch that money again, Markos."

As soon as I was sure she'd left the house I retrieved the excess cash from the shoe and shoved it in my pocket, and I committed myself to spending it as soon as humanly possible. So when I saw the hekamist's daughter hanging around baseball practice the very next day, it seemed like fate. It would be a treat for us—my rainy day surprise.

My mom didn't speak to me again until Win died, three days later.

25

ARI

Two weeks before moving day, a Friday in mid-July, Echo found me at work at the Sweet Shoppe, a tourist spot on the main drag down the block from Markos's family's hardware store.

The best part of the Sweet Shoppe was the cold, which sank into my bones and numbed them. And once I got into a rhythm, time passed quickly. Bend, scoop, plop, extend. Bend, scoop, plop, extend. I didn't have to think about it or anything else. Like the fact that Markos refused to give me five thousand dollars. Like the fact that I botched another practice session that morning and managed to twist my ankle on a wobbly balancé. Like the fact that Diana seemed guarded and mysterious since the bonfire, but claimed nothing was going on.

Echo arrived like a black cloud, a blight on the tourists' pastel lives. I could feel her approaching, though I kept my eyes down on the ice cream case. Rocky road. Peanut brittle. Mint chocolate chip.

A black-painted fingernail tapped on the glass.

"Oh, hi," I said.

"I'm here to collect." Her glare was even more potent than I remembered, fierce enough to melt the ice cream between us, but for some reason I got that partial memory again: lightness, like feathers.

That inexplicable feeling made it easier to pretend to be tough. "I don't have it."

"It's been two weeks," she said.

"Twelve days."

"Sure, argue with me. You must really want everyone to know your secret."

"I don't, but I also don't have five thousand dollars. So I'm kind of in a tricky situation."

"Doesn't seem that tricky to me."

I squeezed the metal handle of the ice cream scoop and rotated my wrist. It cracked and popped from when I'd fallen and bruised it the day before. *Curve*, I told myself, and then Echo and I watched as my wrist bent ninety degrees and my elbow refused to bend at all. That wasn't a curve. It was a dead end. I tried to shake it out, but only succeeded in hitting myself in the side. I could've sworn, for half a second, Echo was going to say something sympathetic.

"Look," she said finally, her expression a hair softer than before. "I'll give you a break. If you can come up with four thousand, we can call it even."

I thought of the money I'd saved working at the Sweet Shoppe, and the money I'd pocketed from not buying new pointe shoes all the time. Still, I didn't even have a quarter of that. "I might be able to get you a thousand."

Echo bit her bottom lip and ran her right hand up and down her left arm. Finally she shook her head. "Not good enough. I need at least four to be sure, and I need it now." She muttered to herself something that sounded like, "Running out of time."

"You should take my thousand and leave me alone. Four thousand imaginary dollars is the same as five thousand imaginary dollars. Might as well make it five hundred thousand. I can't pay."

"How do you think this is going to go?" she asked, leaning onto the glass countertop so she could whisper. There was a line forming behind her, but I didn't dare tell her to leave, even with my manager glaring from the register. "I was at the funeral. It was packed, but I saw you up front with his mom and sister, pretending to be sad. Pretending you gave a shit. Everyone saw you. Everyone felt *so bad* for you. The whole town came out, all of them pitying poor Ari Madrigal. People with real grief. People who were actually sad—who are still sad, and who don't know what to do about it." The tremor in her voice came through despite the whisper. She blinked rapidly and leaned in closer. "What do you think's going to be their reaction when I tell them all that you were faking it? That you took a spell to make things easier for yourself? That you never deserved someone like Win in the first place?"

"Please . . . don't," I said. The pointlessness of asking made me wince.

"It's not up to me. I'm already giving you a break."

"I'm trying!"

"People pity you, but everybody *loved* Win. You may not remember, but I do. Everyone. Loved. Win. Are you ready for people to hate you instead of pity you?"

The people in the line behind her started to grumble. I could see my manager out of the corner of my eye, frowning. "I don't have it."

"Really? No spare insurance money lurking around? Nothing your aunt couldn't lend you?"

"We're moving to New York in two weeks. We need that money."

Her face twisted. "Right. New York."

"So I can dance. I got accepted to the Manhattan Ballet junior corps." I was going to New York. I had to go to New York. I didn't know why I was explaining myself to Echo, but I repeated myself to make the words sound true. "I'm going to be a dancer."

"So get out, then. Leave." She said it like a dare. "Doesn't matter if everyone knows your secret if you're gone, right? Go ahead." I didn't say anything, and she tapped the glass once more for emphasis. "If you're still here, though, you're going to owe me. One more week."

She left, and I should've gone straight back to bend, scoop, plop, extend. The line of customers approached and gave their orders, expecting me to obey. My manager turned back to the register, content now that the black cloud was gone.

But I didn't keep working. My mind raced, totally out of the rhythm. I dropped the scoop into a tub of chocolate and took off after Echo, not even bothering to remove my pink frilly apron.

I followed her past the downtown shops, through the residential neighborhood where Markos and Diana lived, past the high school, across the playing fields, and straight to the old hekamist's house. Echo unlocked the door and went inside.

Echo lived there too.

The hekamist's daughter. She'd said she had one—I remembered her mentioning it, in one of the only full memories I have of the day I got my spell.

I sat across the road and watched the house. Sad, shuffling people came and went, but no Echo. When the door opened, I caught sight of the hekamist.

So that was how Echo knew about my spell. Maybe the whole thing was some sort of con they were running, a mother-daughter grift, the hekamist making spells for people and then the daughter asking them to pay to keep the secret.

At one point, Echo left the house again. But the hekamist kept answering the door, ushering people in and out. Probably offering them a cup of tea.

When it started to get dark, the hekamist opened the door to no one, and stood on the front steps staring at me.

After thirty seconds of eye contact, she began to cross the street. She took every step deliberately, watching me the whole way. I tried to stand, but my balance was all off and my feet tingled painfully, and so I wobbled in the dirt.

"I thought it was you," she said.

"It's me."

"The ballet dancer. Are you ballet dancing again?"

"No. I still can't."

"Traded it in. Lost and gained. Prices paid." She spoke casually, with the intonations of a regular conversation but none of its meaning.

I took a deep breath. "I know what's going on with you and Echo."

"Echo?" The hekamist's face flashed a moment of genuine surprise, as if waking up from a dream. "Have you two met?"

"Come on. Don't make me laugh."

"What's funny?"

"It's not funny. Echo's blackmailing me. She wants five thousand dollars or she says she'll tell everyone that I forgot Win."

The hekamist's eyes widened. She was afraid: good.

I went on, pressing my advantage. "I already paid you five thousand dollars. I should go to the cops."

"The cops?" The hekamist's face sharpened, like clay hardening into cracks and planes. "What would you tell them about Echo?"

I frowned. "That she's blackmailing me, of course. That you both are. What else would I tell them?"

"Oh." Echo's mother sighed the word, and her face relaxed. "Oh . . . Echo, my Echo . . . Secrets are so powerful."

"I know."

"Because if you hadn't kept the spell a secret, Echo would not be able to pressure you for money."

"Yeah, I get it." I started to feel like I'd let the conversation drift off track. "But I don't have any money, so you're both going to leave me alone or I *will* call the cops."

"Yes, of course." She looked through me with an empty smile.

There didn't seem to be anything left to say. I clutched my wrist and shifted on tingling feet. "Okay then."

"Ari Madrigal," the hekamist said as I started to walk away. "You won't give Echo any money?" It almost sounded like she was begging. But that didn't make any sense.

"Right," I said, and kept walking.

My brain told me I should be triumphant, having confronted my enemy and figured out her game. But Echo's mother didn't seem like an enemy, and if she wasn't, then maybe Echo wasn't my enemy, either. So I had the strange, inexplicable sense that I'd been the one who'd been played.

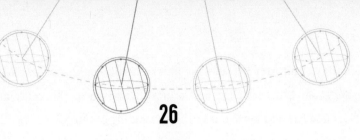

26

KAY

"Kay! You awake?"

"Cal? What time is it?"

"Two thirty-eight. What are you doing?"

"I was asleep."

"Oh yeah." He laughed. "Sorry. I was thinking of you."

"You were?"

"Sure."

"What were you thinking?"

There was a pause on the other end of the line. I held my breath. "I'm not sure, exactly. I just thought: Kay Charpal. And then I called."

"So . . . was there something you wanted to tell me?"

"I guess not. People don't call just to call anymore, do they?"

"Not at two thirty in the morning, at least."

Cal laughed again. He seemed extremely cheerful for two thirty in the morning. "I'll let you go to sleep. Good night, Kay."

I pressed End on my phone and lay back in the dark. I slept

with a comforter because my parents kept the house ice-cold in summer. Mina rebelled and stuffed towels over the vents and opened her windows, but I liked the feeling of the downy warmth all around me. I burrowed in more deeply, but a place under my heart and right above my gut still felt cold.

That call was the spell pushing Cal to me. We talked regularly now; we would soon hang out, too. Ari and Diana would see that I wasn't a throwaway girl to Cal. He thought of *me* in the middle of the night. He wanted to talk to *me*. Exactly as I'd wanted.

Right?

Unhooked.

That was the word the hekamist used to describe my side effects. She said a part of me would dislocate. Unhook. I didn't know what it meant to unhook. Maybe she didn't know, either, or she might have explained it better.

Unhooking could explain this coldness in my chest, more than the air conditioning. Everything I loved most—Ari, Diana, even Mina, having friends who were close, who understood, and all the other things they meant to me—I could pull off like a cloak and hang on a peg. Underneath the cloak there was nothing. The people and things I loved most felt far away and foreign, the cloak beautiful but strange. I could pick up the cloak and try it on, but it still felt like an object, not a part of me.

Unhooked. Had to be. Because if it wasn't my side effects, why wasn't I happy?

Cal kept calling in the middle of the night. He never slept, at least not as far as I could tell.

"Can we talk tomorrow, Cal?"

"But then I'll be awake for the next five hours by myself."

"You could go to sleep."

"Nah. I don't sleep much."

"What's 'not much'?"

"I haven't slept a whole night through since I was twelve years old."

I pulled the comforter all the way over my head and burrowed in. "Why?"

He sighed. "I don't know. I close my eyes like everyone else does. I'm tired, or at least I think I am. And nothing happens. I see the inside of my eyelids. Does that happen to you?"

"No. I fall asleep right away."

"Lucky."

"Except when you call, of course."

"Sorry. I don't want to bother you."

"You're not," I said. At least I didn't think I was bothered. It was hard to tell, sometimes, the difference between excitement and dread. Another thing that had come unhooked? "Do you want to hang out during the day?"

There was a pause. "Why not?" he said. "Come by the store tomorrow morning. We'll pretend to be tourists and go to the carnival."

Great. Me and Cal and—"Can my friends Ari and Diana come, too?"

"Ari Madrigal? Oh man, it sucks so much about Win. Of course she can come."

So we made a plan. A date.

Ari and Diana met us at Waters Hardware. They stood just inside the front door, next to a display of cleaning products, wearing almost identical expressions of discomfort.

I wanted them to come in and join me by the registers, but I could tell they weren't going to, so I went over to them. Cal leaped over the counter to join me and nearly made it without falling, but he was off balance from his jump, and he landed on his knees right in front of Diana and Ari. We all reached forward out of instinct, trying to either stop him from falling—too late— or help him up.

"Ow," he said, smiling, and popped back up without anyone's help.

Diana smiled back at him, but Ari looked as if his lack of coordination was a personal affront to her, and tucked her outstretched hand firmly back under the opposite elbow.

"Can we go?" she asked.

"Jeez, Ari, it's like you're afraid to run into me." Markos Waters appeared from the depths of the store.

"Hey, Markos," Ari said. Diana stepped toward him but stopped short when she saw he wasn't looking at her.

Cal went to punch Markos in the arm but whiffed. "Dude, come out with us, we're going to the carnival."

Everyone but Cal looked appalled at the idea. I knew I should have appreciated his generosity and inclusivity, but part of having best friends meant enjoying that you were a part of an exclusive club. Cal messed that up by inviting other people in.

"You ever find anyone to get you that money?" Markos asked Ari.

There was a moment of confused silence, and then everyone spoke at the same time.

"Money?"

"Don't worry about it."

"What money?"

"Let's just go."

"Did you pay or not?"

"Maybe we should talk about this some other time."

"It's going to get crowded if we don't leave soon. . . ."

"Wait, why do you need money?"

Ari raised her voice. "Everything's fine. I don't need money. Let's just go."

She left the store. Diana waited for a second, looking back and forth between the door and Markos, but then Markos turned back into the depths of the store without saying anything and her shoulders slumped and she joined Ari out on the sidewalk.

Cal grabbed my hand and pulled me to the door. "Come on!" he said.

I pulled back, and he stopped walking. "Don't you think that was weird?"

"What—Markos?"

"Yeah, and Ari asking him for money. Did you know about that?"

Cal shrugged. "Everyone has their secrets."

"But he's your brother."

"I'm not in charge of my siblings. Do you know everything your sister does?"

I pictured Mina at the bonfire, walking away because I told her to mind her own business. Maybe Cal was right and I should expect a certain level of hidden surprises, even with best friends. It didn't feel right, though. It felt as empty and disappointing as his hand holding mine, sweaty even in the air-conditioning of the store.

The four of us went to the carnival, which was set up in a parking lot at the end of the main drag. Cal didn't seem to mind that Ari was surly and snappish and that Diana was withdrawn and distracted. He bought me a stuffed hippo after he failed to win the ring toss five times. He stuck with us all morning and didn't flirt with other girls.

Tourists crowded the carnival in bright colors, laughing loudly. Games and souvenir shops bordered the lot, with a few games and rides in the middle. On one end, there was an arcade with a dozen ancient machines—Skee-Ball, the claw, pinball—and on the other end, high enough to look out over the ocean, stood the Whirlpool, an octopus-like contraption that spun in a circle and side to side and up and down. We waited in line for it. Mostly potheads and dropouts got summer jobs at the carnival, but Cal knew the guy who ran the ride and he promised to sneak us in without tickets.

Cal asked Ari about dancing. She described the program she'd be joining in New York in the fall, and the audition process, and where she and Jess were planning to live. I stood next to Diana.

"You doing okay?" I asked.

"I'm fine," she said.

"Because back at the store you seemed—"

"I said I'm fine, Kay."

"Markos can be such a jerk, seriously."

"Just because you have a Waters boyfriend doesn't mean you're some sort of expert on them," she snapped, then immediately winced. "Sorry. That was awful."

"It's okay," I said. "I'm not an expert."

"It's *not* okay. I shouldn't say stuff like that. You shouldn't let me get away with it."

I didn't say, *So it's my fault when you say mean things to me?* I didn't say anything.

We reached the head of the line and stepped into the tiny cars. Since I was standing with Diana, she and I shared a car, and Cal and Ari shared the one behind us.

"Sometimes I want high school to be over already, so I can get out," Diana said. "It's going to be a strange year."

"I'll be here."

"I was thinking maybe I'll go to boarding school. Be on my own for a while."

From the car behind us, I could hear Ari talking about the Manhattan Ballet. ". . . leave August first, and we're already starting to pack up . . ."

"A girl I know from horse camp goes to a school in Maine. Or I could go someplace else—somewhere I'm a complete stranger."

". . . want to get a handle on the subway, too, so I'm not totally lost the first day . . ."

The Whirlpool started its spin slowly. At first we only went in one big circle, but after a full revolution our cars started turning. The bar across my lap and Diana's creaked.

"You want to leave me here," I said.

"Oh, Kay. That's not it. I want to see what it's like on my own."

The doubly spinning cars lifted up and down, metal groaning. Behind me and all around me as we spun, I heard Ari shriek.

"Say you won't leave me," I said quickly. I could swear the safety bar lifted; I kept a grip on it, pushing it down.

"What?" Diana shouted. Our car shook; the safety bar rattled. I grabbed Diana's hand. It would be so easy for a screw to loosen, for the pothead at the controls to drift off, for springs to rust and break, for electric wires to fray. I'd walked Ari and Diana right onto a machine that could do so much more damage than what a cooler on a beach did to Diana's face.

"You need to say you won't leave!" I shouted.

"We can't get out of the car, the ride's already started!"

I couldn't keep my eyes focused on her; the ride moved too fast. All I could see was red hair and blue sky and bright lights, and the unnaturally loud creaks of the metal as the machine reached its highest speed. "Just say it! Say you won't leave me!"

"Okay, jeez! I won't leave you."

I let go of her hand and closed my eyes. The ride spun and spun.

For the moment I didn't feel unhooked from my feelings. I was too scared.

It might have been irrational, but I had the strong, clear feeling that if Diana and Ari had kept talking about their plans, the spell might've hurt them to keep them here with me.

After we got off the ride, no one seemed to notice anything had changed. I watched Ari and Diana and Cal being themselves, unaware how close they'd come.

It was one thing for the spell to bring me regular doses of Ari and Diana. I wanted to protect them. I cared about them, and they used to care about me. I would be there for them no matter what. But Cal . . . he had never really wanted to be near me. The spell had given him more than a gentle nudge—it shoved with both hands.

The thought rattled me. I'd saved Diana and Ari on the Whirlpool, and I'd always save them because we were best friends, but Cal was different. I mean, for one thing, he was clumsy: it would make it almost too easy for the spell. He'd fall one day, really hurt himself, and it would be my fault for not wanting to hang out with him. But more importantly, I didn't even like him that much, and Ari and Diana seemed totally unimpressed that I'd managed to "date" him, whatever that meant. It had been an impulsive, stupid idea to give him the hook. Now I was stuck with the responsibility.

The next day when he called at two thirty in the morning, I barely spoke.

He talked about nothing for a while until eventually noticing

I wasn't responding. "Is something the matter?" he asked.

"Yes," I started to say, but I couldn't tell him the truth. That he was in some sort of nebulous, ever-present danger because of me. That he wasn't in control of what he was doing. I couldn't risk the spell snapping and doling out punishment.

I had to keep answering the phone in the middle of the night. I had to keep hanging out at the hardware store watching him knock over displays of bug spray and step on rakes. I had to keep doing what he thought he wanted to do. What the spell thought I wanted to do. What neither of us needed or wanted at all.

27

MARKOS

I've never apologized to a girl as much as I had to apologize to Diana. Not because she was mad at me—she wasn't—but because I didn't stop feeling bad.

"I'm sorry again. I don't know what was wrong with me. I was such a dick."

Diana and I were at the diner, a local spot, no tourists, drinking cup after cup of watery coffee. Diana looked down into her mug, her hair falling over her cheeks. "Stop, Markos. It was one stupid day."

I wanted to reach over and brush Diana's hair behind her ear, but clenched my hands around my mug instead, burning them. "I should've gone to the carnival with you. I should've been fucking normal."

"It was too weird. Your brother and Kay . . ."

Later I had asked Cal if he was dating Kay, and he'd laughed and said no. But he'd gone to the carnival with her like it was no big deal. Why the hell couldn't I do the same thing?

"Goddamn Ari and her goddamn money," I said.

"Don't blame Ari. She's going through stuff, too."

"Is that what I'm doing? Going through stuff?"

Diana didn't answer, which was its own answer. I had to blame someone for how bad I felt, for how stupid I'd acted, and there was Ari, "going through stuff." It couldn't have been me being an asshole for no reason.

"Do you think Ari got it somewhere else? The money, I mean?"

"I doubt it."

It had been less than a week since Ari had asked me for five thousand dollars and told me she'd spent what I'd given Win, and though it was embarrassing to admit, it still bothered me. Actually it would've been embarrassing to admit to anyone but Diana. I could vent to her about it all day and she wouldn't mind.

"It pisses me off that she thinks she can come in after however long and ask me for something like that. It's like she thinks because Win loved her, I owe her something."

"There's got to be something else going on," Diana said.

"Like what? Gambling addiction? Bad real estate investment?"

"She must've really needed it, that's all. Maybe it had something to do with New York."

"You give her way too much credit. She's barely talked to you at all this summer."

Diana raised an eyebrow. "You know the reason Ari and I became friends in the first place? She told me this a few years ago. I was the only one in fourth grade who didn't ask her anything about her parents, ever, but who still stuck around. The last thing she wanted to do was talk, and I was always too scared to bring it up, so we've been best friends ever since."

"You . . . don't seem scared anymore."

Diana looked up at me sharply, and I held my breath and leaned carefully back in my seat. Casual. Arms resting on the back of the booth.

"I mean," I said, and forced my voice not to shake. "You're not the worst person in the world to talk to."

I couldn't stop myself from making eye contact and then I was falling into the big dark pit, disappearing, but in a good way.

"Thank you," she said, but it sounded strange and far away, like sonar underwater, pinging in the darkness: There I was. There she was.

I couldn't speak.

Ever since the bonfire I kept seeing her, day after day, and I still didn't touch her. It got to the point where I wasn't pretending to myself that I didn't want to anymore. Sometimes when I was with her I started staring at her—any part, really, like a shoulder—and I went into a total fucking fugue state just thinking about that shoulder, how soft her skin must be and the two freckles and how the shoulder is close to the neck and her mouth and her breasts and how it might taste or how she might shiver if I kissed it right. I mean I was gone. Brain wiped. Desperate.

But I didn't do anything. Maybe the not doing anything made it worse. Maybe this was what it was like for guys who were homely or only talked about video games—maybe they went around hungry all the time, so that by the time they talked to a girl for real they were too starved for touch to get a word out.

I could talk to her—god, I talked and talked like an asshole. But the longer it went on the more it felt simultaneously like I *had* to kiss her and that I'd *never* be able to. And yet instead of doing anything about it—either kissing her, which I was reasonably sure she wanted, or cutting her off and hanging out with someone else, which I knew I didn't want—I kept calling and picking her up and watching TV and getting smoothies.

It was pathetic.

And—okay. I'll be honest, even though this was the most pathetic thing yet. It wasn't entirely true that I hadn't touched her. Nothing serious had happened, but when it was night and we were in my basement watching a movie, we sat next to each other on the couch and we—I can't believe I'm saying this, please avert your eyes—we held hands.

HAND HOLDING. I HELD DIANA NORTH'S TINY SOFT PERFECT FUCKING DELICATE WARM HAND.

DAMN IT!

So we went to the diner, because I knew if I sat in the basement with her hand in mine again I wouldn't be able to enjoy the movie and I wouldn't be able to be anything but a weak coward, so it was better to be out at the diner where talking was what's expected.

Diana smiled at me, a half-smile that made my stomach drop to my knees because it was unexpectedly the most beautiful expression I'd ever seen. "Other than Ari and the money mystery, how was today?"

"Today. Today was medium good. Bad warmed over." What she meant was, how sad was I today. How much did I miss Win. "It sucks, though. Because the days that're not total shitshows, I feel guilty. Like do I deserve to be fine, helping customers, watching TV, drinking this coffee?"

"You do," she said. "What good would it do if you're never allowed to be happy again?"

"What good would anything do? Who says good things have to happen?"

She stirred her water with the straw. "I used to think that there was a fixed amount of good and bad for every person. That they had to balance each other out. That my cat's kidneys failing meant that I was paying for having fun on the weekend or something. That he's sick not because he's old but because—" She looked at me, flushed, and looked down again. "Because I spent time with you."

"I never touched the cat." I had to make a joke or melt into the floor and die, and she rolled her eyes, like she should. "But you know that whole theory's bullshit, right?"

"I don't know. It's sort of what hekamists do. They mix up what you've been given, but there's always a balance."

"That's different from real life. Sometimes things suck ass and they don't get better. Some people have no worries in the entire world forever—there's no balance."

"I mostly agree." She bit her straw and looked at me. "But you should listen to yourself. Just because Win died doesn't mean that you're not allowed to be happy."

I drank my coffee. I didn't let my hands shake. I breathed normally. Looked around the diner—anywhere but at Diana. It was funny to me that I didn't used to think she was pretty. I must've only seen a fraction of her, like looking through dirty glass. She was too beautiful now. And I didn't care what she said. I *didn't* deserve to be happy.

The diner was full of people, and I knew most of them. I could've gone up to any of their tables and started a conversation about nothing and they would've accepted me—no, they would've loved to have me there. The surface Markos could do all the work, and it would have been painless. We wouldn't have to talk about anything serious. We could make up new jokes, instead of missing the ones we used to have. I could ask one of the girls out. Easy, not painful. I wouldn't care enough to be afraid to do anything beyond hand holding.

So why else was I torturing myself with Diana, if I didn't think I should be living in pain?

The room started to feel stifling, and I grabbed a couple dollars from my pocket. "I gotta go," I said.

"Really? But we've only been—"

I was at the door already, ignoring the shouts hello from the other tables and Diana calling my name. Out in the parking lot in the humid night I gulped down air like I was drowning, and I felt a pressure on my hand.

It was Diana. She ran after me. She was holding my hand, looking at me, concerned.

I kept walking to the car, but she didn't let go, and when I got there I was dizzy. Too dizzy to pull my keys from my pocket. The streetlights pulsed and I closed my eyes.

Diana stepped in front of me, between me and the car door, facing me, holding my hand. I could smell her hair and her body and could feel it through the layers of clothes between us. With her free hand she reached into the front pocket of my jeans for my keys. I wasn't breathing. Her breath moved the fibers of my shirt against my chest. She was there. Right there. In between me and the car door. I was a statue—a man trapped in marble, blood pumping, without the strength to break the stone and move.

Holy shit.

It hurt so bad. A hurt that told me I was alive.

Any second she was going to turn and open the car door and the incredible pain would be over, but I didn't want it to be. I wanted to hurt like this forever.

Her pulse beat in my hand.

I guess you could call it self-control keeping me from kissing her, but it was more that I wanted the pain more than I wanted her.

But then it occurred to me that if I leaned forward, this type of pain—the wanting type—might end, but a new pain would begin. The pain and regret and remorse and stupidity of having ruined something wonderful.

And that's what I'm good at—ruining things.

I took a breath and so did she and I leaned in and I kissed

her and she kissed me and the parking lot and the car and the diner and Win all vanished. It was the perfect horrible moment, everything I'd wanted for weeks and everything I was scared of, the beginning and the end all at once.

She kissed back and I could feel her smiling, and that ache for her didn't go away; it grew and grew.

28

ARI

Diana burst into my room at the end of my daily stretches. It was the middle of July. I was running out of time, and the exercises hadn't gotten any better in the two months since the spell. I put on a shrug over my leotard and swallowed down panic. Sometimes if I pushed myself too hard I'd throw up from the stress. But I preferred being sick to the days where I gave up halfway through and curled on the floor in a ball, crying.

Diana dumped her purse on the spare bed and flitted around the room examining every object, as if she hadn't spent fifty percent of the past ten years here. Her humming energy wasn't perfectly happy, but it wasn't sad, either. She seemed on the verge of lots of different emotions all at once, and I wasn't sure if she'd laugh or cry or scream.

"Are you okay?" Diana asked. She looked into my eyes, squinting as if to make out something on the horizon. "We didn't get to talk at the carnival. How's it been going?"

My hand went to my burning wrist. "I'm fine. Fine."

"You don't have to be fine."

I laughed. "Sometimes I wish everyone would be a little less in touch with their feelings and thoughtful and empathetic."

"I can be cold and remote."

"Yeah right. Give it a try."

She crossed her arms over her chest and raised her eyebrows, frowning, but she could only hold the pose for a few seconds before laughing and collapsing backward onto the bed.

"What's up?" I asked.

She hugged her arms around her chest and stared up at the ceiling. "You're going to laugh at me."

"I wouldn't."

"You would about this."

I pinched the sensitive skin inside my elbows. Stupid, stupid Old Ari. Had I laughed at her before? In the year I spent with Win, did I tease her? Make her feel bad about herself? Was I so different with my stupid fancy boyfriend that she stopped depending on me?

I could kill the old me. How dare she treat my best friend like that. How dare she make Diana think she couldn't tell me anything in the world.

"Try me," I said.

She covered her face with her hands and moaned. "I don't think you'd believe me if I told you."

"Told me what?"

She took a deep breath and smiled so that it filled up her

entire face. "I think Markos and I are in love," she said.

I didn't laugh. I couldn't move a muscle from shock.

"Say something," Diana said.

I swallowed. "That's . . . wow."

"You don't believe me." The smile deflated.

"Give me a second, Diana."

"I always believed you when you said you were in love with Win."

I decided it was worth hazarding a guess. "Come on. I never collapsed on your bed and announced we were in love."

Her smile didn't collapse any further, and I knew my guess was on target. Sometimes Old Ari wasn't as mysterious as I thought.

"Tell me what happened," I said.

"We've been spending a lot of time together since the bonfire, and . . ." She stopped and looked at me, lips flattening, huge smile gone for good. "You know what, no. I'm not spilling my guts to you without some answers. Markos told me about the money he gave Win, the money you spent. What did you do with it? Why do you need more? Are you in some sort of trouble?"

The room seemed to chill; I felt a neck muscle pinch. "I can't tell you."

"Come on, Ari. I get not telling Markos. But you can tell me."

"I don't want you to worry about me."

"Oh, please. Shut up already! I'm *supposed* to worry about you. That's what best friends do. God, Ari. Your boyfriend died. You needed money—a lot of it." She picked at the quilt on my bed. "Tell me. Let me make up my own mind if I should worry."

Once in seventh grade Diana and I had stopped for ice cream on the way home from school and then spent an hour on the beach. When we finally reached Diana's house Mrs. North screamed at us. *Every second you're not here I worry*, she'd said, and that had sounded so crazy but also so . . . caring. I imitated her saying that for months and we always laughed, but every time I said it, it was with a twinge, the faint but undeniable knowledge that I made fun of Mrs. North because I feared that no one worried about me like that.

"Don't you trust me?" Diana asked.

"It's bad," I said.

Diana nodded. She leaned forward expectantly, ready to be understanding and supportive. I felt sick, as if I'd been spinning without spotting my turns.

I hadn't heard from Echo since I talked to her mother the hekamist—I might've scared her away. Or maybe she'd come back and blow everything up. I didn't want to live with the threat hanging over me, a ransom I couldn't pay.

My mind felt muddled. Diana seemed to float farther and farther away.

Diana and Markos were in love. I'd never been in love. As far as I knew.

Diana loved Markos. He would break her heart, the bastard, but she'd gotten what she always wanted. She hadn't listened to my advice—she didn't need me. She had red hair and her own strong opinions and we hadn't had movie night in a year and she'd been forced to befriend Kay and now she was asking to worry about me.

Maybe I should let her.

"I took a spell that erased my memory of Win," I said. The words floated out of me easily, lightly. "So I wouldn't have to be sad, I guess. I don't remember anything about him."

Diana jerked back as if I'd hit her. She blinked rapidly. "What are you talking about?"

"I don't remember Win."

She put a hand over her mouth and stared at me. I couldn't tell what was going through her head. Fear? "So you've been lying all summer," she said.

I took a deep breath. "Yeah. It was . . . easier. I guess . . . maybe . . . I was ashamed. I didn't know how to explain why I'd done it, because I didn't remember what made me feel so bad. I thought it would be better to pretend."

Diana stood up and started pacing the length of the room. "You've been lying to us. You're not *suffering.* You've just been avoiding me."

"I didn't know what else to do."

"You could've tried telling me the truth."

"I am telling you—"

"I mean before." She paced again, looking anywhere in the room but at me. "Before you did this. After Win died. You could've told me you were thinking about it. I would've helped you. Talked about it. I would've helped you do whatever you wanted to do. You—you didn't trust me even then."

"I'm so sorry, Diana."

She shook her head, hair whipping from side to side. "You never came to me with problems. You'd talk to Jess or to Win. I was always silly old Diana with her pointless crush, your loyal shadow."

The sting started in the back of my throat and traveled up through my sinuses to my eyes. But I wouldn't cry. I pressed my thumb and forefinger around my left wrist, holding the pain in place. "That's not true. I'm telling you now. Not Jess or Kay or anyone else. I trust you."

Diana stopped, facing away from me. "So you spent Markos's money on a spell."

"Yes." Diana wouldn't face me. I couldn't guess her expression. "Win must've hidden the money in my closet, but I didn't know where it came from—I only found out later it was his, and that he'd gotten it from Markos. The problem was, Win owed it to someone. That person told me that if I didn't pay what Win owed, she would tell everyone I don't remember him."

Diana turned to me. Her eyes were bright and fierce.

"So did you pay her?"

The air leaked out of my lungs. I couldn't remember ever seeing Diana so angry. "No. I followed her. . . . She might leave me alone for a while."

As if she were deflating, Diana sank to the floor next to the bed, anger melting away into despair. "Oh god. What am

I supposed to tell Markos?"

"You don't have to tell him anything."

She glanced up at me, her eyes big and full of disappointment. "But you'll tell him yourself soon, right? Before this blackmailer comes back and tells for you?"

I didn't answer, but I moved from my desk chair to the floor across from Diana. We'd spent hundreds of hours of our lives here in this room. But this felt different, as if we'd been acting before, and now we were real.

Diana didn't say anything else for a long time. She leaned her head back on the mattress and stared up at the ceiling. I tried to follow her gaze and see what she was looking at, but there was nothing there.

"You might not remember Win," she said, finally, "but you should still remember that you and Markos were friends. You gave him a hard time, but you were friends. Now I think he misses you. And it's not fair lying to him like this."

I reached for Diana's hand and held it, even though she looked down at my hand as if it repulsed her. "Please tell me you forgive me, Di. Please."

She stared at my hand holding hers. But then, after a long moment, she nodded.

I nodded back. "I'll tell Markos soon. I promise."

But if I told Markos I'd have to tell everyone, and the girl I used to be—the dancer, the girlfriend, the good person—she'd be gone, replaced by this liar, rotten to the core. So rotten my best friend could barely stand to talk to me or look at me. I thought if I told Diana the truth we'd be close again, the way we always were before. But seeing how I looked through her eyes—seeing that look in everyone else's expressions, forever—

I didn't know if I could do it.

29

KAY

I didn't know if I'd be able to break up with someone. So much of my life had been trying to get people to stay. I couldn't quite imagine telling someone to go away; it seemed impossibly hard, even if Cal hadn't really chosen me to begin with. So I decided to go to the hekamist and get his hook broken, and then I wouldn't have to talk to him or worry about him ever again.

When I heard my parents turn on the TV in the living room late one night, I crept to the front hall where my mother leaves her purse. I pulled out the snakeskin wallet and removed the black AmEx card. If she looked at her bill—which she, on principle, does not—she would assume she'd bought extra fertilizer or dirt or something that month.

I'd tucked the card in my pocket and was returning the wallet when Mina appeared in the doorway behind me.

"What are you doing?" she asked.

"Pizza money," I said. "She won't mind."

"You just ate dinner."

"For tomorrow, duh."

Mina watched me, suspicious, but she let me go.

The old hekamist who'd given me the hook wasn't home.

"Is your mom around?" I asked the girl who answered the door, even though there was nowhere for anyone to hide in their small house.

"She's not available," she said.

"Well, when will she be?"

The girl crossed her arms over her chest. "That depends."

"That's not really good enough for me. I'm a loyal customer."

"Oh yeah? You've got money?"

"Sure," I said.

The girl looked me over, from my lime-green flip-flops to my sundress to my swinging perfect hair. It was a totally normal outfit, especially compared to her biker-esque dirty-looking black coat and asymmetrical short haircut. I didn't know what she was looking for, but she must've found it. "If you have money, I can help you," the girl said. At my doubtful look, she added, almost casually, "I'm a hekamist."

I raised my eyebrows at her. She seemed Mina's age at most. "You are?"

The girl leaned back, tapping her black-nailed hands on the doorframe. "Joined the coven when I was thirteen," she said. "Do you want a spell or not?"

I followed her through the cramped living room and sat at the kitchen table. She bustled around the kitchen making tea.

I pulled the black AmEx out of my jeans pocket and placed it between us on the chipped table.

She glanced over and laughed, though it sounded sad. "What exactly do you want me to do with that?" She picked up the card and twirled it in her fingers. "I can't believe I told you I was a hekamist for nothing. This isn't Barneys. We take cash or nothing, Ms. Lila Charpal."

"It's Kay," I said, then snatched the card out of her hand and crossed my arms over my chest and flared my nostrils. It's a look my mother gives salesladies and doctors when she's dissatisfied, and it covered my embarrassment. "I can get cash."

"I don't work on installment. At least, not for you."

"I don't know what installment is, but I'll get you cash. As long as you can actually deliver."

She sat across from me, mug of tea in her hands. "What do you need?"

So I told her about my spells: the beauty one and then the hook for friendship, and how I'd given the hook to my two best friends and a boy, and how I didn't want him to be in the spell anymore.

The girl—the hekamist—listened and drank her tea.

"There are two ways to do this," the girl said when I had finished. She still hadn't told me her name, and no way was I going to ask for it. "The first is you take a spell to cancel out the effects of the hook. Not a reversal—you won't go back to normal—it's more like another layer of spells over the one you've got."

"What kind of a layer?"

"The hook needs to know who you are in order to hook onto something. So this spell would make you sort of . . . invisible. Not actually invisible. Just harder for people to notice, especially if they don't really know you or care about you. And it would affect everyone, not only your boyfriend."

I shivered. It sounded awful, and I couldn't risk losing Diana or Ari. No. "What's the other way?"

"It's a bit harder. I'd brew something that you'd have to sneak to him to eat. A spell to disconnect from you and really break it."

"Sounds good to me."

"It's dangerous. I can't be sure it would work. Spells protect themselves. They don't want to be broken."

Sounded like the typical hekamist warnings I'd heard every time I'd gotten a spell. "I know."

The hekamist grinned, but not from amusement. "You don't know what other spells he's taken already—you don't know the types of reactions that could take place. Plus if I'm not careful the original spell will lash out at me, and then I'll probably get caught and my mom and I will go to jail until we both go crazy and die."

I shrugged. "You chose to join a coven."

Her eyes flashed and she blinked rapidly. "I saved my mother's life. What the hell have you done?"

"I just meant that you knew the risks when you joined, right?"

"Sure, I knew it was illegal to join and that we'd all go to jail for life if we were caught. But I also knew that the government made it illegal for my mother to grow old in peace. I knew that the legal thing to do would be to watch her fall apart and slowly die by degrees, day by day." She leaned forward, elbows on the table, dark hair dropping over her eyes. "A lot of people say hekamists dying out is for the best."

"Not me," I said.

"Because you've benefitted from us. But do you know what 'dying out' actually means? It's not peaceful, one hekamist by one closing her eyes and drifting off. My mother and all the hekamists her age—they're dying *horribly*. They're dying not knowing who they are. Not recognizing their families. All because people are suddenly afraid of something that's been around for as long as we've had society."

I squeezed my hands together under the table. All the talk of dying made me think of Mina and the shadow of death that used to follow her around. But I didn't want to think of Mina; I was here to get rid of Cal. "I'm just here for a spell."

She flashed a smile, very white teeth in her pale face. "Everyone just wants a spell. So handy, hekamists. What are you going to do when we're all dead?"

"What's your problem?"

"I told you. Aren't you listening?"

"Why are you telling me all this? There's nothing I can do about it."

The hekamist shrugged. "Maybe you caught me on a bad day. Or maybe I'm going crazy, too."

Whether she was crazy or not, I needed her. "Look," I said,

swallowing, "I'm not here to get rich or hurt anyone or do anything else bad, and I'm not here because I care about you or your situation. I won't rat you out and I promise I'll pay you for the work. I'm trying to do the right thing. I doubt Cal wants to be stuck in my spell, anyway."

"Cal?" Echo sat up straight. "It isn't Cal *Waters* you've hooked?"

"Yeah. So?"

She slumped back, frowning. "If you want a spell to take yourself to cancel out your hook completely and you manage to bring me cash, I'd be happy to take the risk, but otherwise—"

"What? Why not do the other thing, and break the spell on Cal directly?"

She picked at the edge of a raggedy black-polished nail. "Like I said. Too risky."

"I thought you were a badass hekamist warrior. You're afraid?"

The hekamist flattened her lips and glared at me, then stood up. "You'll have to find someone else to do your dirty work," she said.

I allowed myself to be herded to the door, past the stained coffee table covered with tea mugs, past the runes scratched into the walls and battered couch sticking into the middle of the room.

I felt like I should've tried harder, offered more money or said something sympathetic, but the whole experience had taken the fight out of me, the way Mina used to sag after doctors' appointments even if they hadn't done anything to her except talk.

"Hey," the hekamist said, peering behind my back toward the road warily. "You said you wanted to do the right thing. Take the spell yourself to rebalance. Let everyone go free."

Everyone would go free, but where would I be? Worse than where I was before. Alone. Invisible.

No. I would have to keep doing this the hard way.

30

MARKOS

It felt like I was buzzing. Like someone'd rigged up an electrical current to run through my skin and if anyone touched me they'd be blasted back a mile. Sometimes it was in my face. Sometimes my chest, my hands. Sometimes other places.

Diana.

I'd hooked up with a lot of girls before her—not as many as my brothers, as they liked to remind me, but a few—and sometimes those girls were memorable for some dirty reason, and sometimes I'd hook up with the same girl more than once because it was convenient or she had an amazing body or a crazy attitude. But I'd never woken up the next morning, and the morning after that, and the morning after that one feeling like this. More alive.

The buzzing didn't go away, either, even though I spent my days in the hardware store copying keys and showing people where the drill bits were. In slow moments—and not so slow moments—we texted back and forth.

How many lug nuts does one man need?!?!

    Is that supposed to be seductive? ☺

I don't have to seduce you, I got you

    Oh? I'd forgotten all about that!

I hadn't.

    Yeah. Me neither.

Gotta go help this dude with his engine starter

    Sounds fun. Call me later?

Miss you

    Miss us

Gross

    You're gross

And when I wasn't doing that—when the customers wandered away and Diana had to go babysit—I talked to myself. Or not exactly to myself. It was that Win voice I heard talking back, the same one I'd been hearing for weeks. I knew it was crazy and I should stop playing pretend, but it was easier to let the voice run than to try to shut it up.

—She's joking but she's right. This is disgusting.

—Why?

—I'm Markos Waters.

—So?

—So I'm letting this girl get to me.

—She's great.

—Yeah.

—She listens. She understands.

—Yeah.

—And the kissing.

—I know.

—So?

—I can't be this guy.

—Why?

—It's not in my DNA.

—That's a weak excuse, Markos. If I were alive I'd kick your ass.

It made me think of Ari and Win together. When we were kids it was me and Win, Win and me. In middle school I started hooking up with girls but me and Win stayed the same. Then in high school, it became me and Win and Ari. Or really me-on-my-own then sometimes also Win-and-Ari. She was annoying at first because I didn't really get it: she wasn't a random girl, she was someone who fundamentally changed who Win was. Not in a bad way. He was more solid around her, more decisive, more purposeful. He took up more space. He was the good parts of himself, but *more*. Ari acted as a Win amplifier.

Once I figured that out, I didn't really have a problem with her. I liked her. Not the way Win liked her. But like a dude. She was cool.

Win, though. It freaked me out that someone I knew so well—better than my brothers, even—could change so much just from being around another person. *I'll never change,* I thought. *I know who I am.*

Ha. Ha.

I was straightening the paint chips when my mother's hekamist sidled up next to me. My first thought was that she was going to yell at me about the stolen six thousand dollars, but that didn't make sense. That was months ago, and Mom would've paid her again, not told her I'd taken it. Then I started to get really paranoid and thought that she could tell all I'd been thinking about Diana and Win and Ari and she had some sort of wise old hekamist life advice about all of it.

"Markos Waters?" she said. She was a large old lady, and whacked out. Smelled like pine needles and forest dirt. Eyes too big and blinky to focus quite right.

I nodded. She picked up a paint chip and looked it up and down. Sort of dreamily, hungrily, like it was a menu. "Can I help you find something?" I asked.

She looked me up and down like I was another paint chip. "I'm very sorry for your loss."

Right. She was a hekamist, but she could still get into the mourner tourism. Schadenfreude. It went like this: People claimed to feel sorry but they were actually relieved and partly fascinated by what the face of loss looked like. *How could he live though this and go on?* they wondered. *He is so completely different from us now.*

"You were a good friend." (How did she know that?) "He seemed the type of person you'd want to remember." (As if I had a choice.) "It's a shame not all of his friends can." (Wait—what?)

"What are you talking about?"

The hekamist covered her mouth with the paint chip, but I could see the smile peeking out of either side. "She didn't tell you. Of course. Funny, funny. That girl—the ballet dancer."

She was almost laughing now, holding her breath to keep it in.

"What did Ari do?" I asked.

"I'm telling you. Be patient." She took a breath and bit the side of the paint chip. "What was it? Oh yes. The dancer forgot Win. Erased him. Silly, so silly, a spell to forget." She took the paint chip out of her mouth, put it back on the rack, and patted my arm.

All the electricity had gone out of my skin.

I barely felt her hand.

Then I was alone. Me and the paint chips. The door bell jangled. The air conditioner kicked on.

I grabbed the metal rack in front of me and pulled. The paint chips crashed to the ground. I stepped around them and walked straight out the door.

My phone buzzed. Another text.

I pressed the touch screen with shaking fingers. Found Diana's number. Listened to the ringing. The pauses between rings stretched out over blocks.

When she answered, there were children screaming in the background. "Hello?"

"Ari paid a hekamist to erase Win. She doesn't remember him at all."

For a second, I heard only the screaming children. I don't

think either of us breathed. Then Diana sighed.

"This sucks. But I am so glad she finally told you."

"What? She didn't—what do you mean *she finally told me?*" The blood rushed out of my head and I leaned over. The weight of my head made me fall to my knees. "She told you. You—you knew."

"A few days ago. I couldn't believe it. I was so angry, Markos. She lied to me—"

"*You* lied to me. You lied to my face. You told me to give her a call, for fuck's sake!" I was screaming, then, on my knees in the middle of the sidewalk, tourists parting like the seas to get around me. The air smelled charged, poisonous.

"I wanted to tell, but she promised—"

"And you believed her? After she told you what she did, you believed a single word she said to you?"

"Markos, I am so sorry—"

"Don't ever call me again. This will be the last time you hear from me, you lying bitch."

I jabbed at the phone to hang up. A call came in, and several texts. My heart bled out my fingers onto the sidewalk. Cement clogged my lungs. I gulped down air.

When I could control the shaking in my hands, I turned the phone off.

I started to head for the Sweet Shoppe where Ari worked but balked. I knew that if I saw her face something terrible would happen. A too-big part of me wanted to hurt her, reach out and bruise her, make her feel, bring back some of the pain she threw out like garbage when she erased my best friend. That anger scared me. Another part of me thought I'd break down. None of it would do any good, anyway.

Nothing would. Not really.

There were so many things that Win and I did together that I somehow thought were safe because Ari had a mental backup. But I was the only one now. Only I remembered Win. All this shit—all this *getting over it*—I was the only one who had to do it. I couldn't let the pain go now, could never get over it. Not when it was only me keeping Win from being forgotten forever.

One moment I was standing in front of the hardware store and the next I was at home. A girl sat on my porch and at first I thought it was Diana and almost took off running. But this girl had dark hair, not Diana's red, and as I got closer I recognized Diana and Ari's beauty-spelled friend—Kay. Katelyn. Something like that. It didn't matter.

She held opposite elbows over her nice chest when she saw me, but then as I got closer she relaxed. I tried to think of something to say that would make her go away quickly, but my mind was blank. I could almost hear the rushing wind between my ears. Or was that a roar?

"Hey. I was looking for Cal," she said.

I stopped a few feet from her. She was between me and the door. But there was nothing inside of the house that was better than anything out here.

"Are you okay?" Kay asked. "You look bad."

"I guess I'm bad, then." I put my hands in my pockets to

keep them from shaking. Everything felt impossibly far away. "I bet you know, too. The three of you being such good friends and all."

"Know what?"

"That Ari took a spell to forget Win. That she's only been pretending to be grief-stricken. She told Diana—you didn't know?"

Kay's mouth dropped open, and an expression filled her generically pretty features that looked almost as pained as the monster eating me up inside. "She was lying to me?"

"To everyone."

"But . . . I'm her best friend."

I laughed at that, and she recoiled as if I'd spit on her. She wasn't a bad person, and she hadn't done anything to me, but I needed to push some of this bad feeling out or it would collapse in on me. "Look, I have a lot of shit I have to take care of, and none of it includes talking to you, so why don't you get out of my face."

She snapped out of her surprise and hurt and put on her generically pretty mask again. But I could see how the mask didn't quite fit, and the anger and the pain pushed on its edges and crevices, threatening to break through. "I'm here to see Cal," she said.

"Why?"

"Because . . . we're friends."

I laughed again. "What, you think you're dating or something?"

"We might be dating."

213

"Yeah, right. Waters boys don't get serious. Don't you know that?"

She stepped closer. As close as a girl had been since the night in the diner parking lot, since Diana—but this wasn't Diana. This girl had black shiny hair and a good face and body but I felt nothing from her. Like a dead zone where your cell phone doesn't get reception, or an ice-cold patch of the ocean.

"Do you ever feel like a pathetic phony?" I asked. "Because everyone knows you've shellacked on some spells. You think we can't remember what you looked like before?"

She flushed with anger or humiliation or whatever and it actually improved her whole plastic appearance. It jolted down my spine, too—not her hotness but what I could do to someone.

I caused that.

"You're the phony," she said. "Trying so hard to seem like you don't care."

I made a face. "So insightful."

"You're only being a dick to me because you're mad at Ari."

"I am mad at Ari, but maybe also I don't like you."

"You wouldn't be such an asshole to me if you knew what I could do," she said.

I laughed. "O great and terrible one, please spare me."

"Shut *up* already!" she said. Then she leaned forward and kissed me.

I should've gotten pissed. Pushed her away. Told her that she wasn't going to prove anything by making out with me. She'd still be a phony and I'd still hate her. I should've come back with something even crueler to crush her properly into oblivion.

But there wasn't anything left in me to get angry.

While I was angry, Ari felt nothing.

While I was in pain, Ari felt nothing.

While I looked for ways to make the pain worse, Ari felt nothing.

While I waited for it to all make sense, Ari felt nothing.

Nothing would ever affect her the way Win's death was killing me.

Now I felt nothing. Or maybe this feeling was everything, like how white is all the colors combined.

"Why'd you do that?" I said. Kay shrugged. I grabbed her arm and pulled her closer and kissed her, hard. She kissed back.

"You're going to regret this," she said when we took a breath.

"I'm looking forward to it," I said.

I didn't care about her—I didn't even like her—which meant that what was happening didn't matter. I wasn't Win, stuck with one girl forever. I was me, the Markos Waters of legend, one of the carefree Waters boys, life of the party, and I sank back into the role with relief. Easier than drowning.

When Kay left a while later, I turned on my phone to text Ari to tell her if I saw her I'd kill her, then I blocked Diana's number and deleted all her messages. I sat in front of the TV with a bottle of Jack Daniel's and proceeded to get shitfaced, which is the temporary, normal, nonhekamist way to obliterate your festering, gut-wrenching memory.

PART III

the
costs

31

KAY

I walked away from the Waterses' house different. The world was different. It was almost dark instead of bright midday, but also the air smelled like fall and the sky pressed down on my shoulders.

And me. Inside. I'd gone over to check in on Cal, do my duty to the spell. Instead I'd kissed his brother.

Markos had been so mad. And so *mean*. I wanted to kiss him to prove that he didn't actually think I was a fake ugly liar. Or at least prove he was as bad as me, and we both knew it.

It didn't even end up proving anything to Markos. It only proved to myself what type of person I was.

A bad one. A person whose best friends hated her and kept secrets from her—for good reason, even if they didn't know it.

That was the problem with my "relationship" with Cal, too. I agreed with Markos; I agreed with Diana and Ari: I didn't belong with someone cheerful and inclusive and popular like Cal. I knew exactly what I looked like inside, and it wasn't girlfriend material.

No. I deserved to be called names by Markos, and disrespected, and tossed aside when it was over. That was who I really was.

A person who had to get a spell to keep her friends.

I walked from Markos's to Ari's. She answered the door wearing her ballet outfit—tights, leotard, gray shrug—but she didn't appear winded or sweaty. She let me in and we sat on the couch in her basement for five minutes without speaking. She was distracted, eyes hollow. We could hear her aunt singing off-key as she walked around the kitchen upstairs.

"I'm kind of having a bad day, Kay," Ari said after a while. "So maybe we do this some other time?"

"What's so bad about it?"

"It's just . . . bad."

"Come on, tell me."

"I'd rather not talk about it."

"Why?" I asked. I pushed my back into the far corner of the couch and my heels into the space between two cushions. "You sad about Win? Because it isn't good to bottle it all up, Ari. You should talk about him more. Let us in. Share some of those precious memories."

Her expression emptied, a beach house left vacant for the winter. "So . . . you heard."

"Yeah, I heard."

"How?"

"Markos told me."

"When did everyone start hanging out with Markos without me?"

I could feel my face heating up. "What do you mean, every-one?"

Ari pressed the heels of her hands into the black shadows under her eyes. "Diana thinks they're dating. That they're in love."

"Who's in love?"

"Markos and Diana."

"Shut up," I said. Ari shrugged. "She never said anything about it to me!"

"Sorry you didn't get the bulletin."

A flash of anger made me forget for a moment how both Ari and Diana had lied to me. "You know, while you were off with Win doing whatever, Diana relied on me. Because you were nowhere to be found."

"I've gathered that."

"She used to get upset about it. That you were abandon-ing her for some boy. But I was there for her." Ari didn't say anything. She wrapped her shrug tighter around her shoulders. "Then, you know what? After a few months she stopped being upset. She moved on. She didn't need you anymore."

Ari flinched, and my bad insides made me smile. "What's your point, Kay?"

"I don't have one. I'm telling you how it was."

"Well, you can stop."

I hugged a throw pillow to my chest. "I don't know if you know this, but you and Diana act like you don't even like me sometimes."

Ari looked up at the ceiling. Part of me hoped she'd deny it, but she wasn't in a denying mood. "It's just that . . . you try too hard."

"I make an effort. I took care of Diana. I take care of you both."

"Yeah. Maybe we don't want to be taken care of."

"Well maybe I don't want to be the pity case you both laugh at."

The words came out before I could decide if they were a good idea. Yet Ari didn't seem offended. She seemed—embarrassed? But I'd told her off. I wasn't nice at all.

Jess belted a high note from the kitchen and we winced. I'd been spending the entire summer—the entire spring, too—making an effort with Ari and Diana. Trying to get them to treat me like a real friend.

But I didn't have to do any of it. No taking care of Diana after her accident. No compliments, no thoughtfulness. I could be as mean as I wanted—I could hook up with Diana's crush and tell Ari what I really felt—and they would still have to be around me. That's what my hook gave me. I had them on the line.

The only reason to make an effort was to prove that my insides weren't totally rotten. And my insides rotted anyway, so the effort was wasted.

"I made an effort," I said again. "At least I don't give up like you do."

She shook her head, her eyes closed. "Sometimes giving up is the smart move."

"Right. Forgetting Win's really going so well, huh?"

The corner of her mouth turned up in a half-smile.

I relaxed back into the couch. Everything was messed up, yeah, and I'd kissed Markos and not checked in with Cal, and if any of them stepped out of line the spell would be there to push them back, violently if necessary, but Ari and I had had our first genuine interaction in months, and it was all because I'd stopped worrying about being a good person (because I wasn't) and stopped worrying about how great Ari was (because she wasn't) and simply said what I thought.

Ari was right. I didn't have to try so hard. I had to let the spell do its work.

32

ARI

Kay was right about one thing: I couldn't give up yet. After she left, I put on civilian clothes and went to Echo and her mother's house. I couldn't dance, Diana barely tolerated me, Markos hated me, even Kay snapped at me, and soon the whole town would look at me like I'd personally turned the wheel of Win's truck. Standing at their door, I braced myself, waiting for one of them to appear so I could unleash my self-righteous fury.

When Echo opened the door, I heard the wailing. It was steady and piercing, a single-note scream.

Echo's face lit up when she saw me, and she waved me in before running back to the kitchen. I didn't know what else to do, so I stepped inside the door. Echo's mother crouched in front of the sofa, face stuck between two cushions. Her curly white hair was all I could see of her head. The noise leaving her was steady and piercing. I didn't know how she was breathing. Other than the noise, she kept suspiciously still, tensed like a single touch would set off an internal spring and the noise and the couch and everything near it would combust.

I kept my back to the front door. Echo opened cabinets and poked into the refrigerator. She produced an apple and an instrument that looked like a large hockey puck.

"What's wrong with her?"

"She's dying."

I froze. "Should we call the hospital?"

"It's not that type of dying. Give me a minute."

Echo put the puck on the kitchen table and the apple on top of it. The apple floated above the puck as if magnetized. She sat in front of the apparatus and stared at the apple, which was slowly turning from side to side.

The air pressure increased like we were in a plane about to land; my ears popped. The air turned hot, too, so that my shirt stuck to my skin. All the while Echo's mother kept screaming wordlessly into the couch. "What are you do—"

"Quiet."

I found my eye drawn to the apple, which I only realized later was because all the light in the room dimmed except for a spotlight over the puck.

Echo leaned into the light. I hadn't noticed until then that she wasn't wearing her usual jacket, only a long-sleeved black T-shirt. She pulled up the sleeve, revealing a row of cuts from her wrist to her shoulder—some of them fresh and not scabbed over.

She picked up a jagged stone and selected a spot. I told myself to run over there and knock her hand away, but I couldn't move. When she cut, she didn't scream or wince. She didn't close her eyes. She watched—and I watched—as blood from the cut dripped down onto the hockey puck. After a few moments of dripping, all the light in the room turned red. I thought I saw a face above the apple, blinking, malignant, and then Echo screamed and I screamed and shut my eyes and covered my head with my arms.

When I opened my eyes, there was silence in the room. Even Echo's mom had stopped crying. She stood at the kitchen table with the apple in her hand, chewing. Echo slumped over, her head next to the puck-like device. Now that the room seemed less like it was going to explode, I could walk over to Echo, checking to make sure she was breathing. She was.

Echo's mother patted her daughter's unmarked arm. "Thank you," she said, then she lay on the couch. The crack of the apple's flesh as her teeth ripped off another piece of fruit reverberated through the room. Echo's arm continued to bleed, red puddling beneath her hair.

Echo was a hekamist.

She shouldn't exist.

All the anger and recrimination that had sounded so good in my head on the way over seemed pointless. My secret was out. There was nothing Echo could do about it now.

I opened and closed a few cabinets until I found a huge pack of gauze and some antiseptic wipes. When I touched the wound with a wipe Echo started awake and blinked twice at me.

"You've got the money?" she said in a low voice, glancing at her mother surreptitiously.

I let my jaw drop for a moment before answering. "Seriously? I came over here to give you shit—Markos knows, which means soon everyone will. I thought you got tired of waiting and told him."

Her shoulders slumped and sank farther into her seat. "Why would I tell Markos? Keeping the secret was my only leverage."

"Well, someone told Markos."

"Maybe he figured out you were lying."

"I've barely hung out with him since Win's funeral. He's had no opportunity to test me on Win trivia."

She sucked in a breath as if I'd pinched her, hard. "It's not a joke, you know. Just because you don't remember doesn't mean a person didn't die."

I held my wrist where it hurt the most. "I know that."

"You can't know. That's the point."

She wiped blood away from the cut on her arm. It was a clean line, despite the rough edges of the stone, still clutched in her hand.

"I told Markos," Echo's mom said from the couch.

Echo and I turned to her. "Mom—why?"

"If you get money you'll leave me." Echo's mom's voice got soft; her eyes closed. The core of the apple rested on her chest. "Couldn't let that happen. Too dangerous for my Echo to be out in the world . . . too many dangers . . ."

"Did you talk to my mom?" Echo asked me.

"Um," I said. "Yes. But . . . you aren't *both* blackmailing me? Together?"

Echo shook her head slowly. "She doesn't want me to go. She worries about me. Shit."

I tried to change the subject. "What kind—I mean—well—what's wrong with her, exactly?"

Echo inclined her head at her mother, now seemingly asleep on the couch, as she started wrapping a bandage around her arm. "This is what happens when we lose our coven. First the mind becomes unbalanced, unreliable. Then there's a period of pain, sudden and devastating. And eventually we stop being able to eat or speak, and . . ." She shrugged. "The more spells you've done, the faster it happens. That's why I'm still okay and she's in the pain part. I've been giving her some spells to take the edge off."

"Why not take one spell and be cured?"

Echo shook her head. "One spell, for that amount of pain, would kill her. The best I can do is dull it temporarily. Buy myself some more time."

"More time for what?"

"To get out of town and convince more hekamists to add us to their coven. To save her life."

"You can't just email them?"

"I'm illegal. Not supposed to exist. If I get caught, everyone in my coven goes to jail. I need to persuade them personally. Maybe even pay them off. What did you think I wanted your money for?"

"Oh." I glanced over at Echo's mom, asleep on the couch. "Oh. She doesn't want to find another coven?"

"She's afraid. That I'll get caught, get taken away. Afraid I'll leave her."

"You are going to leave her, though."

"When we're both still alive in six months, she'll be in better shape to understand why I had to go." She gestured at the small room filled with cheap furniture. "People pay a lot for what we do, but she's always hidden the money, says she doesn't want to call attention to ourselves by spending it, and I've never been able to find it. I'm not sure she knows where it is anymore, now that her mind's going. So I have to earn money myself."

We sat in silence for another few moments. It struck me that Echo had been here the whole time I'd been going to school, living her life in a tiny house, invisible to the rest of us—except when we needed her or her mother.

"So you're a hekamist," I said.

Echo nodded.

"And it's always like that? Spells, I mean?"

"More or less. Food, blood, will." She recited the words like a mantra, then bit off a piece of medical tape with her teeth and attached it to the gauze.

"And it . . . hurts?" I asked.

"Like hell."

"So why do you do it?"

She peered up at me through dark hair matted with blood. "It's not just pain. It's also joy—the power of it. I'm a part of something bigger than me. Something beautiful. I set things right, keep the balance. That always feels good." She sat up, pulling down the sleeve of her shirt over the fresh bandage. "Plus it's my choice. I get to choose to help my mom stop suffering."

"You never regret it?"

She looked for a second like she might snap at me, but seemed to reconsider. "There are moments. When it would be easier . . . not to be a hekamist."

I'd heard hekamists on TV protesting the laws against joining covens, but they never talked about this. They talked about history and natural balance and the free market, and the grand peaceful history of hekame. No "food, blood, will." No pain.

Echo leaned back in her chair. Her hair dripped red onto her cheek, so I handed her some extra gauze and she wrung out handfuls.

"Well, now that the secret's out, I guess we're done, then," she said.

"Yeah. Good luck." I started to creep toward the door, stepping carefully around the awkwardly placed couch and the passed-out older hekamist sleeping on it.

"Hey," Echo said. She chewed on her bottom lip, hesitating. "The night Win died—the night he was going to pay me. Do you really not remember it at all?"

I stared at her, examining every twisted piece of hair and cinched buckle on her boots. Her eyes were light brown, softer than the sharp angles of the rest of her face. I had that not-quite-a-memory feeling again—of buoyancy. Light and air.

"You do seem a little familiar. I don't know what this means, but I have a vague memory of—lightness."

She smiled big then, so big it seemed to crack her face in two, and she started crying.

I could've left then, turned around and walked out the door. But there was nothing out there for me except videos of past performances and friends who didn't trust me. Strangely, Echo reminded me of Diana, or at least the old Diana, who needed me to be the strong one, the leader. Even though she was a hekamist. Even though I was the one who knew a secret about *her*, now. The secret made her real.

I went back to the kitchen and sat down across from her. Echo kept crying, tears gathering at the end of her nose, mixing with blood, and dripping onto her black-sleeved arms, which she'd crossed on the table. I wondered if that was what I would've looked like if I hadn't taken the spell, and was in real mourning.

"I wasn't in love with him or anything," she said after a while.

"Oh. That's okay."

"But he listened, he trusted me. I've been on my own, basically, for a long time. I . . . miss him." She wiped her eyes with her sleeve.

"What was he like?"

She looked down at her sleeve and the fingernails clutching the hem. "He played baseball. He was always kind to his sister."

"I've met her," I said. I remembered a small, pale girl who hugged me fiercely at the funeral. Where was she now? Would Old Ari have sought her out, spent more time with her? Did she miss me?

Echo stood up so abruptly I thought she might pass out. But though she swayed, she stayed upright, grabbing plates and throwing them into the sink. She stowed the puck in a cabinet next to a stack of dented baking sheets. The dirty gauze pads went into the garbage and the clean ones back where they came from. She moved too fast to follow in such a tiny kitchen.

"Win was a good brother," she said. "Not that I have anything to compare him to. I'm an only child, obviously—and I'm not sure how my mom managed to have me, because it's tough for hekamists to have kids. Something about the shared life of a coven isn't conducive to the selfishness of a baby. That's why—it's why most hekamists used to join covens when they were older, back when it was legal to join. They'd wait until they'd already had their kids." She stopped moving in the middle of the kitchen, as if shocked by her own words.

I was shocked, too. No babies. Not ever. I didn't want one then and I doubt she did, either, but it was a tough life sentence to bear.

"But you wanted to know about Win," she said quietly. "Not about me. I wish I had something to tell you. But I knew him so briefly—I didn't get a chance . . ."

I wished I hadn't asked. It was a stupid, thoughtless impulse from that same part of me that studied the tapes of my dance performances, digging up proof of . . . what? The secrets and kisses and looks didn't mean anything to me. It all had no context. I searched for clues about Win clinically, selfishly, while the people who knew him mourned.

"He never even got to use the spell I made him," she said. She glanced at her mom, asleep on the couch, then sat back in her seat at the table and leaned her face into her hands. "I think, well, if he had taken it . . . I don't know. Maybe he wouldn't be dead."

"So the money was for a spell? What type?" She shook her head and wouldn't answer. "How could your spell have prevented an accident?" I pressed.

She didn't say anything. Another secret, then—another thing I didn't know about him.

"I'm sorry for your loss," I said. I didn't know what else to say. She crumpled her head down onto the table again, and I could hear her jagged breathing.

"I hate to admit it, but . . ." She took a deep breath and spoke straight into the tabletop. "I can see why you'd rather forget."

I squeezed my wrist with the opposite hand so hard the muscle ached. "You're probably the only person who will say that."

"People are dicks."

"I bet they'd hate me less if they knew I probably won't ever dance again."

As soon as I said it I wished I could take it back, grab the words out of the air and cram them back in my big stupid mouth. Moving to New York was the only thing I had to look forward to.

But now that everyone knew I'd erased Win, there was no pretending anymore: I hadn't been to class in weeks. I could barely stretch my arms over my head. I'd lost all the blisters and calluses that make you a real dancer, because I wasn't a real dancer.

I couldn't dance.

"How bad is it?"

I pushed back my chair and stood in the middle of the kitchen, feet in fourth position, one arm over my head, one extended in front of me. I saw a pirouette in my mind. I'd done thousands. Easy. Deep breath. Arms out. Weight on the front foot. Let the momentum carry you through the turn. I barely made it halfway before I stumbled into the refrigerator.

Echo looked at my knees and my arms and my torso, calculating. "A brute force spell to fix that much clumsiness would have major side effects."

"That's what your mom told me. Said I'd have extra trouble because of the effects of my previous spells, too."

"A careful hekamist could figure a way to make it work."

"But there are side effects upon side effects. Aren't there?"

She examined me. "It's a risk, for sure. But if it's done right, you'll be a bit of a mess, but basically you."

"And it costs five thousand dollars for a permanent spell, right?"

She shrugged. "When you're a famous ballerina you can pay me back."

My heart jumped in my chest, a wobbly grand jeté. "What?"

"I'll help you. If I can."

Now my heart was leaping in a circle, pirouetting with each landing. Spinning, dizzy, I struggled to stand. "Don't make fun of me, please. I know you must hate me—"

"I don't hate you."

"—but don't mess with me, okay?"

"I'm not making fun of you." She stood, brushing invisible crumbs off the kitchen table. "I'll consider it a favor to Win."

I looked around the room as if I would find someone to tell the news to: everything had changed. I came to Echo furious, ready to blame her for all that had gone wrong this summer. I lost my memory, dance, and my best friends.

But now I had hope that I could get one of them back.

33

WIN

So a better person, a smarter person, a less-fucked-up-in-the-head person would tell you that he ate the damn sandwich, begged and borrowed the money, and then lived happily ever after. But because it's me telling the story, I'm sorry to say it didn't happen like that. You know the ending, anyway: pure tragedy.

First of all, I didn't eat the sandwich. I found a Tupperware container with a snap lid and placed the sandwich in it and then put the container in my underwear drawer. Every day, if I managed to get out of bed, I'd look at it while getting dressed. And every day I decided *not yet*.

Maybe it was what Echo made me promise—that I'd take it rather than kill myself. I figured if I didn't actively want to die while putting on my boxers, I didn't need it yet.

And I started to think more about how permanent the spell was. If I ate this sandwich, I'd be changing the "real" me forever.

Something about my promise to Echo got twisted up in my

brain and I started to think that eating the sandwich would be the same as killing myself. It would kill, permanently, the real Win. I'd be some new happy Win—the Win I saw in yearbook pictures I didn't remember taking, smiling and holding up my baseball glove, or the Win dancing with Ari at Homecoming in the soapy, sparkly dark.

Plus, I hadn't paid Echo yet. It didn't seem fair to take the spell until I did.

Even if I didn't take it, I wanted to pay Echo, help her and her mom, in whatever weak way I could. She'd already put in the effort, after all. And so a few days after Echo gave me the sandwich, I made my first and only attempt to ask Ari for the money.

I picked up Ari and Kara from the dance studio. Everyone else in the pickup lane was a middle-aged mom, and I imagined—or maybe saw, but I can't trust myself on that—them glaring at me suspiciously through their rearview mirrors. I started to shake. My hands rattled the steering wheel and my torso vibrated against the seat and my teeth chattered in my head. They for sure would've stared at me if I'd gotten out of the truck and run for the ocean, which is what the shaking was telling me to do, that or throw up all over the dashboard and smash my head against the steering wheel, and I couldn't hold on—the car was shaking and I was shaking in it, so hard we had to be coming undone. And then Kara opened the passenger door and climbed into the back and a second later Ari sat in the front seat and gave me a kiss that I didn't feel and I put the truck into drive.

Ari and Kara talked to each other, which spared me for a few minutes. I could feel Ari giving me looks, though. Side-eyeing me as we stopped at red lights.

Ari was smart and she noticed things about me, which was scary sometimes. *You seemed mad at lunch. You laughed at that show—must've liked it. What are you worried about?* Things I hadn't noticed myself yet. She'd noticed the shaking for sure. She probably wouldn't be surprised when I asked her for the money; she'd only be surprised when I couldn't tell her why I needed it.

We dropped off Kara at her friend's house. She made smoochie faces at us and Ari stuck out her tongue at her. It amazed me sometimes how Ari could do that—be so free and easy with Kara, laughing, teasing, sticking out her tongue. I had to think it all through, even how to say goodbye to my sister.

"What do you want to do?" Ari asked.

I kept my eyes on the road, but it blurred.

Ari was so happy. It radiated off of her. She didn't even know she was doing it, and that was the weirdest part. She simply *was*.

"Whatever you want to do," I said.

She stretched her arms over her head, overextending the elbows. "I'm a mess. I should probably take a shower before we do anything."

"Okay," I said, and turned toward her house.

She grinned at me. "You forgot, didn't you?"

If I hadn't been thinking of how to bring up five thousand dollars, I would've racked my brain for what I was missing. But all I could do was blink.

"It's our anniversary. One year."

"Oh man." I rubbed my eyes. Last May seemed like a thousand years ago. "I'm sorry."

"Don't apologize. Be lucky you have such a cool girlfriend who doesn't care about stupid stuff like anniversaries."

"I am lucky."

I stopped at another light and she kissed me on the cheek. I believed her when she said she didn't care. But she remembered. If I'd remembered . . . what would I have done? Would it have made me feel any better? Or would the pressure of an Important Day hanging over me be just as bad?

I wouldn't be planning on asking her for a huge sum of money, that was for sure.

The truck shook again. Slightly. Maybe this time it was the wind.

"I can't hang out tonight," I said into the silence. "I'm such an ass. I'm sorry. I think I'm getting a migraine, and—my mom's working the night shift, and Kara—"

"Really?" Ari said. She didn't look disappointed yet, only surprised. But the disappointment would come soon.

"And you know, tonight's not our anniversary," I said.

"Yes, it is."

"No, it's not. You're calculating from that night we were at Markos's. We talked, and walked in the garden? But I'm positive it wasn't until after midnight that we kissed."

She rolled her eyes.

"I'm serious. I'll be ready tomorrow. I'll feel better, and we'll have a really good time, and it'll be the actual anniversary. I mean you wouldn't want to jinx it by celebrating on the wrong day, right?"

We pulled into her driveway. She touched my knee. It could've been someone else's; it even looked far away. "It really doesn't matter about the anniversary, Win. You don't have to feel bad or anything. We're good, you know?"

"It's just a headache," I lied.

She reached up with her other hand and touched the line of my jaw. She studied me, and I noticed her hair pulled tight into a bun, the freckles by her ear, the light brown flecks in her dark brown eyes. I noticed it all, familiar as always. I didn't understand how I could be numb to the entire world, including her hand on my jaw, like a ghost, but I still knew I loved her, knew I didn't want to hurt her.

I wanted the numbness to take away that feeling, too. It wasn't doing any good.

I opened my mouth to ask her for the money to pay Echo, and she kissed me.

I remembered other kisses. Homecoming on the dance floor. Curled up in her room while she cried. I couldn't remember the feeling, but I remembered what I did. And I copied that until she pulled away.

"You're right," she said, smiling at me. "Tomorrow's our anniversary. Of course."

I walked her to her door, where she turned to me and put both hands around my neck. I leaned down to kiss her again, trying to focus on my lips and hers, but there was still no feeling there. I touched the sides of her waist below her breasts, flatter than usual underneath her dance leotard; I pressed my lips harder against hers; I thought about seeing her naked for the first time a few months ago—usually a reliable memory to heat up my numb insides.

But there was nothing. Not a twinge. Not even when she sighed and leaned in and I tasted the lightly salty skin by her temple.

"Headache?" she asked.

"I just need to rest," I said.

"Seriously, Win. You'd tell me if something's wrong?"

I could feel her concern as a physical force, more than I could feel her lips or skin. The problem with this question was that even if I decided to tell her everything, to open myself up like a book and start tearing out pages, I'd have to admit that there were many days—dozens of them—seriously dark times that I never told her about. She'd be hurt about those other days, even if she wanted to help with today. That would be putting my feelings over hers. I wanted to spare hers.

I couldn't be that sick if I wanted to spare her feelings. I didn't need the spell if I could do that much. Right?

"They should move New York closer," she said.

It took me a second to realize she was talking about next year, and her and Jess's big move to the city. "It's not that far," I said.

"It feels far. It feels like another planet."

"It's not another planet. It's New York."

She scowled, her small features fierce. "It's a stupid thing, dancing. You should be able to do it anywhere."

I leaned back so I could see more than her face in close-up. I looked for signs she was going to start sobbing again, like the day she'd gotten into the Manhattan Ballet. I didn't know what I'd do if she did—it might have broken me completely. But her eyes were clear, her skin pale, unflushed. She'd never gotten upset again after that day. It was as if it had never happened. "You have to go to New York," I said.

"I know. Jess is counting on it."

"No, *you* have to go. To dance."

"Sounds like you want to get rid of me."

"No. No! It's only . . . you're so good at it. And you have this thing you can dedicate your life to." I could feel panic creeping in around my edges, vibrating in the air around our heads.

She sighed, dismissing the compliment. "Most people say long distance is stupid."

The panic seized me, like the shaking in the car a thousand times over. "Do you want to break up?"

"Of course not. I thought if you're anxious about it—"

"It's not going to make me less anxious to break up. I mean, it would be awful. I can't imagine it." Breaking up would have meant giving up. "No, I'm fine. I'm going to be fine. You're going to be fine. You're going to dance, and I'm going to . . . It's been a weird day. My head's been all over the place. Tomorrow we'll have an anniversary. I know it's going to be great next year. I'll come down for *both* anniversary days. I'm so excited for you—I'll be there every weekend."

"All right, all right," she said.

"I love you," I said, because I did, and I didn't know how else to tell her except by telling her, even though the words felt stupid and insubstantial, gone as soon as they left my mouth.

She smiled a funny smile. "Duh. I love you, too."

She planted a kiss on my cheek and I turned my head to kiss her for real, as seriously as I could remember how.

When we broke apart I ran for the truck before I could say or do anything else to ruin whatever we had left.

I could never ask Ari for money for the spell. Never.

That truck-shaking panic stayed with me all night, on and on until the dark and silence of three a.m., watching the flash of the alarm clock light on the bedroom wall. Panic gnawed at me until I was worn down to nothing but fibers.

But I didn't feel bad enough to eat the sandwich.

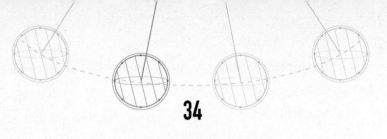

34

KAY

It was a relief to be bad. I didn't have to be nice or funny or kind, and I knew I would never be alone. That heavy cloak of feelings and worries and responsibilities—I could take it off and leave it off. I wasn't scared of the nothing underneath. I felt free. Unhooking was the best thing that could've happened to me.

Even with Mina, who wasn't under the spell, I could let go. She'd already left me, after all. I didn't owe her anything.

On Monday, I went with Mina to her annual checkup at the hospital. I got in the car out of habit, because I always went with Mina to her appointments, but as soon as we were on the road, I remembered: I didn't have to do this.

I could tell as we drove down the familiar streets that Mina thought I'd decided to come with her because I wanted to give her my support, like I used to. She didn't say anything, but she looked at me out of the corner of her eye at stoplights and right-hand turns. She thought I was the same Katelyn who'd come with her to so many appointments in the past. The young, stupid

Katelyn who did whatever she asked, who only cared about cheering her up, who didn't have any other friends or interests.

Just because I hadn't poked myself full of holes and shaved my head like she did didn't mean I hadn't changed, too. I was a different girl now.

After we pulled into the familiar lot and parked in our usual space next to a misshapen hedge, Mina got out and looked at me expectantly. "Ready?"

I leaned against my open car door. "You go," I said. "I'll meet you back here in an hour."

If I'd been the old Katelyn, the look on Mina's face would've ripped out my heart. Surprise, confusion, disappointment, hurt. Things had been tense between us all summer, but nothing I'd done had come close to causing this look.

I didn't care. I didn't have to care.

"Why are you being like this, Katelyn?" she asked, her voice small.

I closed the car door and stared at her. "Really?"

"I barely see you all summer, you're always with your friends, and then when I do see you, you make a point of saying something terrible."

"I'm sorry that me having friends is so inconvenient for you."

She rubbed her shaved head, and I tried to imagine her hair sticking up in every direction in frustrated spikes. I didn't even know what Mina's hair would look like now. "Whatever, I'm late. Do what you want."

She walked toward the oncology wing. I waited for her to

disappear past the double doors, not looking back, before I made my way around the building to the ER.

Lots of people who've gone through stuff I've gone through hate hospitals because they associate them with death and loss and hopelessness. But I think even if Mina had died, which we thought was inevitable for three years, I still would've liked the hospital.

Sure, there's suffering everywhere. But it's also where people go to get well. I loved hearing pages and getting glimpses of freshly stocked linen closets. I loved the special clipboards and the beds with a thousand different levers. I loved the mean nurses too busy to talk to you and the nice ones even when you could tell they were checked out and faking it.

And I loved the doctors. The doctors! They came into a room and owned it. Everyone looked to them for answers, and unless they were brand new, they *knew* the answers. Even when things were hopeless, they were the ones to let us know. They issued proclamations: prescriptions, diagnoses. They wore better clothes than everyone else, and they shook your hand and theirs was dry from so much washing. I loved them. I'd watch what they did, check the charts when they left, try to get Mina to laugh by imitating them.

One time I came into her room after school, took a look at her chart, said something, and Mina laughed—and then ten minutes later a real doctor came in, looked at the chart, and said exactly the same thing. Mina's eyes got huge in her thin, dark face.

"You're going to be a doctor," she said.

"Whatever."

"No, seriously, Katelyn. You've got to."

I didn't believe her. I wasn't that good in school, and doctors had to go to school forever. Besides, the whole reason I liked doctors was because they were so unlike me. I could never walk into a room and own it like a doctor.

Mina let it drop and never brought it up again, which proved my point: wasn't going to happen.

But I remembered enough about my years imitating doctors and keeping Mina company that I knew how to blend in. While Mina was at her appointment, I passed the time trying to diagnose everyone in the ER waiting room. A couple of flus, a kid with a high fever, a middle-aged man with the worst sunburn I'd ever seen. A woman holding a dish towel around her hand got taken back almost immediately. The rest of us sat around.

When I got bored I walked confidently through the swinging doors to the patient rooms. I knew my way around, and I knew that people didn't ask where you were going if you looked like you had a destination. I'd been invisible in these hallways hundreds of times.

They hadn't changed. I walked purposefully past moaning rooms and crying rooms and scarily silent rooms, past the rooms where half a dozen family members forced loud laughter, past many rooms with only a TV blaring. It was all so familiar, but removed. Like walking through a dream.

Since I hadn't bothered to pick a destination, my feet took

me to pediatric oncology out of habit. Mina would be meeting with Dr. Brown in his office, so I turned toward the residents' floor instead.

Once there, my purposeful walk slowed. A few kids hung out in the rec room area watching TV or playing board games. I looked for familiar faces, but of course there wouldn't be any; I hadn't visited in two years, and the kids I remembered would be out by now, like Mina, or dead.

A child stepped in front of me. With the shaved head, I couldn't tell if it was a boy or a girl, and though he (she?) looked around ten, I knew in this place she (he?) was probably a few years older than that. My age when I started coming here with Mina.

"You don't belong here," the kid said.

"Yeah? How do you know?"

"You don't look sick."

"How do you know I'm not visiting someone?"

"Are you?"

I shrugged. "How do you know I'm not a super hot young doctor?"

She looked at me skeptically. (I had decided she was a she.) "Where's your doctor coat?"

"I don't wear one."

"Where'd you go to med school?"

"Northwestern."

"What kind of cancer do I have?"

I looked at her. She was wearing plain green pajamas, long

pants and long sleeves. I couldn't see any scars. It was almost impossible to tell by looking at someone what they had. That was one of the scary things about cancer. You could be walking around, happy, and inside cells were mutating, growing. I suddenly thought of Mina, alone in Dr. Brown's office down the hall, and felt a faint pang.

"Leukemia," I said, because that was a good shot, percentage-wise.

"Nice try. Hepatocellular carcinoma."

I had never heard of that before, but I recognized part of the word. "Ah. The liver," I said, and nodded in a doctorly way.

The girl laughed, a short bark. A couple of the TV-watching kids looked up at us. "I like you," she said. "I'm Hana. If you get caught, you can say you're visiting me."

Cold washed over me, and I took a step back. This was too familiar. I'd been here before, bantering with someone who might or might not get better. "You don't like me. You don't even know me."

Her expression folded in on itself. I noticed this with Mina, too: without hair, emotions lived closer to the surface. "Don't be weird."

"I'm sorry," I said. "Good luck with your hepatocellular carcinoma."

"Hey—where are you going? Wait!"

I didn't look back, and she couldn't catch me.

My heart pounded against my ribs as I made my way back to the ER. Talking to Hana, I'd fallen into an old role. I didn't want to be that girl anymore—the one who cheers you up when you're sick. The one who has nothing better to do than to visit day or night. The one whose entire purpose in life was to support you and help you get better. The one who was left behind. And I *wasn't* her. At least, I didn't have to be. I could walk away.

But as soon as I reached the ER, I thought about where I was.

Paramedics were wheeling in a young guy with a splint around his leg. He had dark hair and for a second I thought *Cal* and then I thought *Diana* and *Ari* and *not here no not here I'm leaving I promise I'm leaving I'm leaving now!*

It was like the Whirlpool at the carnival only much worse. It wouldn't be hard at all for the spell to arrange for them to bump into me at an ER.

My fingernails bit into my palms as I struggled not to panic. But maybe panic was the right reaction.

I ran for the automatic doors, ducking and weaving around sick people and their friends and family, completely abandoning the rules of remaining invisible. A shout came from the intake desk but I didn't stop running until I reached Mina's car in our spot in the lot.

Mina was waiting for me.

"Where were you?" she asked.

"In the ER," I said. I couldn't think of anything else to say. My heart was pounding so hard my vision pulsed.

"Why?"

"It doesn't matter. Can we get out of here? Please?"

Mina played with the studded leather cuff around her forearm.

"Dr. Brown says I'm fine. No sign of the cancer. If you care."

"Oh. Good. Let's go."

Mina half laughed without amusement and didn't look at me as she turned on the car and pulled out of the lot.

The pounding in my chest lessened. I could breathe.

Cal and Diana and Ari hadn't shown up in the ER. Maybe the hook had some sense. Maybe it wasn't as dangerous as I'd thought.

And I was no longer the girl who sat patiently in a visitor's chair and imitated doctors. Hana would forget me before the end of the day. Mina didn't need me. She was fine.

Mina pulled onto the highway, checking her blind spots carefully. She caught my eye. "What's wrong with you, Katelyn?"

"Nothing," I said, grinning for the first time all day. "Actually, everything's perfect."

35

MARKOS

I woke up hungover and with a bitter acid taste in my mouth. For five days in a row.

It reminded me of the day after Win died. I was low from spell side effects and then I drank half a bottle of vodka and tore down the treehouse in the backyard. I was lucky I didn't break my neck, crying and drinking and ripping rotting boards out of the branches, tearing up the skin on my hands, but it was hard to feel lucky about anything when the unluckiest thing in the world had happened.

See, I remembered that horrible last night. The alcohol only dims so much. In the morning everything's crystal clear again.

After the hekamist told me about Ari's memory spell and I kissed Kay, I stopped going to the hardware store. Stopped going anywhere, really, except the living room, kitchen, and bathroom. It was too much trouble to climb the stairs to my room. Besides, there would be another terrible movie on TV or someone to kill in a video game or beer to steal from the fridge instead.

My mom tried to cajole me into doing something, but she was easy to ignore. She'd bring me a hamburger or sit on the couch next to me or shout at me from the doorway. Boring.

"Here's some corn on the cob," she said one night, or day, I wasn't quite sure. She placed a plate on the coffee table next to my bare feet. "You should eat something other than chips."

I pushed the plate away with my heel.

"This Howard Hughes act is getting old, Markos. Eat."

"I'm not eating anything you bring me."

She drew back. "Why not?"

"What if you put a 'get happy' spell in the butter?"

She went white; it felt . . . not good, but satisfying.

"When you stole that money from me," she said, shards of glass in each word, "I let you off easy. I regret that. You've been through a lot, but we are not discussing that money or what it's for or *who* it's for. Ever."

"Like I give a damn." I pulled the smelly fleece blanket over my head to block out the rest of whatever it was she'd come to say.

Then my brothers descended on me, oldest to youngest. Brian came in his uniform and lectured on "manning up" and "letting go." Dev tried to joke with me, going after my fat ass sitting doing nothing, then my wussy feelings getting in the way of life, then the unlikelihood of my ugly face getting a girl even if I did manage to find the shower—and then he stopped, because I threw a stone coaster at the wall next to his head.

When Cal finally came to see me, I was tired of it. I didn't give him a chance to try to cajole me out of my chair. Knowing Cal, his tactic would probably be smiling and tripping over something for a laugh. That was Cal—probably the most easygoing of us. Never held a grudge. Didn't deserve my black mood.

I mean, when we were kids, after our dad died, he went through a period where he scared the shit out of me—jumping off the garage roof onto his skateboard, stealing stuff from the hardware store, trying to impress Brian and Dev's friends by drinking until he puked—but by the time he was in high school and I was in junior high, he'd mellowed. Became a real Waters brother like the rest of them.

And he'd been hanging out with Kay. He'd gone to the carnival with her. She thought they were dating. Just the thought of her stirred a sick feeling in my gut that I quieted with half a can of beer.

Cal looked as shitty as I felt, skin clammy and eyes unfocused. He swayed in the doorway to the living room.

"Leave me alone," I said.

He coughed into his arm, a rattling, wet noise.

"Dude, what's wrong with you?"

"Cold," he said.

"Go take a nap."

"Supposed to talk to you. Because you're so sad."

I threw my half-full can of beer down. It spilled onto the carpet. "I kissed your girlfriend. You gonna do something about it?"

Cal shrugged. "She's not my girlfriend. Haven't even seen her in a week."

I hated how easy it was for him to say that. Like it was obvious. Of course she wasn't his girlfriend. Of course it didn't matter. I wanted to not care, too.

But wanting to not care is just another kind of caring.

"Tell me what's going on. We'll figure it out," Cal said, wiping his nose on his sweatshirt.

Maybe some other guy—maybe Brian or Dev—would've taken him up on the offer. Talked it out. Analyzed the problem. Cried. Felt better. Maybe that would've helped a normal brother feel less alone. Maybe I would've done it, too, if they had bothered to try to reach out to me at any point in the past two months, and if I hadn't been so committed to living on this couch and being pissed at the world.

I thought of my mom's panic at the mention of the spell money. She really didn't want me talking about it. So it was perfect. I didn't know if the money and the spell were for Cal—or what the spell was for at all. But it was just awful enough to throw in his face and see if it stuck. Rag on Cal and piss off Mom, all in one shot.

"It's probably not just a cold," I said. "I bet Mom finally ran out of cash and didn't get you your spells this month."

"My what?"

"Your spells, dummy. It's Sunday, isn't it? So maybe you'll get your spells today. All six-thousand-dollars-a-month's worth. Are they to make you smarter? Because you should up the dosage."

Cal's face filled with confusion. "I don't take any spells."

"Bullshit," I said, almost cheerfully. "Every month Mom pays for them. I've seen the money—stolen it, too. Maybe your spells make you less of a loser. I'd believe that, because you seem sort of desperate. Before she kissed me, you should've heard what Kay said about—"

He lunged across the room at me, arm bent, forearm across my throat, other hand pulled back to punch me in the face. But I didn't grow up with three older brothers for nothing. I relaxed my neck—it hurts worse if you try to brace for it—and waited for the snap and the sting.

When it didn't come, I opened an eye and saw Cal's face twisted in concentration, his punching arm shaking with effort. He grunted. But he couldn't make the arm connect with my face. Even the forearm over my neck seemed to be pulling back involuntarily, as much as he pushed forward with the rest of his body.

"Well, that answers one question," I said. I raised my hands and pushed him away. He stumbled but didn't come back at me.

He couldn't.

His face drained of blood. He *was* the one being spelled. Lucky guess. The spells wouldn't let him hit me, or probably anyone. He looked at me, bewildered, as if I was the one who'd just hit him.

I wished I could tell Diana.

And that was the moment—the shock making me weak-willed—when I thought her name and saw her in my mind and remembered how it felt to sit across from her at the diner or next to her in the car and I missed her, oh god I missed her. I missed Win, too, but there's a different way you miss a dead guy, and not only because I wasn't hooking up with Win. I missed Win stupidly and pointlessly, because part of me understood the situation, which was that death is permanent and life finite and there are no angels, etc., etc. But Diana. I missed Diana like being punched repeatedly in the stomach, because she was out there walking around, talking to people, touching her hair, and worst of all probably miserable and broken because of something I did, because I cut her off completely and I made out with Kay and I did it all knowing I shouldn't.

All this time, Cal was still in the room. Screwed-up Cal who didn't even know he was on horse tranquilizers or whatever.

"Are you crying?" he asked, and I didn't answer, because he had to be able to see for himself, and the question was asked to poke at me.

"I did a stupid thing," I said.

When I looked up I expected him to nod, but he was staring at his hands, turning them over and balling them into fists. He pinched the inside of his left wrist with his right hand, frowning.

"Doesn't matter about your spell," I said. "You don't need to beat the shit out of me because I'm punishing myself plenty."

Cal shook his head. "I can't believe Mom would do this to me."

"She said she was looking out for you."

"For how long?"

"A couple years. At least."

Cal didn't bother trying to cheer me up any more. He left,

and I was alone in the living room again.

But I could never be alone enough, because my brain kept whirring.

—This sucks.

—Yeah.

—I mean it sucks A LOT.

—Never leaving the living room probably makes it suck more.

—But I like it here. It's safe.

—Safe?

—Yeah, safe. Protected.

—Huh. Is it?

36

ARI

I didn't know what else to do, so I went to work at the Sweet Shoppe like normal. But the rhythm of the scooping felt off, and the cold didn't make me numb—it made me shudder.

When Diana came in, I braced my hands along the glass of the display case and thought of Echo's promised spell. If it could let me dance, I could leave for New York as planned—in one week. Everything would be back on track. I could survive one more week if I could dance at the end of it.

"I got your message," she said.

"Thanks for coming by. I wanted to apologize—I know Markos found out about the spell. I didn't have a chance to tell him first."

She shrugged. "You were never going to tell him the truth. You only told me you would to shut me up."

"That's not true."

"It's okay, Ari. You were right about Markos. We weren't in love. Let's just go back to the way things were."

I hated the way her voice sounded, toneless and careful. I hated that Markos had done this to her, and I especially hated that it was exactly what I predicted would happen.

"Do you want an ice cream?" I asked.

"Sure," she said. She would've agreed to anything—ice cream cone, face tattoo, drowning. I filled a waffle cone with Rocky Road and handed it to her.

Diana eyed the ice cream but didn't eat any. "I've been thinking a lot since you told me about your spell. Things have been so weird between us, and I didn't know why."

"It's been tough for me . . . figuring out what to say and what not to."

She shook her head. "It's not that. I think—I *know* things were weird between us before you did this spell. You didn't . . . I had to call Kay. I couldn't rely on you anymore. And I always felt like there was this Ari-Win-Markos club that I wasn't invited to join." She sighed. "A tiny jealous part of me thought that you wanted to keep Markos for yourself, and you didn't want competition."

"Diana, I promise you, I don't think of Markos that way."

"Then why didn't you ask me out with you? The night before Win died, you went out just the three of you. Like you always did. You never included me—and not just that night. All the time."

I squeezed my eyes shut and tried to remember. I could see myself spending time with Markos, having fun—Markos teasing me, Markos getting himself kicked out of restaurants and bowling alleys, Markos singing classic rock at the top of his lungs in the passenger seat of a truck driven by . . . a blank space.

These memories seemed fun, but I saw them mostly from the outside, with no internal monologue, and they jumped and skipped and were as thin as paper. "I don't know why I didn't include you, Diana. I can't remember."

She nodded. "I figured. If you still remembered I would've been afraid to ask. I'm not sure I want to know the answer."

"Was I that bad?"

"You're not bad. You're you. You make a decision and once it's decided that's the way it is forever."

I couldn't tell if that was true—except that the decision to take a spell to erase Win seemed to fit with it.

"I'm really sorry," I said.

She looked at the ice cream and shook her head. "You don't even know what you're apologizing for."

When Jess got home from work I was lying on the living room floor. My back had started spasming during a plié and this was the only thing that stopped it. Even lying down it hurt, but at least it didn't seize up and shake me like a rag doll. (The only thing that comforted me was the thought that Echo's spell would save me. I had to wait long enough for Echo's spell.) I could see Jess's black clogs but nothing else.

"Hi," I said.

She knelt on the ground and wrapped her arms around me, resting her head on the carpeted floor. I could smell the coffee on her clothes and the hair product keeping her short hair pompadoured.

"Hey—what are you doing?" I asked, attempting to shimmy away.

"I'm so, so sorry, Ari," she said into the carpet.

"For what?"

"You must have been hurting so bad."

I closed my eyes. "You heard."

"I heard."

"From who?"

"Some kids at the coffee shop, gossiping. Apparently they heard from Markos and his brothers." I could imagine a group of my classmates—several groups—going over the news with relish. Everyone had seen me at the funeral. Everyone had an opinion about how awful I was. "Then I went to see Rowena. She told me you haven't been to class all summer."

"Oh no, Jess—"

"I should've gone weeks ago." Jess let go of me and rocked back on her heels. "I should've paid more attention. Noticed things. I'm such an idiot."

"You're not an idiot, Jess, come on."

Jess shook her head. "I'm supposed to take care of you."

"You didn't ask for this."

"Does that mean it's okay that I'm bad at it?" Jess rubbed her hands over her eyes. I remembered how she looked the day after I took my spell—she had been crying and wanted to talk. And I went to dance. Pushed her away. "Sometimes I think if your mom could see us now she would've picked someone else for this job."

My wrist pounded and I held my breath to make the pain go away. "Don't say that," I said, but I'm not sure she could hear me, even as close as she was sitting.

"I've always been too quick to believe what's on the surface. If something obvious is off, I can fix it. But if you look fine, I assume that you are fine. That insight—it must be some sort of mothering instinct I didn't get. Katie had it." Katie was my mother; I'd barely heard Jess say her name in years. "She always could tell what everyone was really thinking. But I got a different set of genes."

"If I look fine, I *am* fine, Jess."

"Yeah—even I know that's not true." The lines on Jess's face around her eyes and mouth held the shadows, as if someone had drawn in the grief with wax pencil. "I made you an appointment with Dr. Pitts and I canceled the moving truck."

I propped myself up by my elbows. "You did *what?*"

"You should talk to someone, and I think I've proven that I'm not the greatest at heart-to-heart moments, so—"

"Not that. New York."

The look on her face was so full of pity and guilt I could barely stand it. "We can't go to New York."

"No. We can. You didn't even ask me."

"Can you dance right now, Ari? Show me." I didn't move from my position on the floor. Jess nodded. "Rowena said she hasn't seen you since you fell in class. Right after Win died."

Jess wasn't mad at me. She didn't scream or sound disappointed. Maybe she expected me to be a failure, to suddenly stop doing the one thing I've ever been any good at. I sat up completely and curled my arms around my knees as best I could. "I'll be able to dance soon."

Jess didn't say anything, just looked at me with that horrible, unnatural pity. She reached for my bad wrist and held it; pain thumped along with my heartbeat.

"I'm so sorry I did this to you," she said, and brushed the wrist with her thumb. "Your old spell. It's okay to hurt sometimes. It's okay to have bad memories."

I pulled my wrist out of her grasp and winced as the pain shot to my elbow. "Stop it. You did the right thing."

She only shook her head. "Maybe if I hadn't done that, you wouldn't have felt like you had to forget Win."

"That's not important. New York is important." I didn't agree with Jess that this was all her fault, and that she should've known better or any of that crap. The Win spell was a huge, ugly mistake—but it was my mistake. Not hers. Her mistake would be keeping us from moving. "We have to go to New York."

"Dr. Pitts is expecting you."

"Jess, no. You're overreacting. We're going to New York. Tell me we're going to New York."

"I'll take you to Dr. Pitts first. Then we can talk."

I didn't want to talk to anyone—not her, as strange and sad and wrong as she was acting, and certainly not Dr. Pitts. But I followed her out to the car anyway.

Jess wasn't mad at me like Markos or disappointed like Diana. So why did her pity and love feel like such a burden?

After I explained what I had done, Dr. Pitts sat back in her chair, staring at the wall behind my head. We didn't talk for a long moment. And in the end, I was the one to break the silence. "So you can see why all your attempts to get me to grieve properly might not have worked. But, hey, maybe that's a good thing. You don't have to blame yourself for not fixing me. It wasn't your fault."

She shook her head, wearing her sympathy on her face like stage makeup. I couldn't take it. I preferred when she was needling me into shouting at her. "Ari, we don't 'fix' people in therapy."

"I was joking."

"I don't think you were. That type of attitude—that pain can be fixed—could be what made you go to a hekamist instead of dealing with your feelings."

"Pain *can* be fixed. I'm sure you take Tylenol, Dr. Pitts."

"You really believe that a spell to give yourself brain damage is the same as a Tylenol?"

I ignored the "brain damage" dig. "I'm only saying, I don't think it's a matter of whether or not I *believe* in something. It's true. Take a pill, no more headache. I took a spell, no more grief. I don't know if it's right, but I know that it worked."

"You call not being able to dance working?"

"I'll dance again." I placed my bad wrist against my heart.

Echo's spell. She promised. Any day now. Must be patient.

And still Dr. Pitts exuded a noxious cloud of fake sympathy. Sickening. I don't know how she didn't throw up from it. "How?" she asked.

"I just—I will."

She shook her head. "You don't get to choose to escape something like this, Ari. You can't swallow and push through it. There are always consequences."

"Like having to sit here with you."

Her sympathetic face twitched. If I had to be in this room, I resolved to make an enemy of her. Enemies don't try to figure you out. Enemies leave you alone.

"Look, I don't know what Jess hoped to accomplish by making me come here. I know that this whole thing is totally messed up. I will apologize to Jess, and to Diana, and to Kay, and even to Markos and everyone else in town if you make me. Okay?"

Dr. Pitts just looked at me. Maybe I should've offered to apologize to her, too.

"Let's talk about your parents."

"Why?"

"They died, too."

"I don't remember that."

"You don't remember the fire. But you still might feel that the world is random and dangerous."

"What, so, you think because my parents died in an accident I'm more likely to try to control my life in any way I can? Very astute. I'll be thinking about that while staring up at the three a.m. sky wondering if there's a heaven."

"Have you noticed you often use sarcasm to change the subject?"

I shrugged. "Whatever works."

Dr. Pitts shook her head. "It doesn't work. One day you'll be alone with yourself and you'll have to face the truth."

"What truth?"

"That you've experienced loss. That it's changed you."

I swallowed another sarcastic response. She clasped her hands together and took a deep breath.

"Tell me, Ari. Why is it that you can't seem to talk about your parents?"

"What am I supposed to say?"

"Anything."

"But I barely remember them."

"What do you remember?"

You could fit all the memories I had of my parents into six bars of music. "My mother had thin straight hair, like me. My dad had a goatee."

"Okay."

"We listened to a lot of music together."

Music in the car, music in the house, music out in the backyard. Classical, indie rock, pop, show tunes. When I pictured my parents, I pictured them singing.

"Is that what drew you to dance? The music?"

"Maybe." I remembered the day my dad gave me my first iPod—one of his old ones. He'd left a bunch of his music on it, but I was so thrilled to add my own. I used to fall asleep with the headphones on.

I didn't know if this was true and I had no one to ask, but I suspected that was why I didn't hear the smoke alarm. That was why the house was burning so strongly by the time my dad got me out and then went back for my mom.

But since I'd forgotten that day, I didn't have to know for sure.

"Interesting. Is there anything else you remember about them?" Dr. Pitts asked.

"See, I have to disagree with you. I don't think it is interesting. It's the only stuff I remember but that doesn't mean it's particularly important. We listened to music. So what?"

"Do you feel guilty?"

My mouth went dry. I hadn't said anything about the headphones to her or to anyone else, ever. "No. Guilty about what?"

"That you survived and they didn't."

"I'm not guilty. Stop trying to make me fit some grief checklist."

Dr. Pitts offered me a Kleenex. I wasn't crying, but my face must have looked like I was on the verge. Her gesture only made me swallow painfully, then take a breath and hold it, more determined than ever never to break.

"I'm not trying to impose a theory on you, Ari," she said softly. I didn't need her softness. Didn't need her sympathy. "I'm giving you another way to look at your situation."

"Other than the one where I'm the weak, pathetic jerk who

erased her beloved boyfriend and then lied about it? We're going to blame the dead parents instead?"

"There's more than one way to look at everything. If you know why you feel the way you do, you can better know how to deal with your emotions."

"But I don't want to know," I said without thinking.

Dr. Pitts sat silently for a long moment, letting the words hover in the air.

"You don't want to know what, Ari?"

"Nothing. I was being contrary."

"What don't you want to know? Yourself?"

"Doesn't mean anything. It just came out."

"Please tell me. You don't want to know . . ."

"I don't want to know why I did it! Why I erased Win. I don't want to know any of it."

Dr. Pitts's composed expression shifted, and I think she was genuinely curious when she asked, "Why?"

Because I was scared if I looked too closely, I would discover I'd changed in ways I had no control over. Old Ari seemed like a different person from me. Abandoning Diana, choosing a boy over everything, including dance. Even Older Ari—the little Ari, the one with a hand-me-down iPod and singing parents—she wasn't me, either, since I'd taken away the memory of the fire. But those were changes I'd planned for, changes I'd chosen, even if I no longer understood why I'd made the choice. I didn't want to know what other changes had taken place without my knowledge or permission.

I wanted to be a predictable set of reactions to a finite set of situations; I wanted to know that I was a girl who would always make the same choices she'd made before. The thought of changing suddenly and randomly scared me down to my marrow.

I smiled at Dr. Pitts, even though the smile hurt my face. "Because it's better in the dark."

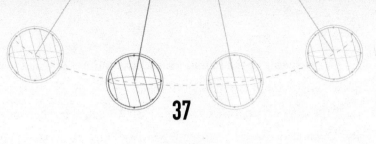

37

KAY

The late summer light cast long shadows onto the deck. Diana lay curled in a ball in the hammock on one end, and Ari had pulled a deck chair next to her. Out on the lawn, the automatic sprinklers ticked as they shot tiny rainbows into the sky. My mother was somewhere near the edge of the property in her dirty gardening outfit, which she practically lived in. She'd be out there until it was too dark to see. My dad, who spent most weeks in Boston being a CEO, joked that the garden was her third child, only the real joke was that the garden was her *only* child.

I pocketed my phone, with its messages from Cal. I hadn't actually talked to him or seen him in much longer than three days, but I got his texts and voicemails, and I assumed that was enough, or the spell would shove him my way. The longer it went since I'd seen him, the less I wanted to, especially since his texts had started to get super weird.

"Come on," I said. "It's the middle of summer. Let's go do something."

Diana swung in the hammock silently, and Ari adjusted her neck. "We're not in the mood," she said.

"You guys are depressing," I said. "So Ari lied about her spell and Diana had a secret boyfriend. Now we know about the spell and Markos is gone. So what?"

Ari raised her head halfway. "Nice, Kay. What do you want from us?"

"I want you to snap out of it!" I said. Diana sighed deeper into the hammock and Ari rolled her eyes. "Ari, you once said to me that you were awesome, and you weren't friends with anyone who wasn't awesome, too."

"I don't think I put it like that. . . ."

"All I'm saying is, you're still Ari Madrigal and Diana North. So act like it."

They didn't answer, but before I could press them to get up and do something, the doorbell rang six times in a row, as if someone was leaning his or her whole weight into it. I left them on the deck and ran through the house to get it.

Cal stood on the front steps, with gray skin, sunken cheeks, and hair so greasy it looked like ink. "Oh, hey, Kay," he said when he saw me, then sank down onto the top step.

I closed the door behind me and sat across from him. "What happened to you?"

"I've been sick. Where have you been? You haven't answered any of my texts."

"Oh." Maybe the spell needed me to actually answer him. Whoops. "Sorry about that."

"I don't know who else to talk to. I stopped eating at home for now, which means I've been sick and starving, until I realized I could just go grocery shopping and keep the food locked up, but that's not even the problem."

He spoke normally, as if I should understand the words, but I didn't. I glanced back into the house. "So what *is* the problem?"

"It's my head. And this spell."

I sucked in a breath and scrambled to my feet. "I don't know what you're talking about."

He laughed, which turned into a bitter cough. "I don't know what I'm talking about, either. I thought it was just that I couldn't hit Markos, but things are shifting around in my head, like the paint's running, or dirty windows are smashing up, and I can't tell what's real and what's—"

"You tried to hit Markos?"

"He's sulking. I think he wanted me to hit him. I might be able to now. I haven't tried."

"What spell are you talking about?"

"I don't know. A spell. That's what I'm trying to say."

I backed toward the door. "Well, I don't know either. But you'll feel better now, okay, Cal? We'll talk later. You can call me in the middle of the night, I promise to pick up."

Cal shook his head. "That's the other thing. I've been sleeping right through the night."

"Good!"

"No, not good. I always thought I had insomnia. . . ." He

shook his head, almost angrily, and crossed his arms over his chest. "Don't know why I came here. I won't bother you anymore."

I watched him walk away, clenching my teeth as he went down the steps, expecting to see him trip and fall. Then I unhooked the worry and hung it up with all the rest of them; they were not useful to me. Cal didn't trip, anyway. He walked away fine. He was sick, but he'd be all right now that we'd talked.

On my way back through the house to the deck, I could hear laughter. Maybe my pep talk had worked; maybe Ari and Diana were ready to let bygones be bygones and go back to normal. Then, as I got closer, I heard three voices instead of just two. And I knew the third voice.

"—found that it was totally different, and scary sometimes, and crowded and unfamiliar. I was lonely, too."

"But it was worth it?" Ari's voice.

"Oh, yeah. It's good to be lonely. You get to know yourself."

Tears stung the back of my eyes and I clamped my hand over my mouth. Mina didn't know anything about being alone.

"I sound like such a cliché when I talk about it, but I don't think I understood before how big the world was. And how old. I saw forts that had been around for centuries. Mountains that had been there for eons." She laughed a little bit. "It was sort of comforting to be around all these places and people who didn't care that I'd been sick, and who didn't look at me as if I were about to die."

"I know what you mean," Ari said. "Not that people think I'm going to die. But my whole life—everyone's looked at me like I'm fragile. Like I might start sobbing my guts out any second." She paused. "Except when I'm dancing."

"I don't look at you like that," Diana said.

"And that's why I love you."

I knew I should stop listening and walk out there. The spell wasn't supposed to bring me my friends so that Mina could hang out with them. But I leaned on a kitchen chair and held my breath.

"Did you ever actually sob your guts out?" Mina asked.

"No!" Ari's voice dripped scorn.

"I cry enough for both of us," Diana said.

"Crying's not as bad as it sounds. I cried in India for a week. Around the third or fourth month, I was totally overwhelmed with the trains and the weird hostels and everyone looking at me like I should know Hindi, and I missed home. And then I'd feel guilty for being annoyed, because I'd made it, I was out, not sick, living my dream, so who cared if I was uncomfortable, right? But you can't go around peaceful and grateful and zen every second of the day. It's just not possible."

"I love that you guys are talking about *letting* yourselves cry," Diana said, and I could hear the tears in her voice, as if talking about crying was enough for them to spring to life. "Like there's a moment in your lives when you say 'oh, I'm so upset, but I think I'll not cry, not today.'"

"Diana!" Ari said, and there was scuffling and laughing, and

I could tell that Ari had thrown herself into the hammock with Diana. The sky was completely dark now. I'd been hiding way too long; they should have at least wondered where I'd gone by now. But they hadn't.

I pushed the chair I was holding, which clattered to the ground, and rushed onto the deck. Diana and Ari looked up from the hammock where they lay head to toe. Mina sat in a deck chair, the lights from the house glinting off her eyebrow piercing. I started talking before she could make another sound. "Hey guys, sorry about that. Oh, Mina, what are you doing here?"

"Just saying hello."

"Well, hello. We were kind of in the middle of something, though."

"No we weren't," Ari said. "Mina, are you back for good or just home for the summer?"

Mina leaned back in her chair, making herself comfortable. "Finished my freshman year at University of Michigan this May. Should be a junior, but chemo slows you down on the APs."

"As does backpacking around the world," I said, but they all took my cheery tone at face value. Mina, who should've known what I meant, smiled at me.

"I wasn't aware there was a schedule in place," she said, completely missing the point for the millionth time.

Here's the point: it wasn't just cancer that could take people away from you. Sometimes it was fucking India, too. Mina got better and then she left me. That's all there was to it.

"Who was at the door?" Mina asked.

"Cal."

All the muscles in Diana's face stopped moving. "Are you still dating him?"

"You were *dating* Cal Waters?" Mina asked.

"No—I mean, yes, maybe we were, but we're not anymore."

"Oh my god, Katelyn, I can't believe you didn't tell me."

"Nothing to tell." *Except that I kissed his brother, Diana—sorry about that.*

"He's *way* too old for you, Katelyn. It's creepy."

"Thanks for your concern."

"So what did he want? You didn't break up just now, did you?" Mina asked.

"No, of course not." They all looked at me, expecting more detail. But how could I explain that he was sick and didn't know why but *had* to see me? "He . . . he said Markos tried to punch him."

"What? Why?" Ari asked. Diana looked as if she wanted to melt through the hammock and into the ground.

"He said Markos was sulking. Maybe . . . maybe he misses Di. That would be good, right? Because he cares?"

Diana's face crumpled, and she turned it toward the ropes of the hammock.

"Cal came over here to tell you that Markos misses Diana?" Ari asked.

"Um . . . yeah." I knew that didn't make sense, but I couldn't think of anything else that would. "Hey, so, listen—you all are coming out for my birthday dinner, right?"

"Jeez, Kay," Ari said.

"What?"

"Sensitivity." Ari pointed at Diana, who had started crying silently. For a moment I felt awful, like a failure of a human being, but then I thought of the spell and how it was working fine and how it didn't care if I was good or bad and I felt better.

"I'm definitely coming to your dinner," Mina said.

I rolled my eyes. "You're not invited."

"Sure I am," Mina said. "You just said 'you all.' I'm part of 'you all.'"

"Yeah," Ari said, grinning. "She's 'you all,' too. Right, Diana?"

Diana wiped her eyes and gave Mina a shaky smile. "She's as 'you all' as I am."

I took a deep breath. Birthdays used to be our thing, me and Mina. We would eat cake and do each other's makeup. She would write me a story that made me laugh, and she'd read it to me, doing all the voices. Even when she was sickest. Even the year she gave me four stories and told me that if she wasn't there next year I should read them one a year and pretend she was doing the voices, and she apologized for not having time to write more but she was too tired, and we cried and fell asleep in her bed.

If she wrote me a story this year—which she wouldn't; she hadn't in years—I would scream and run away.

But it didn't matter that Mina horned her way into dinner,

and it didn't matter that Mina bonded with Ari and Diana, because she would inevitably leave—that was what Mina did. It didn't matter that Cal was a little bit crazy and I had kissed Diana's crush and lied to her and made her cry and that I couldn't hang out in hospitals or on carnival rides. None of that mattered.

The spell worked, and nothing mattered at all.

38

MARKOS

I'm the only one of my brothers who has no memory of our dad. None. Not even something hazy like being lifted onto a giant's shoulders or some other touching Hallmark moment. I was two and a half when he died of a heart attack. Cal was six, Dev eight, Brian ten.

I don't want pity or weeping or group hugs about it. It's a fact: I am the youngest. I never had a dad.

The missing-a-dad-I-never-knew part isn't what messed me up, though. That's, like, okay—he seemed like a great guy and it would've been nice but I managed to be basically fine anyway. The part that got to me was that the rest of them—Brian and Dev and Cal—got to be in this club together. The Remember When Dad Club. As in, *Remember when Dad made us boiled hot dogs every night for a week?* Or *Remember when Dad built the treehouse in the backyard?* Even next-youngest Cal, six years old when Dad died, remembered the Christmas everyone got Legos and we all went to Legoland. My brothers all got to pool those memories together, trade them back and forth. They helped each other reinforce the ones they already had stored. But I was no help with that. Even when I was in these stories, I was mostly asleep on Mom's lap or crying horribly in the background.

In a way it felt like we were in two different families: the three of them, who once had two parents, and me, who's only ever had one.

And what I wanted, more than Dad, was to be let into that family, and be one of the ones who had two parents. I wanted it so bad. I watched them and kept trying over and over to belong with them. The Waters brothers.

I got pretty good at pretending to be one of them. Confident, funny, flirty but never serious. Steady Bs and the occasional C. Pick a sport, be a team player. Don't get angry, or sad, or impatient, or excited. Stay cool. They could tell I was a fraud and they gave me shit for it, but no one on the outside could ever tell that I didn't belong.

The weird thing—or, I don't know, maybe it wasn't all that weird if you thought about it—was that I hadn't thought about my dad much at all this whole summer. You'd think being confronted by the specter of death and grief and all that shit I might've spared a couple minutes for Dad. He was my first major loss, but like I said, it's not much of a loss when there's nothing there to remember.

After I found out Ari erased Win, I started thinking about my little soft baby brain that could barely handle eating and shitting, let alone the death of a person. Ari was like baby me, babbling and oblivious. She couldn't remember someone who should've meant everything to her, like I couldn't remember my dad.

She and I, we had been a family of our own: those who loved Win. I was finally a member of an exclusive club—what I'd always wanted with my brothers. And then she'd gone and had herself purposely thrown out of the group.

I could understand now why my brothers had closed off that part of themselves from me. It wasn't because they were selfish or mean. They wished I could be in the club, too, to better hold the shared memories. But you're either in or you're not. You can't fake it.

The worst thing is to be alone with it.

When she showed up in my living room, I was lying on the couch wrapped tightly in a red fleece blanket, watching a blond man demonstrate amazing 100-percent-guaranteed, stronger-than-steel ceramic knives, set of twelve for $49.99. She turned off the TV and stood in front of me, scowling.

Part of me wanted to leap off the couch and strangle her for forgetting Win, but the rest of me was too exhausted to move.

"What the hell are you doing here?" I asked.

"I heard you were sulking. I wanted to see it for myself."

"What? From who?"

Ari didn't answer. I saw her looking over the couch and half-empty bottles of Gatorade and my face, which was probably greasy and pale, not that I'd looked in a mirror in a long while.

"Why did you mess with Diana?" she asked.

I swallowed. As bad as I looked, she looked terrible, too,

dark circles under her eyes and hands bent awkwardly at her sides, not lithe and bendable like she used to be.

"She thought you were being real," Ari said. "You must have gone to a lot of effort to convince her. Why bother?"

"Shut *up*," I said. "Shut the fuck up, Ari. Me and Diana, that's not the issue. You *forgot Win*. You went in and ripped him out like a cancer. But you weren't going to die from the memory of him. He wasn't a cancer. He . . . *loved* you. And you didn't care."

"I think I must've loved him a lot to do what I did."

"That is such pathetic bullshit."

She shrugged. "You're right," she said. "Old Ari was full of shit."

My eyes closed, but the blackness didn't mean she was gone. I could sense her there, breathing. I didn't know what to say, so we stewed in silence.

"Tell me why you broke Diana's heart," she said.

I opened my eyes. "What do you care?"

"She's my friend."

"You're a shitty friend, which I think we've already established."

"And you're being more of an asshole than usual. Why'd you do it? Was it only so you could feel loved and special for five minutes? That's inhumane."

I sat up straighter on the couch, blanket bunched around my shoulders. "That's who I am, Ari, in case your memory needs refreshing. I'm the one who messes around. I'm not serious. What did she expect?"

She kicked my shin. It hurt, but the pain was sharp and red and satisfying. She stumbled, as if kicking me knocked her off balance.

"I get that you're mad at me," she said. "Hell, I'm mad at me, too. But breaking Diana's heart is a stupid way to get revenge."

I froze for what felt like years, and then I burst out laughing. Nothing had been that genuinely funny in weeks.

And then I had the feeling, for a fleeting moment, that the Ari I used to be friends with was the same one as the one in front of me now, and any second she would start laughing, too. And she'd sit down and we'd make fun of daytime TV together, and she'd tell my brothers to leave me alone, and I'd make her snort soda out her nose.

But she didn't laugh. She wasn't that girl.

"This isn't only about you, you psycho," I said, pretty nicely, all things considered. "Why don't you tell me, though, just for fun—what is it that you want me to do? Because here are the options: I leave Diana alone, which is pretty much what I was doing before you showed up. Or I apologize, and I'm not sure I see the point in that. She would know I didn't mean it and that you'd made me."

Those were the best options she could've hoped for, but she still looked disappointed. "I want you to be different," she said.

I snorted, though it was no longer amusing. "Yeah, well, that makes two of us." I turned the TV back on.

"Markos . . ." she started, raising her voice to be heard over the infomercial, but oddly hesitant. "Why do you think I did it?"

Because you're a bitch.

Because you never loved Win.

Because you were weak.

"You spared yourself," I said.

She shook her head, but I knew I was right.

"If you really loved him, you would've wanted the memories and the pain. You excused yourself from being a human being."

I didn't look at her. My eyes followed the slice of a knife down the screen.

"What do you know about love?" she asked.

When I didn't answer, she finally left me alone.

But something she'd said wormed its way into my head and I couldn't get it out. It made the infomercial seem stupid; it made my plan to stay on the couch and never leave seem childish.

She wanted me to be different. Well, I wanted to be different, too. For real, like different down to the DNA. I wanted to be someone I'd never met before. I wanted to be someone who'd never met *me*.

I went upstairs, took a shower, and fell asleep in my own bed. The next morning I snuck out of the house before anyone else woke up and started walking to Diana's.

—She's going to slam the door in my face.

—Think positive.

—She's going to throw a lamp at me and then slam the door in my face.

—Or maybe she'll listen.

—Yeah, right. It's like I told Ari: I'm not the apology guy.

Diana knows that. She knows me.

—And that's bad?

—Yeah. Because I ruined it all like I always knew I would from the night of the bonfire. There were only ever two options: stay away, or complete devastation. I went through door B.

—Why even go over there, then?

—Because I need to.

—Why?

—Because . . . maybe she'll forgive me.

—But you said—

—If there's even a chance she might forgive me, I have to try.

—And why would she?

—Because she knows me.

39

WIN

Echo started waiting for me after baseball. Actually, she watched our entire baseball practices, a black dot along the third base line, and then she'd loiter by my truck after practice. If I came out with Markos or some of the other guys, she'd fade away. But if I came out alone, she'd get in the passenger-side door and we'd talk.

She wasn't exactly pressuring me for the money. She wanted to know, first and foremost, if I'd taken the spell, and then, because I always said no, she wanted to know how I was.

And so I told her. I told her about black days and sleepless nights, and lying to Ari to save her more pain, and not asking for the money I knew I needed to ask for, and the worry on my mom's face and the confusion on Kara's. I told her that I wanted the spell more than anything, but the problem was, I couldn't want anything properly, and so that weak wanting wasn't enough to actually make me take it. The fact that the spell was right there in my sock drawer didn't make it any more accessible. Ari was right there in front of me. My real life was right there. None of it came easily.

"I can't force you to take it," she said one afternoon. She sat in the passenger seat with her back against the door, head leaning to the side on the headrest. "But I wish you would."

"I will. I will." I shrugged out of my letter jacket and tossed it in the backseat. The truck got warm with two people sitting in it and the engine off. "I should pay you first, though."

Echo watched me take off the jacket and tried to press herself deeper into the car door, farther away from me. "I told you not to worry about that. You'll probably be able to figure out a way to get the money faster after you take it, anyway."

"But then once you have the money, you'll leave me here to go off and be a hero," I said, trying to joke. "Maybe I don't want to pay because I enjoy our chats."

Echo didn't laugh. Her neck and cheeks turned red and she stared at the glove compartment.

I tried not to move. I'd said something terrible without even knowing it.

"I'm sorry," I said.

She didn't respond.

"I really do like our chats," I said. "You're the only person I actually talk to. Everyone else, it's too hard."

She still didn't say anything, but she stopped glaring at the glove compartment and looked at me. Her eyes were so clear and warm and sad I had to look away.

"What is it?" I asked. "Please tell me. I'm an ass, I know. I've made you mad."

"I'm not mad. It's—I want you to take the spell. I want you to feel better. But . . . I'm not sure if I want you to give me the money. Not anymore."

"Oh," I said.

She meant she wanted to be in the truck with me, checking up on me. She meant she wanted to stick around town, put off her trip, not seek out any more hekamists and covens to save her mom and herself.

For me.

She reached out and took my hand, which was tapping nervously against the steering wheel. Her skin was cool. I exhaled, which created a vacuum in my chest that meant I had to breathe in right away, deeply, completely, and the air smelled like the leather of Echo's jacket and the lavender in her shampoo and I raised my head and turned to her and she was right there and if I moved an inch I would be kissing her.

For a second I thought I would do it. I felt the possibility consuming me, an electric bolt from my eyes to my toes, all of me suddenly aware of this girl's proximity and the reality of her body underneath her layers of black jacket now pressing closer to my own.

Then my hand jerked out of hers and I pulled back and away and breathed through my mouth so I would not smell the leather and lavender again. I covered my eyes with my palms to go back to numbness and darkness. The back of my head hit my window, which was a jolt of pain that was nothing compared to how much I hated myself in that moment.

I did not kiss her. But it didn't matter. I wanted to kiss her, and that was bad enough.

"I'm sorry," I said.

She was breathing hard, too. That's all I heard in the car— that and my heart banging on my chest. "I'm sorry, too," she said.

"I can't."

"I know."

"But you—I like you—"

"No, no. Please don't say any of that."

"I appreciate all you've done for me—"

"Definitely do not say *that*. Seriously, Win, let's not talk. Let's be totally silent and not speak and you drive me home and neither of us ever mentions this ever again. Okay?"

I nodded, and I turned on the car. I had to roll down a window because the air outside had gotten cooler and the inside of the car's windows had steamed up. The seconds we spent waiting for them to clear were the longest seconds in the world, each one a thousand heartbeats or more.

I looped around the athletic fields to drop her off and then drove myself home. The whole time I was sure that *now* I would take the spell, that surely *now* I was such a miserable, pathetic excuse for a human being I had to take it—there was no other choice.

At home I took the sandwich out of my drawer and stared at it. If I took it and it worked, the next day I could be back to normal. I'd probably continue to feel guilty, but at least I could kiss Ari and really feel it again, the way I felt the voltage of Echo's almost-kiss.

I didn't deserve either of them.

I thought about it. And I put the spell back again.

40

ARI

Echo called soon after I left Markos's. I'd been walking in circles around his neighborhood, killing time before Kay's birthday dinner, turning over the idea of Win in my head. The few things I knew about him, the little clues I'd learned. How much Markos missed him. How I'd changed when I was with him. They formed the outline of a person, defined by his effect on others, and together didn't add up to a real human being.

Markos said if I'd really loved Win, I would've wanted to remember. I thought about my parents. Perhaps I didn't love them enough. Perhaps if I'd cared more I could've kept the memory of the fire and built up a scab around it. Then at least I'd have the scar to show for all the pain.

It occurred to me that it was August first.

I was supposed to be in New York, but I couldn't prove to Jess that I could dance, so she'd never called the movers back after canceling them. She'd stopped putting things in boxes, too. Dishes and books appeared back on their shelves overnight.

Echo's voice was bright in my ear. A strange contrast to the thoughts of Win and New York.

"Can you come by?" Echo asked.

"Now?"

"I've practiced a couple of times and I think I'm ready to make your spell." She sounded excited, almost giddy, and I was excited, too, but I also couldn't help picturing her arm covered with cuts and the sound of her screaming.

"I'll be right there," I said and started to run, then slowed so I wouldn't trip in the middle of the road.

Echo described what she planned for my spell, the phases of the moon and the type of food, and how she was going to try to limit the side effects by giving me just enough grace.

"And the side effects?"

"It's a physical spell, so it'll have a mental side effect. Grace and control and power . . . you might be more emotional than usual, maybe? Hard to say, especially because it's compounded."

I wanted to be excited about everything she was saying, but something nagged at me. Some part of the outline of Win that I couldn't fill in. Finally I interrupted her.

"Tell me what kind of spell you were making for Win."

She paused. "I don't think he'd want me to."

"Why? Was it a love spell?" If Win had spelled me into loving him, that would explain what I'd done—completely changed my goals and life for him.

"No. It had nothing to do with you."

I tried not to be disappointed. "But he was going to give

you five thousand dollars for it—that had to be something important. Expensive, so it was a permanent spell, right?" No response. "Did I know what it was, before I forgot him? Or was it a secret then?"

"You didn't know."

So Win had secrets. If Old Ari had known that, would she still have gone to so much trouble to forget him?

"Ari? You still there?"

"Why did it take you so long to blackmail me?" I asked.

There was a pause on the other end of the phone. "What do you mean?"

"Win died at the end of May. I got my spell a week later. But you didn't come to find me until the bonfire on July third."

My steps slowed as the pause got longer and longer. "I couldn't really think about anything for the first couple of weeks."

"After Win died?"

"Yeah. I . . . It wasn't easy."

"Why not?"

Her voice faded almost to a whisper. "The way I grew up . . . I never had a friend before. I'd never told anyone I was a hekamist. I wasn't even supposed to answer the door when my mom wasn't around."

"But you opened for Win."

"I started to get desperate. My mom was fading. I needed to make money that she wouldn't hide or destroy—so I told him. I didn't expect . . ." She breathed into the phone. "I didn't know how it would feel to tell someone. To have someone know you.

He knew me. With my mom so sick . . . he was the only one who did."

I stopped walking. Something bitter churned in my stomach. She had stolen my grief, even if I'd given up all rights to it. "You know what, I can't come over right now," I said. "I have to meet my friends for dinner."

"Oh. Okay."

"But thank you. Thank you for making this spell."

"It's okay."

"My friend's been looking forward to this dinner, otherwise I'd ditch. I swear."

"Don't apologize. I'll see you later."

"I'm so sorry," I said again anyway, even though the more I said it the less convincing it sounded. "I have to pick up Diana, we're going to meet up with Kay at the restaurant. I'm probably already late, so—"

"Wait," Echo interrupted. Her voice stopped wavering; she sounded like herself. "Your friend's name is Kay?"

"Yeah. Kay Charpal."

"Pretty Indian girl? Naïve? A little needy?"

"Basically." Echo didn't respond. "Do you . . . know her?"

She sighed, a long whoosh of air into the phone. "Yeah, I know her. You've been hooked."

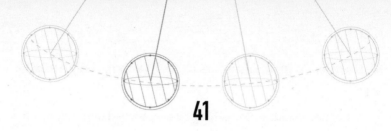

41

KAY

For my birthday, my friends found out about the hook.

It was Monday, and we were supposed to meet at the lobster place in town where you have to wear a bib and share buckets of seafood and they keep bringing you sides of potatoes. They were only open in the summer, when you could get fresh seafood and there were enough tourists to make it worthwhile. It was one of those quiet, dry nights, not too hot, moon shining down like a spotlight through the restaurant windows. I was the last one of us to turn seventeen; in fact, Diana would be eighteen in two months, so we'd all be the same age for a short window. Everything was lining up.

Mina and I waited an hour for Ari and Diana. They didn't text or email or call; I thought I might've told them the wrong time. Finally we ordered, and I texted them under the table.

"Maybe they've gotten held up somewhere," Mina said, attempting to be kind.

I bristled at her pity. They didn't get held up. They couldn't get held up. Eventually the hook would bring them to me, because it worked. It always worked.

The first one to show up wasn't even invited.

Cal Waters stood at the door to the restaurant, blinking and looking around the room. He still looked terrible: thinner, twitchy, sweating. I waved him over; what else could I do? He'd only look worse if I ignored him. When he reached us he stank of tequila.

"Hi, Cal, I'm Mina," Mina said, smiling and reaching out her hand. "We were in eighth grade algebra together?"

He looked at her outstretched hand but kept his own by his side.

"What are you doing here?" I asked.

He opened and closed his mouth without speaking. "I don't know. I just . . . sort of ended up here."

Behind Cal, I could see the door open, and Ari and Diana stepped through. I jumped up, pushing drunk Cal aside. "Ari! Di!"

Ari turned to me, her face set in anger. She grabbed Diana by the arm and dragged her to our table. Diana seemed to be in shock.

"Ari Madrigal," Cal whispered, taking a step back.

"Where have you guys been?" I asked.

Ari glared. "Cut the shit, Kay. We know about the spell."

"You do?" Cal slurred. He'd gone even paler under the thin sheen of sweat.

Ari barely glanced at him, nose wrinkling. "Yeah. We know

Kay gave us a hook and we aren't allowed to leave her. You, me, and Diana."

"Oh," Cal said, swaying slightly. "Oh, that's not good."

"What're you talking about, Ari?" Mina asked from her seat in the booth.

Ari explained how her hekamist friend had told her what I'd told the hekamist, that day I'd tried to get her to undo Cal's part of the spell.

"Gee, thanks," Cal said. "More spells."

"Oh my god," Mina said.

I sat back in the booth and crossed my arms over my chest. "So what?"

"So I want to go to New York and dance. Diana wants to be able to drive out of town without bashing her face in." Ari gestured at Di, who stared at a point on the wall and didn't seem to notice. Ari looked briefly worried, then turned to me, anger back in place. "It isn't right."

"What do you want me to do about it?"

"Break the spell. Let us go."

"Breaking spells is nearly impossible. Don't you know that?" I asked. Ari flushed and pressed her wrist against the edge of the table. "And anyway I don't want to break it. We're friends."

"No, we're not."

"We've all made mistakes. Diana lied about being with Markos. You lied about forgetting Win—and we forgave you. So forgive me and let's move on."

Mina shook her head in disbelief. "I can't believe you did this."

"What do you even care, Mina?" Too loud. The tables next to us turned and stared.

Ari shot a look at Mina. "You better watch out Kay hasn't given you the hook, too, because if you try to go to India again, you'll probably end up back in the hospital."

Mina stopped breathing, went still.

The waiter approached the table with a cupcake crowded with candles, but when he saw our faces, he blew out the candles himself and backed away slowly.

Everyone seemed to be waiting for me to say something, but I knew whatever I said would be wrong.

"Happy birthday to me," I said.

"Something's still wrong," Cal said. He exhaled alcohol over the whole table. "Not you and your hook. Something else. I'm so . . . hungry. D'you have anything to eat?"

"Shut *up*, Cal," I said.

"Might not be a memory," he said to Ari as if she'd asked him a question. "Might not be. I could be delusional, schizophrenic. I can't tell." He looked back and forth between our faces as if not quite seeing us, stopping on mine. "Did you give Markos a hook, too?"

My stomach dropped. "No, of course not. Cal, why don't you go home?"

Diana grabbed Cal's sleeve and stepped closer to him. He didn't seem to notice. "Why did you ask if she spelled Markos?"

"Because they kissed. And now Markos is a shut-in."

Diana and Ari looked at him and then at each other, then,

simultaneously, at me. I saw in their eyes every shred of possible understanding and forgiveness falling away; as flimsy as it was, it flaked off like the thinnest gold leaf. Underneath, there was nothing but cold, ugly concrete. All the anxieties I'd unhooked jumped and flew at me, making it hard to breathe.

"I don't know what he's talking about," I said.

"They kissed," Cal insisted, then burped. "Markos said so. He wouldn't lie to me."

I bit the side of my mouth and wished again for some wit, to know what to say and how to say it so that they'd understand and forgive me. "If it is true—which I'm not saying it is—but if he's telling the truth, it was before I knew Diana was with Markos. If she'd told me they were together—"

"What the hell, Kay?"

"Ari, don't," Diana said.

Ari ignored her, getting louder by the second. "You claim to be this perfect friend who's always here for us, but meanwhile you're spelling us and kissing Diana's crush—it's sick. *You're* sick."

"Please stop," Diana said. People at surrounding tables whispered to their waiters, pointing in our direction.

"Do you even know what being a friend is? Because I may have forgotten a lot in the past year but I know enough not to do something so monumentally stupid to the nicest, most loyal best friend you've ever been lucky enough to—"

"Shut up, Ari!" Diana said. Her face was bright red. She still held Cal's sleeve, as if she'd forgotten to let go. "Stop defending me. You're not some paragon of perfect friendship."

Ari flushed and drew herself up taller. "I'm not as bad as her." She pointed at me.

"Think about it, though. It doesn't matter what Kay did. Markos would've still broken up with me because I lied to him about your stupid spell."

Ari stepped back and stumbled into the booth. "You blame *me* for what Markos did?"

Diana took a shaky breath. "You'll always be my best friend, Ari. But sometimes you're not very good at it." Diana turned to Cal and pulled on his arm. "Come on. I'll hail you a cab." Cal allowed himself to be led out of the restaurant.

I wished I could follow them. During the conversation the place had become drab and unromantic, with cheap tablecloths and tacky seafaring decoration. I should've picked someplace else to eat. Someplace less beachy, less summery. A bistro with white tablecloths and classical music playing. Maybe none of this would've happened if I'd chosen differently.

Ari and I faced each other across the booth. "I tried to be a good friend," I said. Ari snorted and I spoke faster to stop her from speaking over me. "I did. I love you guys. I've been trying to help you all summer." My voice warbled, which I hated. I didn't have to explain anything to her, but I did anyway. "I've been staying near. Even when you ignored me or made fun of me, I knew I had to stick around. And maybe—maybe one day everything would go back to normal. You'd appreciate me. We'd be real friends."

It was humiliating down to my bones, as if I'd burned off clothes and skin and muscle to get to the truth. Tears stung behind my eyes, more from anger than from sadness, and I held them back.

Ari shook her head. "Diana's mad but she and I will be fine. You're delusional if you think it'll be the same with you."

Ouch.

Unhook it. Hang it away.

I stood up. Mina stood, too, but I refused to look at her, and she let me leave the restaurant alone.

I left Ari and Mina stewing in the restaurant, hating me. Cal and Diana, waiting for a cab on the street, hating me. Fine. I hated them, too.

Only I didn't really hate them.

All the feelings I'd unhooked were still there. I could unhook them but that didn't mean they were gone. Somewhere in me, I was ashamed. They'd seen the worst part of me, the truest part. I could pretend that it was good enough to order them around and get them to do what I wanted, the birthday dinner and sitting sullenly in my backyard, but what I really wanted them to realize was how much they missed me. And I couldn't force that.

Instead, I punished them. I was true to my word and didn't call any of them for four days.

Knowing what I did about the spell, I knew that what happened then was partly, if not fully, my fault.

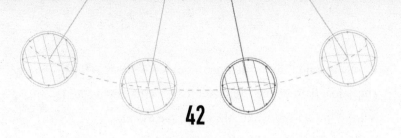

42

MARKOS

It was so early the heat hadn't sunk into the ground yet, and the papers were being delivered by a middle-aged man in a truck. There were no other cars on the road, and the quiet made the buzz of cicadas even louder. When I got to Diana's house, her mother answered the door in her housecoat and broke into a huge grin, like I was delivering a sweepstakes win. Diana must not have told her what I'd done. I hated her for not screaming at me.

Instead she called for Diana and tried to make small talk with me, but I turned my face into stone and stared past her, waiting for Diana to appear.

She did, finally, wearing a tank top and pajama shorts, her hair up in a ponytail, her face—looking at me—after more than a week—a blank. Like I was no one. No anger. No lamp thrown at my head. Nothing.

For a terrible second I thought she'd gotten a spell to erase her memory of me, but then she asked her mother "Can we have a second?" and when her mom left I caught a flash—barely there—of pain before the blank mask came down again.

"What do you want, Markos?" she asked.

"I'm sorry," I said. "I'm so sorry. I was an asshole—I can't even believe how much of an asshole—and I need to tell you I'm sorry."

"You kissed Kay."

"It was a stupid mistake."

"You swore at me. You haven't talked to me for almost two weeks."

She listed my crimes quietly, much more devastating than if she'd screamed at me. "I'm sorry, Diana."

She took a breath and straightened her spine. "Okay. I forgive you."

My mouth probably flopped open and closed a dozen times. "You . . . do?"

"Yeah. Thanks for coming by. It's good of you. Bye."

She started to close the door, but I put out a hand to stop it. She looked at the hand and looked at me and I felt like a slug, or maybe a slug that died and was decomposing on her front steps. "So—wait a second. We can be friends again?"

"I don't think so."

"But you said you forgave me."

"Yeah."

"Doesn't seem like true forgiveness if you never want to see me again."

Her eyes went fiery. "Are you here to lecture me on how to

properly forgive someone? That seems a strange topic for you of all people."

I didn't have the brainpower to deduce what she meant by me *of all people.* "I'm not here to lecture you, no. I'm here so you can yell and scream at me for fucking up your life."

She appeared to grow five inches, her eyes level with mine. "Don't flatter yourself, Markos. I'll get over it."

"You've got to give me a second chance!"

"Why?" she asked, sounding a lot like that Win-voice in my head.

"Because, I—" I stopped, swallowed, and had one of those moments where you see yourself from up above and you look like such a pathetic loser, begging and pleading. And yet I'd gotten this far. I had to keep going. No bullshit. Honesty.

Even though honesty sucked.

"Because I miss you and I can't stop thinking about you and I actually sort of need you in order to keep living, like I'm scared of who I'm going to become without you around because that guy, the guy I was, was such a mess." She opened her mouth as if to argue, so I kept talking, not because I thought I'd convince her but because I wanted to hold back her inevitable no. "And actually if I'm being completely honest, which I am, or at least I'm trying to be, I really think I might sort of love you, but I don't know because that's not something I know anything about. And I've been trying to figure out what Win would say, which is a losing game, but he was a better guy than I am so I think he'd say that this is love and that I should tell you, so I am. I love you. I think."

I forced myself to make eye contact and had to stop talking because she was crying. It hit me like a baseball in the solar plexus: I made her cry. The look on her face was because of me.

No way was this good. I may have had no prior experience confessing love, but I doubted gut-wrenching tears were the optimal response.

"Please leave me alone, Markos," she said. "I can't be responsible for you being a good person. Why can't you just *be* a good person?"

I took a step back from the door, stumbling. I shuddered, suddenly cold. I tried to take a breath but a sharp pain in my chest made me wheeze.

"I . . . I told you the truth," I said.

"Thank you for that."

She closed the door.

I was kneeling on her front lawn.

I had to get up or her mother would come out and find me.

I had to get up so Diana wouldn't look out her front window and see me kneeling.

I had to get up to find a bottle of Maker's Mark to start forgetting what happened here.

I had to get up.

I had to.

43

WIN

After what happened with Echo in my truck, I knew I had to get the money. I couldn't keep things going the way they were. Pretty soon I'd make a mistake so big that I'd never be able to get back to where I wanted to be.

In the end, it wasn't hard to get at all. We were at Markos's playing video games. I didn't even pause the game.

"If I needed money," I said, "could you lend it to me?"

"How much?"

Neither of us looked away from the screen. Markos machine-gunned a couple of pedestrians.

"Five thousand."

He didn't say anything right away, and I thought he might laugh, in which case I would have to laugh, and then I'd be paying off Echo in quarters I found underneath soda machines for the next thirty years.

"Okay," Markos said. "You really need it?"

"Yeah."

"Okay then."

Then on Monday he handed me the envelope in between fourth and fifth periods. I put it in my locker and felt it beating like a heart all day.

But then what did I do? Did I go to Echo's house and hand it over right away? Did I finally feel like I had permission to bite into the sandwich slowly growing stale in my sock drawer? Did I do anything at all?

No.

First I took it home, emptied the bills out of the envelope onto my bed, and stared at the pile—more money than I'd ever seen in my life, all in one place. It was so much *more* than I'd imagined it would be. A towering stack. Twenties, mostly, but also some wrinkly tens and fives and ones and a fake-looking hundred—fake-looking because a hundred-dollar bill was one of those things that only fictional rich people in movies ever had in their wallet.

Five thousand dollars could buy Kara braces. It could get my mom a new (used) car, to replace the one that kept stalling out at intersections. If I put it in a savings account it could make more money *just sitting there*. Five thousand dollars would make my mother so happy, or at least relieve her of worry for a few days or weeks. I could help her—not be a burden for once.

But I was planning on using it to make myself happy instead.

So selfish. Such a waste.

The same five thousand dollars could help Echo get out

of town, find other hekamists, and convince them to save her mother's life. Save her own life, too. Save mine.

So how was I supposed to weigh it? My mother and Kara versus Echo and her mother—it didn't seem fair to choose. Or should I have ignored all that and just chosen for me?

I stuffed the money back into the envelope. I heard my mother at the front door, calling my name. I tucked the envelope into my waistband and pulled down my shirt.

If she found the money on me or in my room, she'd want to know where I had gotten it. She would assume something terrible: drugs or thievery or worse. She'd blame herself for being a bad mom. She'd want to talk about it, and get me to tell her what it meant.

And that, in the end, is what decided it. How would I explain to her where I'd gotten the sudden windfall? She'd be humiliated if she knew I took it from Markos. It would ruin the happy feeling of giving her something to help make her life easier.

Later that night, I went to Ari's. While she was talking to her aunt in the kitchen, I hid the envelope at the very back of her closet in a half-crumpled empty shoebox. I knew I could always retrieve it from the box if necessary and my mom wouldn't accidentally find it and ask questions. Keeping it with Ari and out of my house made me feel less like a selfish dick, less like I'd chosen myself over my family. I could put the money almost out of my mind completely.

Getting close to the end here. The final wrap-up. I had the

money, the spell, I had Markos and Ari and Echo, everything's seconds away from resolving perfectly—the pop-up fly to end the inning sailing straight for me.

It's the calm before it all falls apart.

PART IV

all
things

44

ARI

Three days after Kay's birthday (three days after the day I was *supposed* to move to New York), I fell over while trying to fouetté in my bedroom. I hadn't talked to Diana or Kay since that dinner, and I'd been avoiding Jess and her suddenly endless supply of well-meaning hugs since she made me go to Dr. Pitts. I hadn't gone to Echo's house, either, even though I knew she said she was ready to make me the spell—something about our last conversation had unsettled me, not knowing what she and Win had been cooking up, not knowing how I was supposed to react. So in my little isolated bubble I had a lot of time to worry that every stubbed toe, missed stair, and paper cut was the work of a malicious spell.

When I fell, I landed on my bed, pushing the mattress out of alignment with the box spring. A journal that had been stuck in between fell out onto the floor, an unfamiliar book hidden in an unfamiliar spot full of very familiar handwriting. I rubbed my hip where I'd landed and sat on the floor to read it.

Looking at the journal, I could dredge up a memory of placing it under the bed, in that distant, removed way I recalled a lot of the past year. I could not remember having written anything in the book, but it was full of my handwriting. I opened the notebook with the same curiosity that made me stare at the dance videos: maybe this would finally explain why I'd done what I'd done.

But the journal didn't explain. Not exactly.

In the front of the book there was the jagged edge of a page ripped out—where I had written the note to myself the night I took my spell. Then, near the middle, a few pages were written in cramped letters.

Skipped dance today to hang out with Win. Not even on purpose—forgot to go. Didn't miss it until Rowena called the house. So tired of Rowena and buns and perfection. So tired.

Win says it's a gift to be good at something as good as I am at dance. And that I'd regret it if I didn't go to New York. But Win is being Good Boyfriend Win and I know he'll miss me. He's been so strange. Sadder than usual. I'm worried. Won't say what it is. And I have my own worries. Jess is so excited. Applying for jobs by the dozen. Talking about Greenwich Village and MoMA and concerts in Central Park. Going to New York is how I pay her back for the past nine years. Get her out of here. Can't imagine six hours a day, so far from Win. I used to dream about it but now it seems such a waste.

When I finished reading I realized I was sitting on the edge of the bed squeezing my wrist so tight my hand had started to turn red. The pain was a hammer banging rhythmically on a metal spike. Old Ari's words hit so hard I got dizzy.

She didn't love to dance.

I didn't love to dance.

I went cold all over, like being dunked.

I had assumed that she and I had most things in common. She had Win and I didn't, but we shared dance. Something so important couldn't change so much. Right?

Unless there was something about my relationship with Win that made me not want to dance. Or not need to dance. Because that's how I'd always thought of it before, a need.

Jess thought the spell had saved me—the one that took away the memory of the fire. But she was wrong. *Dance* had lifted me out of the pit of my parents' death. Without it, I'd still be down there, wandering blindly, looking for escape.

I checked the time. An advanced ballet class would be getting out soon. I got in the car and drove to the studio, then ducked my head under the wheel and hid until all the students left.

Rowena was the last one out, locking the door behind her, heading to the only other car in the lot.

I almost fell in my rush out of the car, unfolding clumsy limbs. She didn't seem startled to see me, but then again she's always been unflappable.

"Ariadne. How lovely to see you." Her eyes flicked to my legs, my arms—I clenched and didn't move so that I wouldn't give myself away. (I had a flash of memory of how it used to feel to dance, with every part of me in sync and under control, and with that flash a sudden sureness that I would never feel that way again, no matter what Echo's spell might fix.) "You're looking well."

"I'm okay," I said. "You heard—about my memory spell."

She nodded. "I spoke with Jess. And the girls—such gossips. But I understand, now, about your difficulty. Side effects, yes?"

"Did I . . . Rowena, did I want to keep dancing? Before Win died?"

Rowena leaned a little bit against her car door, tired but still precise, straight-backed, poised. "No," she said. "No, I don't think so."

"Because of Win?" I asked, bitterness twisting my mouth.

"Not exactly. Mind you, you never spoke of this directly. But you changed." She smiled. "I am quite used to my girls changing; it can be lovely to see someone discover the type of person they're going to be."

"Even if that person wants to give up dance?"

"Even if. There are many things a person could be that are as important as a dancer. Or more so. Goals shift. They change. You were as talented as always, and the Manhattan Ballet saw that at their Institute last summer, but over the course of the year your heart went out of it."

A wave of shame passed through me. "I gave up."

"A dancer's world can be very narrow. Yours expanded." She looked off into the thin scrub lining the parking lot, as if seeing great forests and mountains and rivers. "Then after Win passed away and you came back—I was happy to see you, of course, but not surprised that your body didn't want to obey. I had the reasoning wrong, but it did make sense, at least to me."

I could tell Rowena considered this the end of her speech, but I couldn't let her go while I was struggling to make sense of it all. "So . . . even if I think I want to dance right now . . . if I meet some guy, in six months I'll probably change again?"

"I don't know," Rowena said. "Perhaps there was an alchemy unique to you and Win. But I will say to fear change is the most hopeless fear one can harbor. Change will happen, Ariadne. Injuries. Loves. Deaths. There's never a moment where you're finished, that's it, all changes over. Change is forever."

I knew I should've thanked her—for caring about me, for teaching me, for noticing me—but if I opened my mouth I would've cried, so I backed away to my car, nodding at her helplessly. She nodded back.

I drove out of the studio's parking lot for what I knew would be the last time.

45

MARKOS

Every night that I spent sitting in Diana's front yard, staring up at her window, I descended several rungs to a new, disturbing low. And yet I kept doing it, night after night. If my brothers knew what I was doing they'd lock me in my room for my own good, but I didn't show up for breakfast anymore, so I didn't have to listen to them decide how I should live my life.

I arrived at Diana's yard soon after it got dark, and stayed until I fell asleep. Usually I'd wake up before daylight and wander home, sleepwalk through the day, and then do it all again. The vigil didn't have a purpose or a goal. It was what I had to do.

It didn't feel like I was making a statement. Not like I was trying to prove to Diana how much I loved her or anything. There was no hope that a voice would whisper in her ear, *See there? That guy wasting his nights in your yard? He must really be serious.* I didn't feel more serious than I did the day before. It was relaxing, actually. That probably makes me sound insane.

I sat with my back against an oak tree and ate packaged

foods and drank Gatorade. The first night, Diana's mom came out a few minutes after I'd settled myself. She glanced at my picnic with distaste, and at me with pity. To be pitied by a mom. The new levels of humiliation were almost funny, sometimes.

"Markos, honey? What's going on?"

I considered not answering her, but it was her house, and I didn't need her calling the cops on me. Diana had told me how protective she was. "Nothing."

"Because I don't think Diana wants to see you."

"I know. That's why I didn't ring the doorbell."

"So . . . you're going to stay out here?"

"Yeah."

"Why?"

Because otherwise I might never leave my house again. "Maybe she'll change her mind."

Mrs. North nodded. "Well, yes, and I hope she does . . . but maybe it would be better for you to wait for her to call? At home?"

"I'd rather wait here."

She nodded again, then picked a leaf off the tree above her head and worried it through her fingers. "It's nice to see your dedication, of course, it's just that . . . it seems like a lot of trouble to go to."

I leaned back into the bark of the tree and closed my eyes. It was almost as if she was trying to bait me, but I was underneath too many layers of shit to be roused by something so stupid. "Ignore me, Mrs. North. I won't bother you or Diana or Mr.

North. I'm only going to sit here for a while."

After a second she shrugged and turned back to the house, dropping her leaf and brushing her hands like she was brushing away me and her daughter's problems.

—She should've kicked me out.

—Why?

—I'm a menace.

—So leave.

—But I won't hurt her again.

—Who says you won't?

—I do.

—People hurt each other. It's what they do. Nobody can decide they will never hurt again.

—But I'll try not to. Doesn't that count for anything?

—Is that why you're sitting out here? To prove something?

—No. I just can't think of anything better to do.

—So . . . staring at a window it is.

—Staring at a window.

—What's going to happen?

—She'll either come out and talk to me—

—Unlikely.

—Or I'll stop wanting to sit here. I'll get up and not care anymore. Either one would be fine.

The next night I found a blanket under the tree, presumably left by Diana's mom. This was the person who'd cared for Diana her whole life. It was weirdly comforting that this same person was now taking care of me.

It seemed, under the tree wrapped in the blanket with nothing to do but think, that I only had bad signs and bad memories to sort through and catalog. There were the mistakes I made, like kissing Kay, or the betrayals by others, like Ari spelling away Win and Diana lying about it. Then there were the memories that I thought were good at the time but have since turned rotten: anything Win-related, which meant my entire life, practically, from age five onward, and the more recent memories of spending time with Diana, from the diner parking lot continuing backward to the bonfire. All of those were tainted, too burning hot to touch.

I tried to think of nothing. Meditate, I guess you'd say. But my mind wouldn't empty. No blank room to escape to.

I could only talk to myself and imagine futures less terrible than the one I was destined for.

I imagined dozing off under the tree and waking up with Diana curled up next to me.

I imagined walking into the hardware store and seeing my brothers and mom cleaning the place out, organizing everything into clearly labeled sections and rows that didn't dead-end and backtrack.

I imagined a different set of brothers: ones who understood me like Win had.

I imagined falling asleep and waking up back in May, before any of this happened, and returning the money I stole from my mother, meaning no spells from that young hekamist, no last night on the beach, and no funeral.

In that one—the time-traveling miracle—I imagined insisting to Ari that she bring Diana along when we hung out. I imagined that back then I wasn't who I knew I was—and that I would've given Diana a chance and not screwed around on her and somehow we all would've been happy.

Yeah, right.

The rest of the time, I waited and watched.

On Friday, the fourth night I'd spent in Diana's yard, my phone rang just as I got settled. It was Brian. I leaned my head back into a groove in the tree and answered it.

"What."

"Markos, where are you?"

"Out."

He sighed. I could hear the sounds of phones ringing and chatting in the background; he must've been at work. "Cal's missing."

"What do you mean?"

"I mean we can't find him, dumbass."

"He'll probably be home in the morning."

"No one's seen him since before dinner last night. He didn't open up the store. Mom's freaking out."

I knocked my head back into the tree's trunk: *thump, thump, thump*. "So what do you want me to do about it?"

"Help Dev look. He's checking out the beach. I get out in an hour and I'll join you."

"Do it yourself. You're the cop," I said, and I knew I sounded like a dick, but I didn't want to leave my post.

"I'm sorry," Brian said, not sorry at all. "Am I interrupting something? Are you performing open heart surgery? If so, I can call back."

"Come on, Brian . . ."

"Mom said you've been staying out all night and not talking to her when you're home. Nobody's said anything, but maybe we should. This isn't cool, Markos. It's time to grow the fuck up. Be a member of the family. It's not adorable to be the baby anymore when you're eighteen years old."

I thumped my head on the trunk too hard and winced. "I'm seventeen."

"Just do this one thing, Markos. Cut the attitude and help find your brother. Then you can go back to whatever important moping you had planned."

I looked up at Diana's window. The light was on. If she peeked out through the curtains, I wouldn't go. If I saw her shadow on the wall, I wouldn't go. If the curtains moved even the tiniest inch, I wouldn't go.

"Markos? You there?"

I stared at the window, wishing so hard. Hoping.

But the curtain never moved, and I never saw her face.

"Fine," I said, and hung up.

I tried not to look at Diana's window as I walked away, but I couldn't help imagining that I saw the curtain twitch out of the corner of my eye. Of course when I stopped at the end of her driveway and looked back, there was nobody there.

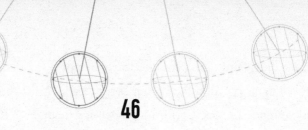

46

KAY

When I couldn't hold out any longer and tried to reach Diana and Ari on Friday night, Ari wouldn't talk to me for more than a few seconds, and Diana wouldn't pick up the phone. I left her message after message, but she never called me back.

Hey, it's Kay. Just calling to . . . yeah. Let's talk.

Diana, it's Kay. I was thinking about you. Call me.

We don't have to hang out. You don't have to talk to me. Only text me that you're okay.

Me again. Call me.

Call me.

When you get this, call me.

Ari wasn't much help. Her sigh came through the phone loud and clear. "I don't want to talk to you, Kay."

"But Diana . . ."

"She probably doesn't want to talk to you, either."

"She has to. Every three days. What if she tried to leave town and something happened to her? What if she's hurt and she can't come see me?"

"It seems more likely that she's pissed at you," Ari said. "Maybe you should respect her choice."

"You don't get it—she doesn't have a choice."

There was a long pause on the other end of the line. I could hear how the words sounded, and they sounded bad, but it didn't make them any less true.

"Have you talked to her?" I asked.

There was another, differently weighted pause. "No. Things have been . . . weird. In case you haven't noticed."

"So you don't know," I said, almost shouting. "You don't know if she's okay or not! You don't know and you don't care what happens to her!"

Ari's voice turned ice cold. "That's not true."

"So call her yourself. Please? I get ignoring me, but she should pick up for you. . . ."

"I'm not your errand girl."

"But I only want to know she's okay! Ari? Hello? Are you there?"

She'd hung up on me.

Mina had walked in on me talking to Ari and stood there, watching. We were in the dark kitchen standing around the granite island. Mom and Dad were out to dinner, so there were four untouched twenties sitting on the island that we were supposed to use for takeout. Typical parental overkill.

"What?" I asked.

"Nothing."

"If you're going to yell at me, yell. Don't stand there judging."

"Maybe you should leave them alone."

I waved her away. "I can't."

"It seems like Diana doesn't want to talk to you."

"She has to talk to me."

"It's probably tough for her. I barely want to talk to you, and you're my sister."

"So don't!" I snapped. "Stop pretending you care and leave me alone."

"I care," she said.

"Yeah, right."

"I can't believe you gave them that spell. What were you thinking, Kay?"

Despite everything that had happened and the fact that I really didn't care what she thought anymore, something pinched right behind my heart. "It's not that different from the beauty spell. It means I don't have to be alone."

"You took a beauty spell?"

I rolled my eyes. She had to be kidding. "I wrote you and told you about it. Obviously you were too busy to notice."

She shook her head. "You never told me that."

"I did! What, you think I got gorgeous overnight?"

"You were always pretty," she said.

"Don't be stupid."

"You're my sweet sister. Everyone would love you if they got to know you."

"Are you not paying attention? I'm not sweet little Katelyn.

I'm the bad guy. I hurt people. I'm a life-ruiner."

Mina uncrossed her arms and took a step around the island to get closer to me. I took a step back. "You're not a bad guy."

"Really? If I'm so great, why would you leave me?"

All the air was sucked right out of the room. Mina didn't say anything.

"I was useful when you were sick," I said. My voice came out hard like the bar of iron through Mina's eyebrow. "I was convenient. But now that you're okay, who cares about stupid, ugly, friendless Katelyn?"

Mina clutched her left arm with her right hand. That was the IV arm. It used to get so sore she couldn't accidentally bump against anything without screaming.

"That's not what happened," she said.

"Liar. It is. You got better and couldn't *wait* to get out of here. To change everything about yourself." I knew I should take a breath to calm down but I felt too full already; I had to let more out. "So I changed, too. I changed my face. And I found my own friends. Ones who wouldn't leave me on a whim. Ones who couldn't leave me."

I pulled up Diana's number again, muttering "Pick up, pick up," under my breath. Mina left me alone in the kitchen and went out the back door of the house. She started her car and was gone before I could run to the window. *Fine,* I thought, *get out.* I didn't need her distracting me.

Hey, Diana, it's Kay. Duh. I'm . . . worried about you. Please call . . . yeah.

So many things could have happened. A sudden flu, a slippery step. Leaving the gas on or dropping the blow dryer in the tub. Diana could step off the curb without looking, or get into a fight with a stranger without knowing why.

All because I'd pushed her away.

47

ARI

Diana's cell went straight to voicemail. Mrs. North picked up the landline.

"I wonder if you could tell me where Diana is?" I asked her, just after dusk on Friday night. I stood in my kitchen, peering out the back window as if Diana might emerge from the neighbors' yard.

"Oh, Ari. I'm really not sure she would want me to tell you."

"But you know where she is?"

"She needs some time. You can understand."

"Mrs. North," I said, trying to slow my words, overenunciating. "You've known me practically my whole life. Can you please just tell me where Diana went?"

There was a pause on the other end. "I believe she went to try to find Markos."

"Markos?" I said. I nearly laughed in surprise, though it wasn't funny. "Why on earth would she do that?"

"Well . . . maybe she's forgiven him."

No. Diana wasn't that stupid. Markos had kissed Kay and broken her heart. "That's impossible."

"Markos has been working hard to earn her forgiveness. Not everyone would do that."

I heard a slight admonishment in her words, though her tone was mild. "Not everyone would kiss someone else and break off all contact with her, either."

There was a pause, and Mrs. North's voice chilled. "Do you need me to talk to your aunt?"

"I'm fine," I said. "Thanks for telling me about Markos."

"Talk to Diana tomorrow. I'm sure you'll be able to work everything out then."

I threw the phone down on the kitchen counter. From the living room, Jess called out, "Everything all right?" and I said, "Sure!" with such insincerity I sounded demented.

"Your mom and I used to fight like this," Jess said, stepping into the kitchen. "She was the cool older sister. She never wanted me tagging along."

"That's not how it is with me and Diana," I said.

"I know. You used to be the one who would go out and leave *her* at home alone. Now it's the other way around." Jess grinned. "When Katie had you, I got to be the cool one, going out, flirting with girls, calling her in the middle of the night. It was so different for me I may have rubbed it in her face a little bit. Diana's probably just doing the same thing."

The question I wanted to ask—*Why are you choosing this exact moment to start reminiscing about my dead mother, when we've spent the last nine years pretending she never existed?*—was replaced by a different one entirely: "Jess, how did Win make me ditch Diana and want to stop dancing?"

Jess looked surprised for a minute, as if she'd forgotten about my spell—or maybe she hadn't known about Old Ari's dancing change of heart. "Nobody's ever made you do anything, Ari."

That wasn't an answer at all.

I picked up the phone and called Markos.

48

MARKOS

Cal wasn't at the beach, the gym, or any of the shops along the main drag. Dev had already checked the hardware store and Cal's friends' houses. Dev joked as he and I went in and out of coffee shops and bars and bank lobbies, but as it got darker and Brian joined us, we stopped joking. I couldn't tell by looking at them if they were really worried or just pretending.

I worried about Cal—sure. I wasn't a monster. Not so worried I'd freak out and start handing out flyers at the bus stop, but he was my brother—the nice one. The one mom had been spelling. He'd been sick the last time I'd seen him, days ago, and my working theory was that he'd passed out somewhere.

But I'd have to be an idiot not to notice that they never put out any search parties for me when I'd gone to Diana's. They let me disappear. It put a halt on my worry, made me pull away even as they were dragging me back in.

Brian led us around town, to the alleys and back streets I'd never thought to explore but that he seemed intimately familiar with. Bums with brown paper bags, street kids, people obviously fucked up on alcohol or drugs or spells. There was a whole secondary seedy town underneath the one I knew. Everyone knew Brian; no one had seen Cal.

I got the call from Ari as we checked the last open hole-in-the-wall bar and started to head for Brian's squad car at the end of the block. I let it ring until it went to voicemail, and then it started right up again.

I hated Ari. I never wanted to talk to her again. She'd fucked over my best friend.

But my best friend had loved her.

—She can go to hell.

—Don't be that way.

—Fine, then. Tell me what to do.

—See what she's calling about, at least.

—But she's the worst.

—She's not. You know that.

—I'm still angry, though.

—Fine, be angry. But forgive her.

—What if I can't?

—You can.

—What if I don't want to?

—Shut up and do the right thing, dumbass.

I answered the phone. "What do you want?"

"Are you at your store?" she asked. Her voice seemed higher-pitched than usual.

"No. Why?"

"Diana's bike's here. She's not answering her phone. The door's locked, though, so I don't know how she'd get in. I don't know *why* she'd go in, either, if it wasn't to find you."

I stopped walking, letting Brian and Dev get into Brian's car without me. "Diana's not at home?"

"No, she left to find you, according to her mom."

I could tell from her tone she thought finding me was the stupidest thing Diana could've ever thought to do. And for a second I agreed with her—the deal was, Diana would stay in place, and I would sit and wait for her.

Only I'd left my spot, and so she'd left, too. She didn't get it. What, did she think me in her yard was *her* looking after *me?*

And then Brian honked his horn for me to get in the car and I knew why I'd been coming to her house in a way I hadn't known before. It wasn't so much that I thought she'd forgive me, or that I was doing penance. It was my version of Diana GPS: As long as I knew where she was, she wasn't quite lost to me. Actually it was that I knew where I was: I was at her side.

But now she was lost. And so was I.

49

KAY

I didn't fall sleep. I lay on my bed with my phone resting on my chest, waiting for Diana to call and let me know she was okay— waiting for her to save herself, if she could. I watched the room darken and the light from passing cars flash on the ceiling for hours, and she still hadn't called. I wondered if the hook could accidentally kill her in its attempt to keep her near me.

It's a blunt instrument, I reminded myself. It keeps people close and that's all it does. Maybe it couldn't calibrate finely enough to stop pushing them back to me before it was too late.

After midnight I heard Mina's car in the driveway, and then a few minutes later she tiptoed into my room and sat on the edge of my bed.

"Did she call?" she asked.

I shook my head.

"No luck on my end, either. Went to every diner and bar within twenty miles."

"You were out looking for her?"

"Checked a few beaches, too, but no one had seen a teenage girl with ultra-red hair."

"Why would you—"

"You were worried. I wanted to help."

I turned onto my side and curled into the fetal position. "She's got to be hurt or trapped somewhere. She can't contact me. The spell would work, otherwise. It always works."

Mina plucked a feather from the comforter. "I don't know her very well. But she seems . . . like a regular girl."

"What does that mean?"

"You really thought a spell was the only way to be friends with her?"

I put my phone up against my heart, letting it warm me. "If my own sister wanted to get away from me, why would anyone else stick around?"

"Katelyn." She tugged at my blanket, waited until I was looking right at her before continuing. "When did I try to get away?"

"As soon as you got better you were gone. Globetrotting without me. We used to talk about traveling together, but I guess that was dying-girl talk—not a real promise."

"You had school."

"So did you. But you didn't go. The whole plan changed. You changed. Look at you."

She bit her lip ring and shifted in her safety-pinned shirt. "When we found out the cancer was in remission . . . Yeah, I guess you're right, in a way. I thought the rules had changed. They changed so I could live." She frowned, remembering. "I had to jump at the chance. For the first time in years, I wasn't dying. You don't know—"

"No, I get it. I don't know how hard it is to be sick and all that." I took a breath and whispered, "I wanted you to get better, Mina. That's all I wanted. For years. Mom and Dad spent all their time on you, and so did I, because I loved you." I tried to breathe again but couldn't because of the snot leaking from my nose. "This is the horrible selfish stuff I shouldn't even be feeling. But I do feel this way. So it's like I told you, I'm horrible."

"I will still be your best friend, no matter how horrible you are."

You know when someone says something super nice and heartfelt, and you know it's true and she has no reason to lie, but instead of lifting you up it curdles and twists unbearably?

Mina did that. I should've been happy that my sister bothered to take the time with me—it should've washed away the past two years, or at least made them slightly less awful.

But Diana was out there somewhere, in trouble, because of me. Not to mention Ari and Cal—they were all potentially in danger. From something I'd done to them.

I don't think even Mina would want to be my friend if I got Diana hurt. Or killed.

Or maybe she would stand by me, always understanding, loyal forever—but I didn't want to be someone who she had to forgive every second of every day. I wanted to be better than that. Deserving. Someone who she would be proud to stand next to for the rest of our lives.

My phone buzzed with a text. I knew it wasn't Diana, and I knew what I was going to do before I even read it. It was from Ari:

Come to the hardware store NOW.

Mina read it over my shoulder. "I need you to drive me somewhere," I said.

"Let me guess . . ."

I shook my head. "I have to stop somewhere first."

Mina nodded and held my hand.

It would be okay. I would fix what the hook had broken.

50

MARKOS

I left my brothers and ran to the hardware store, which wasn't easy after two weeks of living on Fritos and beer. By the time I got there it was officially the middle of the night, and the street was deserted, stores all dark and shuttered. You could hear the ocean hitting the sand a couple of blocks away. Ari unfolded herself from where she was sitting, tucked in the store's doorway. She stumbled and nearly fell, catching herself with a hand on the "WA" of the "WATERS" label on the glass door.

I thought I'd be furious to see her again, but it was a relief. For a second it didn't matter that she'd forgotten Win—she cared about Diana as much as I did. That was something.

"You look like shit," she said, her voice cracking.

"Thanks. Why don't you fall down some more?"

"If you're lucky. I fall like a goddamn angel."

I got out my keys and gestured for her to get out of the way of the door.

"You really think she's here?" I asked.

"Can't hurt to check."

I propped open the door with a brick. "Dev went through a couple hours ago when we were looking for Cal and said it was empty."

Ari blinked several times. "Cal's missing, too?" I couldn't read her face in the darkness. I was going to answer but she reached out and grabbed my arm, hard. "Do you smell that?" she asked, and as soon as she did I could: a dry, sharp chemical scent coming from inside the store.

Not good.

"Diana!" I called as soon as we stepped through the store's door. The smell got stronger inside, and there was something in the air—something that got in your throat and made you cough like you'd inhaled fifty cigarettes. "Diana, you here?"

Ari stood close behind me. I knew she didn't like the store, and for once I couldn't blame her: it looked menacing in the dark of night, the uneven rows crowding in and strange shapes materializing out of the darkness, the smell of fumes in the air. We walked as quickly as we could up and down aisles, calling Diana's name.

"So you can't find Cal?" Ari asked.

"No. I don't know what's going on with him. I found out my mom pays an old hekamist every month to spell him—has been paying her six thousand dollars a month for years."

"Six thousand dollars!" Ari's eyes practically bugged out of her face. "That's more than I've ever heard anyone pay for a permanent spell. And that's every *month*? What for?"

I hadn't realized it was so expensive. The only spell I'd ever bought was the one on Win's last night. "He can't hurt people. Couldn't hit me. But maybe if it's that much money, it's for something else, too."

"Huh. That's so weird, because Kay's spell—"

I winced. "Can we please not talk about Kay?"

She was silent for a second, thinking, and we reached the end of another aisle before she spoke again. "Hey, can I ask you . . ." She breathed out through her nose, frustrated. I've never known her to ask permission to ask a question, so I braced myself for whatever it could be. "You really like Diana?"

I looked straight ahead. "I'm in love with her," I said.

She didn't say anything for another couple of steps. Then she tripped over a stray gardening hose and hissed. "I'm sorry," she said.

Some heavy, sad feeling in my chest broke loose and banged around my heart.

"I mean for everything. I'm really sorry."

"Yeah, I got it."

She was not forgiven. Not yet. But I fell into step next to her easier now. If I closed a part of my mind, I could believe Ari and I were friends again, like before. If I didn't look to the left, I could imagine Win next to us, silently a part of the group.

We saw a ring of light around the almost-hidden door to the woodshop. Ari saw it, too, and grabbed my arm.

"Diana?" I called. "You back here?"

I opened the door with my free hand—it stung my skin. The

woodshop was so bright I had to blink to see. It wasn't only the fluorescent lights; some of the scrap bins lining the walls were on fire.

"Shit—we have to get out of here," I said, backing away from the door. It wouldn't be long before the rest of the woodshop caught fire, and then the rest of the store—we'd be stuck here.

Behind me, Ari sucked in a breath and pushed past me, running straight into the burning woodshop. I started to call her an idiot then saw what she saw: Diana, behind the chain link fence of the cage where we usually kept the welder.

My heart pounded against my ribs, *no no no no no no no*, and the shelves of wood and tools and fire closed in and towered above me.

When Diana saw us, she scrambled to her feet and started crying and talking at the same time. But I couldn't hear anything she was saying over the rushing in my ears.

I ran across the shop, stumbling, and grabbed the chain link and shook it—actually kind of surprised when it didn't crumble in my hands. *The key the key the key the key*—I knew where the key was, by the door, on a hook by the woodshop door, had to get the key to unlock the cage so Diana—

Diana was crying. Ari pressed her hand through the holes in the fence, reaching for her. "I was looking for you," Diana said to me. "You weren't under the tree. I went looking for you."

I wrenched myself away and ran for the door, where I knew the key would be. The scrap bins burned and I could see where the end of a stack of two-by-fours had started to get black and smoky. I slipped on something on the floor—paint thinner? Alcohol? The floors all shined—someone had covered the place with it.

At the door I reached for the key on the hook even when I could see perfectly clearly that there was no key hanging there. Someone had taken it.

I kept saying "someone" in my mind but there was really only ever one person who could've done it, gotten in the hardware store after Dev checked it, known where the key was kept, locked her in and set the place on fire—even though I couldn't imagine why and I didn't want to believe.

Tools hung on a pegboard to my left. Fire licked at the bottom of it, but it wasn't burning yet. (It would burn soon. The whole place would be ablaze. And Diana locked in the cage.) I took a deep breath, coughing on smoke, and grabbed a crowbar from its spot.

It was red hot; it burned my hand. I screamed and dropped it, then used my shirt wrapped around my left hand to carry it back to Diana.

She stood behind the fence watching me, tears streaking down her face.

She didn't hate me. Okay.

I was breathing too fast. Wood shavings and paint thinner and something like sulfur filled my nose; there wasn't enough air. I wedged the crowbar into the padlock—but the bar slipped from my hand and clattered to the ground. I bent down to pick it up again—I could barely stand to tear my eyes from Diana for a second—when Ari shouted and I turned.

Cal stood in the doorway to the woodshop. He had his silver lighter in one hand and a bottle of paint thinner in the other.

"Give me the key!" I yelled. It was hard to hear words, and I didn't think it was just me; the flames had gotten louder, the burning more intense.

Cal started walking toward us and I looked at Diana. "It's okay, it's okay, we'll get you out—"

"Markos, no—you've got to get out of here—"

"I'm not leaving without you."

Cal stopped a few feet away and put the can down. He didn't say anything. I didn't look too closely at his face—there was something strange happening with his eyes—and I didn't let myself think of anything except that he had the key.

"Hurry up hurry up! The key!"

"I'm not under a spell anymore," Cal said.

Diana sucked in a breath and I turned to look at her. Which meant I missed the moment that Cal picked up my dropped crowbar; missed him winding up and swinging; saw nothing but Diana's wide-eyed panic before the pain hit and the whole world turned black.

51

ARI

"Cal, no!" I shouted, but he'd already swung. The crowbar hit Markos's head solidly, straight on, and he collapsed. Cal dropped the crowbar and covered his eyes with both hands, pressing the lighter into his eye socket. Markos's body lay unmoving on the ground, and Diana knelt inside the cage and whispered to him. Spots of fire licked at wood and walls.

"Why'd you do that?" I asked.

"Because I couldn't before," Cal said into his hands. "And it's his fault that I can *remember*." He said the word as if it tasted bad.

My heart felt strangely light, beating its way out of my chest, and the room pitched sideways as I tried to breathe normally through the smoke. Something was seriously wrong with Cal. But more importantly, I needed to open the cage and get Diana and Markos out before the fire spread.

"Cal . . . the key . . ." I said, keeping my eye on the crowbar in case he came after me next.

Cal looked up.

His eyes . . .

He looked so much like Markos, only shattered. Like behind his eyes, a cornered animal peered out instead of a person.

He tried to take a deep breath but it got caught in his throat and he gasped. "I used to be angry," he said. I couldn't even tell if he knew who I was, or if he understood what he was saying. "Angry about my dad, about everything—but I haven't been angry in nine years." He blinked and whatever wild thing had taken up residence inside him shifted, pushing its way to the front, all rage and blindness. "Do you know what that's like? No emotions? It's not being able to breathe, but also not remembering what breathing even *is*. But now I can, only it's—too much. Too big. You understand?"

I didn't try to answer. Something caught his eye on the wall—the security monitor, with its dozens of camera angles throughout the store. Most were dark, but the view of the entrance had enough streetlight to make out two people walking through the propped-open door. One of them had a long swinging coat and short hair.

Cal made a noise, something between a cry and a scream, and ran out of the burning shop.

"Ari," Diana said. "The fire."

I snapped into action, grabbing a dropcloth from underneath one of the machines and using it to smother the fires—the two-by-fours and piles of scrap. The flames hadn't joined together into one big blaze yet. I felt cold, even, but I suspected that was some sort of shock, the sweat on my skin chilling like shards of ice.

It took me a second to realize that as I was running from fire to fire, Diana kept saying my name. "No—Ari. No," she said. She knelt behind the chain link as close as she could to knocked-out Markos, but she looked up at me with the saddest expression I'd ever seen.

"Don't worry," I said. "We'll get out. Echo's here now. She'll find us. It's okay."

"No, Ari. The fire. Not *this* fire."

"The fire?" The only other fire I could think of was the fire that burned down my house when I was eight. Diana never brought it up. We never talked about it. It was in the past.

"I came here to try to find Markos," Diana said. "The door was open so I walked in. I could smell the kerosene or oil or whatever this is—found my way back here—Cal was dousing the place. I tried to stop him and he freaked out. Put me in here."

I pressed my chest, pushing my racing heart back into my rib cage. Wished I could push it through to the other side.

"I thought it was Kay's hook that was making him act so odd. But if it was the hook it would've brought us both to Kay, and he was keeping us away. So I thought—the only way to interfere with a hook is another spell, right? So he must have other spells."

"Yes," I said. "Markos said he's been taking them for years."

Diana went silent. I tried to think.

Hekamists make spells temporary so people keep coming back month after month. You pay a little bit of money to them regularly, a steady stream. Markos told me his mother had been paying for Cal's spells for years—but a huge pile of money every month, not just a little.

Nine years, Cal said. Nine years since he was last angry.

I felt close to understanding something bigger than me. I pulled at my hair and squeezed my eyes shut.

Nine years. So he would've been eleven when it started. Just a kid in junior high. I tried to remember what he was like then. When he was eleven, I was seven.

So maybe he got in a couple of fights in junior high. He might have gotten in trouble for pranks. Big deal. Nothing to warrant an anti-violence spell, nothing he would need to forget. It's not like he killed anybody.

My hand jerked to my face.

The ground dropped open, but if I didn't look down, I wouldn't fall.

No.

"The key," I heard myself say to Diana. "I have to get the key from . . ."

I couldn't say his name.

One big barrel of scrap wood kept burning but the rest only smoked. I could leave this room and find him—find out if this terrible suspicion was true.

I ran for the door. On the way I stumbled on nothing, all the way to my knees, crack, right on the floor.

In class, before Rowena arrived, we used to make fun of the girls with bruised knees and shins and hips. Dancers weren't supposed to walk into desks or trip up the stairs. Sometimes we got bruises from certain movements or being dropped in a pas de deux, but that wasn't the same thing. Those were badges of honor. There was a difference between civilian bruises, which were stupid and avoidable, and battle scars.

Since taking the memory spell I'd become a civilian, covered with bruises. I had thought the bruises were a mistake, and that if everything were right again, my skin would look as clean and smooth as the dancer I was inside my head.

But no—these bruises were my battle scars now. I'd earned them. My outsides matched my insides, nothing clean and smooth about them.

For a second before I got up again, I thought the best thing to do would be to stay exactly where I was and wait for Echo to find us—someone else could be the hero and save us all. Then tomorrow, if I was still alive, I could go to a hekamist with every last penny of my Sweet Shoppe savings and my parents' life insurance money—all of our moving funds for New York—and have her pluck this memory from my mind. Cal Waters. The terrible thing he might have done. The secret his mother and Echo's mom kept for years. Markos knocked out on the floor. Diana whispering his name over and over. The smell of fire and paint thinner and oil. I'd even rub out Kay for good measure.

I didn't want to know the truth.

Only thing was, if I did erase it all, who knows who I would be then and what I might want.

My damn spells. They scraped me away layer by layer. Cut out my parents' deaths and fill the empty space with dancing.

Cut out Win and the need for dance poured in again. What other deeply held but now forgotten desires were underneath those?

Dig down farther and farther, discarding desires like old clothes. Eventually there had to be a point where I wanted nothing at all.

But I hadn't reached that point yet.

52

MARKOS

When I lay blacked out on the floor of the shop, I didn't exactly dream. But it wasn't pure blankness, either. I floated in and out of my body in waves. In—pain, panic. Out—numbness, nothing. In and out. For moments in between, breaths and heartbeats at a time, I knew where I was and what had happened.

I knew the smell of the shop, wood and oil and charcoal, something crackling like spice.

I knew I was in trouble. I knew we all were.

I knew Ari was hurt and wasn't moving, but I also knew that she would eventually get up and keep going, because she would never leave me and Diana trapped here to burn.

I knew Ari was my friend.

I knew what Cal had done.

I knew the story. Ari's dad brought her out of the burning house, then went back for her mom, who had passed out from the smoke. Then the house collapsed on them. The person who lit the fire wasn't a drifter or robber, as we'd always imagined, not someone random and faceless. The person who did this was someone I'd known my entire life. One of my older brothers, who I idolized. One of the Waters brothers, which meant something.

I also knew I wasn't dead, because I didn't see Win and my dad in some sort of mystical vision urging me to walk into the light.

I had to get up.

—Get up get up get up GET UP!

—Can't.

—Don't be such a baby. Who knows what your brother's going to do next?

—I don't.

—So what are you going to do to prepare?

—Lie here. Wait.

—Well that sounds like an A+ plan.

—Not my choice.

—What about Diana?

—What about her?

—You going to lie there when she needs you?

—Diana.

—Yes, Diana. You love her. Remember?

—Right. Yes. I have to get up. Have to help her.

—Well, you can't.

—Hey, fuck you. I have to.

—Some things aren't possible.

—She needs me! I have to get up!

—I'm sorry, Markos.

In those fleeting moments, the part of me that wasn't fighting against my lifeless body thought that this was it, the worst thing that was going to happen. Cal had knocked me out. Now someone would show up, take him away, and take care of us. I thought for sure that what he'd done in the past was the worst of it; that getting it all out in the open would be good in the end; that one day we'd all be able to get past this.

I was wrong.

53

KAY

Echo and I walked right in through the propped-open hardware store door. Mina waited out in the car; I had promised we would only be a minute.

I followed Echo through the dark aisles. She wouldn't have been able to follow me. This is what "balance" meant, to a heka-mist, and what Echo had told me would happen when Mina and I went to her house for the spell. She put a layer on top of my hook, not to break it, but to counter its effects. There was nothing left for the hook to hook into. If someone really loved me, if she was able to look carefully and recognize the real me, she could see me—I hadn't actually disappeared—but for everyone else I'd become a part of the background. I was invisible, except not in a cool superhero way—more like an I'm-screaming-and-waving-and-nobody-notices-me nightmare.

Worse than that was the feeling. The side effects of this new spell. My hook had let me unhook my worries, and my conscience felt clear. Now . . . how to describe it? I was a vacuum, sucking up emotions. Every time one came anywhere near me, it sank its teeth into me—into my whole body. I felt *everything*.

I needed to see Diana, to make sure she was okay and that it had been worth it. Echo had insisted on coming along. And since I hadn't actually paid Echo yet—I had only my parents' eighty dollars of pizza money, which she'd taken as a deposit—I wasn't in a position to argue with her. Once we'd seen Diana for ourselves and Echo had done whatever it was she came here to do, I could go home with Mina—Mina, who could still see me; Mina, who loved me—and cry forever.

In the store, we heard something scuffling and crashing around corners, and we smelled smoke and alcohol, but we didn't see Ari or Diana anywhere. It got darker and darker—I held up my cell phone for light—until we reached an open door next to a rack of paint chips.

Inside the interior room, which was full of huge power tools and slabs of wood, smoke made us cough, and it took a second to see Markos collapsed on the floor, and Diana kneeling in a chain link cage next to him. The walls and benches were half-burned, and flames still licked the lip of a metal barrel of scrap. Close to where we stood, Ari had wrapped herself into a tiny ball on the floor and was crying.

"Oh my god," I said.

Diana looked up—her eyes drifted away from me, no longer hooked—and she addressed Echo. "He's hurt—Cal hit him—and he hasn't woken up," she said.

I ran over, slipping on the wet floor, and took Markos's wrist.

His pulse was shallow and uneven. If he'd opened his eyes they would be dilated and unfocused, I was sure of it. Concussion at the very least. His skull felt almost pulpy where he'd been hit, but I hoped that was from the bruising. I didn't know what to do if Cal had smashed his skull in; it probably meant Markos was dying slowly right in front of us.

I didn't say any of that out loud. No one would've heard me if I had, anyway.

"Ari?" Echo asked. "Ari? Are you okay?"

Ari didn't answer her, and Diana pressed her forehead into a gap in the chain link. Her breathing was shallow and her skin sweaty and flushed; it seemed like she might be hyperventilating and running a fever. "Are you the one who spelled Cal?" Diana asked Echo.

Echo stiffened and looked at Ari, alarmed. Ari didn't move from her crouch.

Someone spelled Cal?

"My mother made Cal's spells," Echo said softly. "Cal's mom came to us when I was ten, not yet a hekamist. She was terrified. I'd never seen an adult so scared in my life. I didn't know what was going on. I thought it was good that we were helping that poor woman."

"What are you talking about?" I asked, but no one answered. I thought about trying to carry Markos out to Mina in the car, but he was too heavy, and if his injury was bad it could be terrible to move him. It might loosen something that needed to stay in place.

Plus Diana would still be stuck there. I looked around for something that I could use to pick the lock, or cut the chain link. Not that I had any idea how to do either of those things.

"I didn't find out what we were really doing until years later, after I'd joined the coven," Echo said. I wished she'd stop talking and do something. She was a hekamist; she should have a lockbreaker spell or some other brilliant idea on hand. A fire extinguisher, maybe—I looked around the woodshop but didn't see one, so I got up and started pushing aside tools to see if one was hiding in a corner. "I thought it was awful, but necessary. Mom believed Cal's spells were our protection, in case people found out about me. Money to live on—not that she let us spend much of it—and a family in the community that needed us. I think that she's regretted making me a hekamist since the day we did it. She wishes she had been strong enough to die and save me." Echo's smile seemed forced and bloodless. "We have different ideas about that."

As she talked I gave up my search and circled back around to Diana. I thought about running out into the rest of the store and trying to find a fire extinguisher or a wire cutter—but I wouldn't know where to look or if I'd ever be able to find anything, and I knew I'd get lost and might not be able to find my way back. Instead I got out my phone and called for an ambulance as calmly and firmly as I could. I hoped the spell wouldn't work through phones, or 911 would forget about me as soon as I got off the line.

While I was calling, Ari unfolded from her crouch, swaying on her feet. I couldn't see her face; she was looking at Echo so her back was to me. Echo's eyes followed Ari's every jerky move-ment. When Ari slapped her, the crack of it made us all—except Markos—jump. Echo held her cheek but didn't fight back.

"What's going on?" I asked Diana, hoping and praying that just this one question could be heard and answered.

"Among other things?" She tried to breathe deeply. "Nine years ago, Cal burned down Ari's house."

"Oh," I said.

The sadness and sympathy were too strong, like all my emo-tions now. I could feel tears filling my eyes, not just for Ari and her parents but for Echo and her mom, for Markos lying busted on the floor, for Diana trapped, and for all of us broken by spells.

I reached out and took Diana's hand through the cage. She held Markos's with her other one.

She didn't look at me. Probably forgot I was there. That hurt, too, very badly, but I would get through it, I would wait with her until I was sure she was going to be okay.

I'd made myself powerless, invisible, inconsequential, in order to save Diana from my spell, but it turned out I wasn't the dangerous one after all. Now all I could do was keep my eye on her until help came.

I hoped it was worth it.

54

ARI

Echo's skin, always pale, seemed clear and fragile as glass in the shop's harsh bare-bulb light. When I slapped her and the bright red hand mark appeared, it only made the whiteness seem brighter. She swallowed and did not break eye contact.

"You knew this about my parents and you still blackmailed me."

"I . . . You don't understand. I'd been alone for nearly twenty years. Win was important to me. I was . . . upset . . . about what you did to him."

"Why do people say I did it *to* Win?" I asked. "I did it to myself. No one can do anything to Win anymore."

"That's not how it feels."

"Things you do to yourself do have an effect on other people," Kay said from where she was kneeling with Markos and Diana. I hadn't noticed she was there, and it was hard to focus on her. Even her voice sounded muffled.

Echo wrapped her black-clad arms around her stomach. "I

have done some bad things, and I've done some good. But the world isn't fair."

"That's all you have to say?"

Echo exhaled and spoke gently. "There's nothing I can say to make it not true." She reached into one of the many pockets of her jacket and pulled out a plastic sandwich bag. It was filled with crackers and cheese; she held it out to me warily, as if I might swat it out of her hand. "I made you your spell."

"Is that supposed to be an apology? Here's your dancing spell, everything's better now?"

"Everything's *not* better. Win's still dead. Your parents are dead. My mom will be dead in a few weeks, since I don't have the money to leave her and get a new coven." She shook the bag; the cheese smeared the plastic. "But you can dance again, if you want. I promise."

I took a step closer to where she stood near the door to the woodshop. She did not flinch away, just left the plastic bag hanging in the air between us.

I turned from her and stared out the woodshop's door into the mess of a store as if trying to clear it all away with my mind. Wanting to erase what was right in front of me. Wishing to deny the truth.

Cal was out there.

The person who killed my parents.

There it was: the thing I'd been trying to avoid thinking about. The thing I wished more than anything not to be true, but that Echo had confirmed wholly and completely.

I lost my parents.

It was a long time ago. It was today. It was all the time. I couldn't escape it. I couldn't contain it. They'd been taken from me, and I missed them, and the hole in my heart was a fatal wound.

I shuddered and saw that I was holding my sore wrist. For once, I didn't feel the usual isolated ache. Instead the pain covered all my skin, paper-thin, and sank into muscle and bone and blood.

It didn't make it any better that the memory of the day they'd died had been removed. In fact, it was worse. Instead of knowing exactly what terrible thing had happened, I imagined a thousand different ways of it happening, each worse than the last. I saw them die over and over, their faces surprised or angry or sad. I wore my headphones or I didn't. I slowed them down or I didn't. I cried or I didn't. In each one, Cal ran from the house and hid. He'd been hiding ever since. Until now.

Now I knew what had really happened.

55

WIN

My last night on earth, a Saturday, began like many others. I picked up Ari and Markos and we went to the beach in my truck. It was raining and tourist season wouldn't start for another couple of weeks, so we had the place to ourselves.

It had been a bad day. I hadn't left my room, not even to eat, and so my tongue felt fat and heavy in my mouth, my stomach pinched with hunger, and my mind filled with sludge. Like the wet sand that worked its way between our toes as we picked our way down the shore.

"Remind me why we aren't at the diner or someone's clean, dry basement?" Ari asked. Her shirt was wet and sticking to her body in a way I know I should've found attractive—Markos took a couple of long looks—but it seemed clinical, like a diagram of a female body in health class.

"I've arranged a special treat," Markos said. "Trust me, you'll thank me later."

Ari sighed and swung my arm over her shoulder. Knowing

Markos, his surprise could've been legitimately great—a barbecue dinner, or a nighttime whale-watching cruise—or it could have been nothing at all, and he wanted to own us for the evening.

It could've even been that he wanted to cheer me up.

Ari and Markos riffed back and forth as the sun started to go down. Since it was raining, there was no subtle sunset; it got grayer and grayer until it was black, and Markos flipped on a flashlight.

"It was a dark and stormy night," he said, pointing the light at his chin.

Ari grabbed it from him. "And a douchebag prowled the beach, slowly drowning his friends to death."

Ari handed the flashlight to me and I looked into the bulb. It was my turn to continue the scary story, but all I could think to say was the scary truth, so I didn't say anything. I shone the light at Markos: grinning, confident, reliable Markos, hair blackened by rain and falling into his eyes. Then I shone it at Ari: funny, dedicated, tough Ari, skin even more glowing with rain dripping over it and the flashlight making her squint. I couldn't see it then, but I see now: they loved me. Wholly, completely. And not like Kara and my mom. Ari and Markos loved me because they *chose* me. How incredible.

At the time I saw their faces and felt their love like a burden. As if each of them had installed their own iron ring around my heart, and when they wanted to punish me all they had to do was make eye contact and the iron would cinch a little tighter.

So I flipped off the light.

Markos "hey"ed and grabbed it from me in the sudden dark. Dark on the beach, this far out, was different from dark in town. The ocean was pure blackness and suddenly loud, like the light had been keeping it in check and now it could scream. The dunes seemed endless, a desert to cross back to cars and people and life.

"Dude, we need the light," Markos said, half laughing, as he fiddled with the button. "That's how she's going to find us."

"She?" I said as Markos's beam hit a girl's figure not ten feet away. Ari screamed and I grabbed her hand, but not to comfort her—to steady myself. The girl now stepping closer to our small circle was Echo.

"Hey, you're here," Markos said. He immediately adopted the tone he took with waiters and cleaning ladies and other service staff: self-important, chummy. "You've got it?"

Echo held up a bag filled with three small, round white pastries. "As you ordered, sir," she said.

Markos laughed and grabbed the bag out of her hands, but she wasn't amused. She kept staring at me. I must've looked terrified, because she shook her head slightly.

"What are they, Markos?" Ari asked. She didn't sound entirely pleased.

"Why don't you try one and find out?" Markos said. He opened the bag and ate a pastry in one bite, then handed the package to Ari.

We watched him, all of us—even Echo. He crossed his arms over his chest, waiting. At first it happened so slowly I didn't notice. But then I heard Ari gasp, and I shook myself out of my fog, because Markos was floating five feet above the ground and rising fast.

At ten feet he let out a yell and zoomed over our heads, swimming through the air.

"You've only got a few minutes, so don't go too high," Echo said, but Markos was already climbing, flapping his arms like a butterfly and disappearing into the dark and rain.

"Get up here, Win!" he called.

Ari looked at the bag and then at Echo. "Are these safe?"

Echo shrugged. "They'll let you become impervious to gravity for a while. Nothing about that sounds safe to me."

"And side effects?"

"Unpleasant. But since it's a temporary spell, they won't last long."

"I have a memory spell from way back. Will the side effects be a problem?"

Echo considered her. I had a brief, terrified worry that she would lie to Ari to hurt her—I thought of nearly kissing Echo in the truck, and what Echo must think of Ari, my girlfriend—but then I shook it off. Echo wouldn't do that, even if she was jealous. "No. You should be fine."

Markos whooped and Ari looked at me, eyes sparkling. "Well?" she said.

"How could we not?" I asked.

Ari laughed, trying to sound unworried, and ate her pastry. "Mascarpone. Delicious."

"Thank you," Echo said.

Ari handed me the bag from shoulder height. "Holy shit! Win, hurry up!"

She spun away into the sky. Already she was more graceful than Markos. Her ballet training showed as she twirled and tumbled in the rain. I opened the bag, but Echo grabbed it out of my hands before I could fish out the last pastry.

"What the hell?"

"Have you taken your other one yet?" she asked quietly. I shook my head. "Then you can't do this, Win. The side effects—"

"Come on!" I said. It came as something of a shock that I wanted to fly. I hadn't wanted anything in so long. "I'll take the other spell as soon as I get home."

"Please trust me."

"You said it wouldn't mess with Ari's side effects. Why am I different?"

She looked at me for a long moment, rain making her hair stick to her forehead so that her eyes seemed bigger. "Because you are."

I reached for the bag but she turned away, quicker than me in the wet sand. Markos yelped and then landed nearby with a thud.

He hoisted himself to his feet, swayed, and then barfed. On his side now, he moaned. "I feel like shit," he said.

"It'll wear off," Echo told him.

"Oh man. Fuck you. Seriously, fuck you."

"The spell makes you weightless physically. Mentally, it

brings you down. Way down." She said it loud enough for Markos to hear, but she was staring straight at me.

"What am I supposed to tell them?" I muttered. Ari buzzed by my head, lightly tapping me with her pointed toe. Markos swore loudly, a string of uninterrupted curses.

"Not my problem. I can't let you have this." She shook the bag.

"What, because of some sort of hekamist's code of ethics?" I meant it sarcastically, but she nodded.

"Something like that."

"Please for the love of god kill me!" Markos shouted. Echo looked at me pointedly.

"But Markos paid you for three. . . ."

"I'll take it out of your tab."

Ari floated to the ground, as graceful as always, until both feet touched sand. Then she shuddered and sank to her knees. Very slowly she lowered her forehead straight down until it rested on the sand, like someone praying.

"I hate you, Markos," Ari said.

"You're welcome."

"I'm going to hold my breath until I stop breathing forever."

"Ari?" I said.

"I hate you, too, Win."

Something flared in my chest, and it took a second to figure out why my back clenched up and my jaw ached. I was angry. Not at Echo for denying me flight. At my supposed friends, for— what? Co-opting my sadness?

Aching and moaning on the ground, wailing and gnashing their teeth. This wasn't the same as Ari's freakout over the Manhattan Ballet, which at least was genuine, even if it didn't last very long. This felt like a parody of what I was living, day in, day out. I knew they weren't doing it on purpose, but it didn't matter. They took what was horrible and secret and *mine* and lurched around like drunks, proclaiming it to the world.

And what was worse, they got to fly. I never got to fly, so why did I feel like shit? Where's the balance in that?

"I have your money," I said to Echo.

Her face lit up and she grabbed my wrist from excitement. I thought she might try to kiss me, and so I yanked my hand away.

"I've got to go get it."

"Let's go, then."

Yes, I thought. Let's go to Ari's house, distract Ari, and get the money from the back of Ari's closet. Then let's go to the shitty house at the edge of town, into my tiny hole of a bedroom that smells like sweaty socks, dig below my underwear, open the Tupperware container, and scarf down that cheese sandwich. I had reached that point. This was it. The lowest moment. Enough.

I walked over to Ari and touched her shoulder. She moaned, and I whispered into her ear. "Ari, I forgot something at your place."

"So go get it."

"Why don't you come? The fun's over."

"Seriously, your voice is like nails on a chalkboard. Go get your whatever."

"You could come—"

"I said go away!" she shouted. "Leave me alone. I don't want you here, Win."

"Would you shut the hell up already?" Markos said, then coughed so hard he nearly barfed again.

I left her and went back to Echo. "I can't leave them here like this."

"I can stay with them. Go get it and come back." She grinned and hugged me quickly, a flash of arms in the dark.

I handed her the flashlight and bent over Ari again, intending to kiss her on the cheek. Before I could, she threw a handful of sand in my eyes. "Get out of here!" she screeched, then covered her head with her arms and wailed.

I didn't try again. That was the goodbye I felt I deserved, even if, somewhere distant in my brain, I knew it was just her side effects talking.

I walked to the truck in the dark. It felt farther than it should have, like the parking lot was shrinking away with every step, but eventually I reached it and my truck and started toward Ari's.

The road to Ari's. This is the important part. No witnesses, only me. A road I'd driven hundreds of times before. It was a wet night, yes, but the road was empty. No other cars. No animals, no nothing.

Did I have a moment of weakness? See the tree and let go of the wheel? Could I have planned this, somewhere, in a dark recess of my mind, while Ari and Markos floated overhead and Echo watched me too closely?

That's one way this could've ended. The other is the randomness of the universe: something so small so as to be functionally unmeasurable distracted me and a series of inevitable events pulled me toward the tree. No human intention or reason had any part in it.

Or it could've ended through hekame. I'd been joined in the truck by something invisible, fathomless and unmovable. And that thing pushed my arms. A force bore down on them and turned the wheel to the left, off the road, into a tree. Straight into oblivion.

But those are only theories. Only I know what happened.

In the moment that the crash became inevitable and unavoidable, I had enough time to notice the tree and my course, and to remember Mom and Kara and Ari and Markos perfect and loved and to hope that I had somewhere to go after this—somewhere where I was weightless, careless, free—before the truck crashed.

One of the strangest parts of being depressed is how it affects memory. When I was depressed, I couldn't remember anything particularly happy ever happening to me. Things I had previously assumed were happy seemed false and empty. The good past faded epically far away, and the good present, well, that was pretty much an oxymoron.

But when I hit the tree, all that cleared away—the sadness filter my memory had been set to—and I remembered moments of pure happiness.

Playing catch with Markos as kids.

Holding Kara when she came home from the hospital.

Ari laughing at something I'd said.

Birthday cakes. Big wins. Stupid jokes. Surprise As.

Lying in a sleeping bag in the backyard. Which house, it didn't matter, because the sky was the same at all of them, vast and cold, twinkling brightly, beautiful and remote.

For a second I remembered it all and loved it all with my whole heart.

And then I died.

56

ARI

I took the bag from Echo's outstretched hand.

It wasn't a spell to forget, like I had hoped for, and it wouldn't fix anything Cal had done, but it was something. It would get me out of town.

"If this works," I said to Echo, pressing the plastic together between my fingers, "you can come with me to New York, stay on the couch in our shitty apartment. There's got to be a ton of hekamists in New York, right?"

Echo touched her face where I had hit her. "Why would you do that for me?"

"Because . . . otherwise me taking this spell is charity. And I don't need your pity."

That wasn't the only reason, of course—there was the fact that she'd probably die if I didn't help her, and the fact that I owed her doubly for this because I'd stolen Win's money, and the fact that I liked her, despite myself. She'd kept Cal's secret, she'd tried to blackmail me, but she'd also tried to help, even though she had no reason to. Plus she cared about Win and I used to care about Win, so she must have good taste.

She looked at me for a long moment. For a second we didn't worry about Cal out in the store or Diana in the cage or Markos still knocked out on the floor. She smiled tentatively, as if I might change my mind. "It'll work. You'll be beautiful."

I pulled open the seal on the plastic bag and several things happened at once.

Kay pushed Echo into a stack of buckets and tackled me to the ground, grabbing the bag from my hand.

Just as the shelf behind me—right where I had been standing—creaked and toppled over, sending a pile of PVC pipes clattering to the floor.

When the pipes stopped rolling, I pushed Kay off me. Echo groaned and sat up. "What the hell?"

Kay spoke frantically, words tumbling over one another. Though she wasn't whispering I had to lean in close and concentrate extra hard in order to make out the words. "I figured it out. There's got to be a spell. Echo's spell. I mean the spell *affecting* Echo. A hook!" Kay flapped her arms in frustration. "Remember when you and Diana tried to leave me at the bonfire, and Diana busted her face?"

"Your hook's balanced out now," Echo said.

"And thanks so much for that," Kay said, bitterness souring the words. "But I'm not talking about me. I think there's a spell affecting Echo. A hook. One that her mom gave her, probably years and years ago. Think about it—that's why Echo can't seem to get anyone to pay her for their spells, why she doesn't just leave. It's exactly like my spell—it keeps her close to her mom."

Echo frowned. "My mom wouldn't do that."

"But Echo—all your bad luck," I said. "What if it's not luck?"

Echo kicked a piece of pipe and it rolled away. "She wouldn't. Hekamists don't spell other hekamists."

"You give your mom spells for her pain," I said.

"That's different. That's for her own good." Echo's eyes widened when she heard her words out loud.

"She would've thought she was protecting you," Kay said.

"Keeping you from being discovered and going to jail," I added.

"Watching over you. Because she cares about you." Kay sounded defensive.

"Wait—hold on," I said. "All I did was offer you our couch in New York if the spell works, and the shelf fell down on us. So if someone tries to help you, or gives you a way out . . ." I stopped, looking at the plastic bag in Kay's hand.

A little thing—the thing that would let me dance again and go to New York as planned. I wasn't attached to Kay's hook anymore, so that wouldn't keep me in Cape Cod.

And if I left, Echo could leave, too.

She'd been close to leaving once before. She'd told me she was waiting for Win to pay her the night that he died.

I leaned across the fallen pipes and grabbed Echo's arm. "Echo—Win owed you money, right?"

She sucked in a sharp breath. "Oh." Her chin shook, which

made her look ten years younger. "Win was on his way to bring me the money when he crashed."

"If you had his money, you could go," Kay said.

"So if there was a hook on me . . . Win . . ." She hugged her arms close to her chest, as if to keep her heart inside her body.

"It could be a coincidence," I pointed out.

"That's how hooks *work*," Kay said. "With coincidences and luck and chance. Your mom told me that when I got mine."

"Oh god." Echo took a deep, shuddering breath. "I killed him."

We'd never know. Not for sure. No one was there with him in the truck; no hekamist could do a forensic analysis and tell us the truth. But it felt true, like how Cal setting the fire at my house felt true, like how Kay's hook explained so much about my friendship with her.

"Everything I've done has backfired," Echo said. She stared at her hands and spoke in a monotone. "Every spell I've ever done has made things worse."

I knew that feeling. I was about to tell her it wasn't her fault, and that I had made plenty of the terrible decisions that brought us here, too, but we heard sirens in the distance, and Kay grabbed our arms.

"They're not going to be able to find us back here," Kay said.

She started for the woodshop's door, my spell still clutched in her hand. I was still trying to decide if I should follow her or stay with Diana and Markos when she stopped suddenly and backed up, stumbling over fallen PVC pipes.

Cal walked in after her.

That blank look on his face. He'd forgotten so much—to have it all come crashing back at once, every terrible feeling and thought, must've made him lose it.

Or maybe he was always a little bit off, and this was his real personality finally clawing its way to the surface, freed from the cage of spells he'd been given.

He held out an arm, his silver lighter in his fist. With a metal snap, he lit the flame.

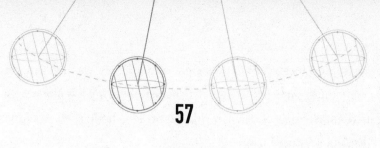

57

KAY

I stepped right up to Cal and took the lighter from him.

It wasn't particularly brave. In the hour since I'd balanced out my hook, I'd almost gotten used to being mostly invisible, and I figured he wouldn't notice me. Sure enough, he had to blink a couple of times before his eyes—his strange, wild eyes—focused on my face.

"You don't need that, Cal."

He frowned, those terrible eyes darting all over the room, a bird crashing against windows looking for the sky. "You shouldn't have spelled me," he said distantly, as if recalling a dream.

"I'm sorry. I screwed up. I thought being alone was the worst thing that could happen to me, but it wasn't."

It didn't matter that I meant that sincerely, and for Diana and Ari, too, because he didn't have to listen and neither did they. He shoved me by the shoulders—hard—and ran from one end of the woodshop to the other, jumping nimbly over benches and around hulking pieces of machinery, digging through smoldering piles of scrap and tossing PVC pipe right and left. He was looking for something. Another lighter? I clenched his in my fist along with Ari's spell in its plastic bag. Maybe my anti-hook spell wouldn't let him see that I had it.

It wouldn't be long before he found something that would work just as well, though. I thought about running, but I couldn't leave them all. I thought about trying to get him to give Echo some money, so we could trigger her mom's hook and rain hellfire on him like the hook had done to Win, but there was no time. Plus, spells were unpredictable. I remembered hanging out in the ER expecting my hook to kick in and send one of my friends through the doors. They never showed. No one could know how far we had to push before the spell fought back.

Ari shrank against the wall away from Cal as he tore through the room, and Echo stood in front of her protectively. I glanced at the security monitor and saw cops shining flashlights through the closed front door. Cal must've doubled around behind me and Echo and locked the door after we came in.

That chilled me more than the darkness in his eyes or the lighter fluid. It said to me that he wasn't simply unhinged, but that he knew what he was doing, and he didn't want us to leave or be rescued. He wanted us to burn with him.

As he ran by Markos's motionless body he knocked over a tin of lighter fluid. It spread quickly, seeping underneath where Markos lay and under the edge of Diana's cage. She let it soak the knees of her jeans.

He made a noise—a cry of some kind, almost a howl—and

flicked the switch on a knee-high box with a rubber pipe running out of it, sitting just outside the cage where Diana was trapped. The pipe ended in a handheld trigger and a thin neck like the stem of a flower, and he clicked it once—twice—before the flower blazed to life. Blue and yellow. Too bright to look at.

I didn't think. I ran straight at Cal, hugging him around the stomach and trying to tackle him. But he was taller than me, and stronger, and I didn't want to hurt him—I just wanted to stop him. I managed to push him against the wall. He dropped the welder and it went out before it could touch any of the lighter fluid, but he grabbed a two-by-four leaning there, and as I scratched and kicked and flailed, the two-by-four swung and hit me in the side. I dropped to my knees. Then it caught me right in the chest with a crack.

Couldn't breathe.

Fell to the ground and gasped for air.

I expected another hit from the two-by-four and welcomed it because I knew it would knock me out, and I wouldn't have to feel my broken ribs and aching side, and I wouldn't have to see Cal burn down the store and us in it.

Instead, lighter fluid seeped all around me. Up my nose. Stinging my eyes.

Ari yelled at Cal—yelled for the EMTs, somewhere out in the store—begged him not to do it—told him we would forget, that we would all take a spell with him, go back to the way things were, if that was what he wanted.

He didn't respond. Nothing in him could hear her.

Breathing in fumes, lightheaded. The room shimmered.

Turned my head, and Cal picked up the Zippo from where I'd dropped it. Visible again.

Dizzy. Lighter fluid on my clothes, in my hair. Couldn't get up.

I couldn't see Ari or Echo. Markos lying next to me, not moving. Diana on the other side of him screaming.

I rested my head in a puddle. Took a breath and my chest crackled. Ribs broken. No air.

I felt empty, floaty, like there was nothing left of me but a paper shell. Wouldn't hurt to burn to death. A *whoosh* and then nothing, like a scrap of newsprint.

So much for making things right and reversing the hook. So much for spells.

They couldn't be counted on when it mattered. Spells would always find a way to trick you, to use your weaknesses against you, to come up with the ugliest possible solution to your problem. They were blunt instruments—but then again so were planks and flames. Fists and hammers. So were words and kisses.

Cal held the yellow flame of the Zippo far from his body. It came closer, a tiny sun, and I had to close my eyes.

58

ARI

"What's in the bag?" Cal asked.

He held the Zippo a foot from Kay's head, which was soaked in lighter fluid. I smelled barbecues and bonfires. Burned flesh.

If I ran I knew I'd trip and fall and get lost in the store before finding the door to the outside. I knew the place would burn down with me and Diana and everyone else in it.

Cal looked at my dancing spell, lying on the floor where Kay must've dropped it.

"It's—it's a spell," I said.

Kay raised an arm and pushed the bag toward him.

"What does it do?" Cal asked.

"It'll make you forget," I said more steadily. "Like I forgot Win."

He picked up the bag. Something flashed from the depths of his dead, blank eyes. Something alive—something that hurt—a flash of the person Cal had been, trying to claw its way out.

He blinked at the spell. The bright hot room lit up his face and the hope and desire and anger and fear in it.

Get ready.

I looked for Echo, and she was kneeling over something in the corner, muttering to herself.

Diana's mouth moved, and she shook the chain link.

Kay turned her head and managed to half roll over to watch.

Tears streamed down Cal's face, no longer a terrifying blank, but broken, in agony and relief. He opened the bag and emptied most of the contents into his mouth. Chewed and swallowed.

A beat of silence, the Zippo still lit in one hand.

He made a strangled noise and his expression twisted. "What the hell . . ." He turned and crashed into a machine. "What did you—this isn't—"

I ran to him, slipping on the lighter fluid. I landed hard on my knee and it twisted beneath me. Something snapped. Pain shot up my thigh to my back, but I dragged myself up and threw my entire body at Cal, knocking him down. I dug my knees, even the one that felt loose and shaking with pain, into his back.

There was a *whoosh*, and fire burst from the spot where he'd been standing. He had been holding the lighter—it was a live flame. Markos was still unconscious. Kay could barely turn over. Diana was locked in the cage. We would burn up quickly from the fluid in our clothes and hair and mouths.

An easy way for Echo's mom's hook to eliminate the threat of Echo leaving would be for it to kill us all.

Echo—where was Echo?

59

MARKOS

Breathe in.

Heat and fire. A table saw caught on fire, then a stack of plywood. Flames licked the sides of my head and chest and legs, but I couldn't move.

Breathe out.

Diana tried to reach me. I could hear her crying. I opened my eyes.

She wanted to pull me away from the flames. She pressed the fire out on the side of the cage with her shirt. The room brightened like we were back at the July third bonfire.

Breathe in.

My head hurt. Cal had hit me in the head. My brother.

Breathe out.

It was hot. So hot.

Breathe in.

Out of nowhere, the room chilled and darkened. The flames seemed to freeze in place. The air pounded with the heartbeat of a creature much larger than us. In the corner, a single spot of light revealed Echo with her arm raised over a scrap of paper. She'd pushed up her sleeve, ripped off one of many bandages, and torn at the skin until a cut oozed over the paper.

The room seemed to shudder and something flashed in the smoke above Echo's head. She screamed, and a second later the room was as hot and bright as ever. Echo stuffed the paper, wet with blood, into her mouth and swallowed.

Breathe out.

60

KAY

"What did you do?" Ari asked Echo as she dug her knees into Cal's back, pulling his arms together past where they would normally stretch.

Blinking took effort. The smoke stung. I wondered what Echo's new spell was for, in a remote corner of my mind that wasn't in pain on the floor about to burn to death.

Echo looked dazed for a moment, then she snapped into action. She ran to the chain link cage and ripped the lock off in one quick motion. Diana stumbled out, coughing from the smoke.

"You got him?" Echo said to Ari. Ari nodded, though when she stood, pulling Cal up with her, she could only put weight on one leg. Echo turned next to Markos, smothering the flames covering his chest with her long black coat and hoisting him easily onto her shoulder. She went straight for the door to the wood-shop, with Ari limping and dragging a moaning Cal behind her, and Diana shuffling last. Away from me and this hellish room.

Forgotten. The spell to layer over the hook worked so well.

I took a breath and tried to push myself upright.

The pain in my chest made me cry out. I couldn't get enough air.

Diana heard me and turned around. She came back. She offered me her hand. I almost pulled her over, but then I was standing and coughing and gasping. I leaned on her, she leaned on me, and together we hobbled out of the burning woodshop.

Smoke had already started to fill the aisles of the rest of the store. I couldn't tell my way around. We followed the sound of Echo crashing. She didn't try to maneuver her way around the twists and turns; she kicked over shelving units and ripped up displays, taking the direct route to the door. Behind her, Ari dragged Cal, and Diana and I helped each other pick our way as quickly as possible over the mountains of junk. We passed the EMTs, but Echo didn't stop, and they followed us to the exit, shouting, asking if we were okay, trying to figure out where the smoke was coming from.

The lock on the door had been smashed by the EMTs, but instead of pushing it open, Echo's single kick sent glass and metal flying. We stumbled out onto the street.

61

ARI

Ambulances and fire trucks and police cars swarmed the street, the lights turning it bright as day. EMTs and cops swirled around us, shouting questions; firemen ran into the store with hoses. I refused to let go of Cal's arm until an EMT pried my hand away; another EMT led him to an ambulance as he clutched his head and cried. I watched him, and my EMT had to repeat herself half a dozen times before I could answer.

"I'm fine," I said, but she frowned and examined my bruises, fresh and old, as if I might be lying to her. She seemed particularly concerned about my knee. She said I might have torn my ACL. I heard her with only a part of my mind.

I was fine. None of my scars came from that night; none of my wounds were visible.

In the lights and confusion, I lost sight of Cal, and part of me wished I would never have to see him again. Dr. Pitts would say I was avoiding facing my trauma. Or she'd say it was healthy to move on. Either way, she'd have lots to say the next time I saw her.

On the ground near where Cal had been taken away from me I spotted a smushed sandwich bag filled with crumbs: the remnants of the spell Echo had made for me, the one Cal had taken because I told him it would make him forget. My spell. My gracefulness. My future. I didn't know how long it would last—or even if there was enough power left in the remaining crumbs to do anything at all—but I couldn't leave it there.

I clenched my teeth, put my weight onto my injured knee, and kicked the bag into the gutter and down the sewer grate.

Diana followed Markos into an ambulance—the first to leave, sirens flashing. Echo stood next to Kay and Mina, sentry-like, as Kay sat on the curb and held her ribs, gasping, and Mina held her hand and leaned Kay's head on her shoulder. "Do you need me to get an EMT?" I asked.

Kay shook her head. "They'll get to me." She spoke in between shallow breaths. "What was in that spell he took?"

Echo answered. "Gracefulness. He'll be a beautiful dancer." With a huge exhale she sat on the ground, her sudden burst of energy and strength spent. Her arm was bleeding thick streams of blood onto the sidewalk: the fresh cut, and several others from earlier. She looked extraordinarily pale. When she spoke, her voice faded, word by word. "And it'll mess him up. More than he already is."

"What about you?" I asked.

"Don't worry about me," she said, then closed her eyes and slumped over onto her side.

"Echo?" She didn't respond. I dropped to my knees—my

poor busted knees—and shook her shoulder. Kay reached for Echo's wrist to check her pulse, and I held her other hand, just to hold it. The fire blew the windows out of the store with a crash, and she didn't flinch. "Echo!"

Her eyes didn't open, but she managed to murmur loud enough for me to hear. "It's okay, Ari. It was too late for me and my mom. Not with the hook."

"You could rebalance like you did to Kay—"

"Too many spells. Too many side effects. No more spells." She exhaled. "No way out."

"Echo, no—"

"Tell my mom I'm sorry, but it was too late."

"No, it's not," I said. "Echo, listen—you can still come with me to New York. Take your mom with you! Find hekamists together. Or if I don't go to New York we'll still find a way to save you." I heard more sirens in the distance, and still Echo didn't move. "You probably shouldn't stay here to be questioned—you should get up. They'll find you, they'll find out about you, put you and your mom in jail. Please, Echo—you've got to get away. Echo—come on—"

No lightning fell from the sky to destroy me. My heart didn't stop. And that's when I got really scared.

Her mother's hook didn't work anymore.

Faintly, from far off, I heard someone calling my name.

"Ari? Ari!" Jess ran toward me, and I let go of Echo's hand.

I tried to run to meet Jess but my knee would barely let me stand. She reached me and hugged me, almost knocking me back onto the sidewalk, and I buried my head in her shirt.

"It's okay, it's okay," Jess said.

"I'm sorry," I said.

"Shhhh."

No one came to hug Echo. No one came to carry her home.

Echo was in a coma on the way to the hospital, and she died a few hours later. Loss of blood, they said. But doctors don't really understand hekame—not like I do, with my multiple spells. Echo made herself a spell that allowed her to break though doors, snap locks with her hands, and rip apart metal cabinets. The side effects of something like that would be disastrous.

The spell made her superhuman, ever so briefly. To balance that, she had to know what she'd give up.

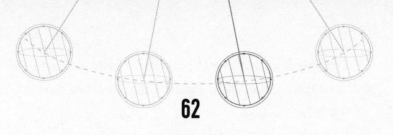

62

MARKOS

The smell woke me up. *(Someone left meat on the grill too long.)* Then the hurt. *(I am a white-hot metal knife of pain.)* I tried to will myself back into unconsciousness, but it was like running headfirst into a brick wall. So instead I opened my eyes.

"Hello," Diana said.

"You're okay," I said—barely. My vocal cords crackled.

She held my hand, which set off such pain that part of my vision went white, but I never would've told her even if I could.

"Cal?" I said, or at least shaped my mouth into the word. I couldn't hear very well because of the sirens. We were moving. An ambulance.

"In another ambulance," she said. He'd set fire to the hardware store. Would they arrest him for arson? For Ari's house, nine years ago? Either way it was a relief, not only that he'd been caught and we'd gotten away, but also that he was alive. Dead is so permanent. You can't actually summon the dead for pep talks, or to see what they think about your situation.

The ambulance went over a pothole and I started to fade—or the world did, at least, Diana and the paramedics and the pain.

—Win?

I wanted to tell Diana I was sorry, and that even if she never wanted to see me again, I would still be sorry, but I couldn't open my mouth, so I squeezed her hand.

—Win?

I couldn't see the real world anymore, but a room in my mind opened up, bright and cool, and I decided to lie down and rest in there because everywhere else was so noisy. But I kept the door open, so I could come back when it calmed down.

—Goodbye, Win.

Severe concussion. Second-degree burns on my face and legs. Third-degree burns on my hands. Part of my right eyebrow would never grow back, though they promised me the angry, puckered skin on my cheeks and nose would fade. I wouldn't look so much like my brothers anymore. An unmatched set.

"You're lucky your skull didn't crack," the doctors said.

Yeah. Lucky.

Diana slept in the chair next to my hospital bed. Her shirt was half-burned and her hair a tangled, charred mess. They'd given her fluids and a sedative, but she seemed mostly fine for someone who'd been locked in a cage and nearly burned to death. Better than the rest of us, for sure.

When my mind wouldn't stop racing and I couldn't sleep I'd turn my head and watch her breathing, shifting slightly in her chair, red hairs curling at the back of her neck. I *was* lucky.

I couldn't tell how long passed before Brian, Dev, and my mom showed up. Brian was out of uniform but he had on his full Cop Face, hardened and watchful. Dev wore pajamas and watched Brian and Mom with a lost expression. Mom—I couldn't look at her. She had rivers of tears running down her cheeks and agony filled her face. Diana took one look at all of us and slipped out of the room, closing the door carefully behind her.

"Oh my god, Markos," my mom said, crying more when she took in the bandages, the hospital bed, the IV running to my right hand. "I told you not to talk about the spell. I begged you. Why didn't you listen?"

"Me?" It hurt when I breathed in; the doctors had failed to catalog a few broken ribs, probably from when Echo got me out of there. "Cal set the fire."

"Only because you told him—"

"I mean the one nine years ago. The one that killed people."

"Accidentally." Her face twisted, as if she could hear how that sounded. "He was a boy. A good boy. He was acting out, and he made a mistake. Set off some fireworks—I don't know why it was the Madrigals, and it was terrible—a terrible accident—but it didn't have to be his whole life. They would've taken him away from us, Markos. He would've grown up in juvenile detention. That would've changed him. Ruined him. But instead I helped him—he started over."

She clutched the end of my bed, arms shaking. "All that money . . . all your dad's insurance money and money from the store, for all those years. It was for nothing now. He remembers. He told the EMTs on the way here—he's telling the nurses, he's telling everyone. Everything I did for him . . . for all of you . . . was for *nothing*."

"Look at me, Mom." I raised my broken hand and tried to gesture at my burns. "He did this to me."

She closed her eyes rather than look at me. "I would've saved you, too, you know. I would've done the same for any of you."

I swallowed with difficulty. "You would've spelled me— without my knowledge—for the rest of my adult life?"

"I *gave* him a life. I gave it to all of you." She kept crying, snot mixing with the tears and dripping onto her shirt. "Why did you have to *ruin* it?"

She seemed to totter, and both Dev and Brian—and me, reflexively, from lying down—moved to help her stand. She was crying too hard to talk anymore and so she allowed herself to be led out of the room by Dev, leaving me alone with Brian.

Brian watched them go.

"They're going to prosecute her for obstruction of justice," he said, as if to himself. "I resigned."

My stomach sank. "She's going to jail?"

"They want to do something. Statute of limitations is up on the Madrigals' fire, so this is all they have."

"I didn't think . . ."

"Of course you didn't." When he turned to me, his face had lost some of the cop stiffness. "Why didn't you tell me what was going on?"

"You didn't want to know."

"That's not—"

"Sure, you want to know now—now that something's happened." I took as deep a breath as I could and tried to speak quickly before he could interrupt. "But back before—when you thought I was pissed and sad about Win—you wanted me to shut up and be cool."

His eye twitched. "I wanted you to be happy. That's what everyone wants for their family."

"Yeah. Exactly."

He looked out the window into the just-rising sun. "You've always been so angry with us. I never understood why. You didn't have a bad life, you know."

I wanted to tell him that the life he and my brothers had given me wasn't ever truly mine. But even though he was trying his hardest to listen, I didn't think he'd understand.

He exhaled. "We could've fixed it together, if we'd known. But not now." My eyes drifted closed; it didn't block out his voice, which stayed eerily calm. "You really have no idea what you've done, Markos. We had each other's backs, but do you think anyone's going to have your back again, after this? After what you did to me and Dev and Mom and Cal?"

I kept my eyes closed. It was easier not to see him. To think of him only as a voice. "I think you should go."

"I'm your brother."

"Just go away, Brian."

I kept my eyes closed until I heard footsteps and the door

close. I couldn't be sure if that was it—if it was over, if I was no longer a Waters, if we were done. I'd asked him to leave and he'd left. It seemed too easy.

But not easy at all. Because now I was alone.

When I opened my eyes, Diana was standing in Brian's place at the head of the bed, looking at me.

"Are you okay?" she asked.

"No," I said. "Everyone I love is either dead or hates me."

She smiled for a second and then her face crumpled like she was going to cry.

"Diana—what's wrong?"

Her eyes flitted over my face—my burns, underneath the bandages. Probably full of pus and blood, stinking of rot. I was hideous, obviously. But it shouldn't have made her that weepy.

"Where are your parents? What did they say?"

She shook her head. "They checked in on me while you were asleep. They're worried, but it's okay. They understand."

"Understand what?" I'd been pumped full of drugs so that nothing hurt physically, but it still tore me up to look at her and see her upset. "Please. Tell me."

She took a shuddering breath and came around the side of the bed, where she sat carefully, without touching any of my damaged skin, and then curled up on her side next to me and rested her head on my pillow next to my bandaged face. "I'm scared, because"—she swallowed—"because I'm going to trust you again and that's totally terrifying."

I held my breath and managed to raise my arm so that she

could lean her head onto an unburned part of my chest. She could probably hear my heart beating all over the place, but for the first time in hours I smelled something other than lighter fluid and flesh and gauze and hospital. I smelled her hair.

The only thing that could make her leave was me. It had always been that way since the night of the bonfire, when I could've crushed her spirit or made her night, and I chose to do neither. The fate of this—us—was in my hands. I could make it work or fuck it up again.

The difference now was that it wasn't only her fate at stake anymore. It was also mine.

"I'm scared, too," I said.

She must've understood all that because her breath lost that hesitant catch and she settled into my chest more comfortably.

And I was happy. So happy.

At that moment, I would've spent the rest of my life in the hospital wrapped in bandages if it meant I could have her head next to mine forever.

But all the same, I felt my chest caving in, because I missed Win.

It hurt that I could not tell him about this. That he wasn't here to see it. It killed that I couldn't talk to him anymore.

I had loved him so much. I never imagined that I would have to grow up without him.

Was I a coward for admitting it? I don't know. It felt brave, actually, no longer keeping up appearances.

I cried all over Diana's red hair, heart breaking with the bigness of Win gone, and she didn't move away. She stayed with me all night.

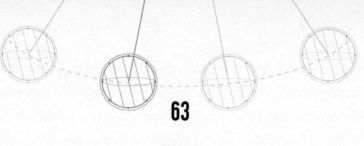

63

KAY

I could tell you about the aftermath. How we went to the hospital—the big, familiar hospital—and they patched us up. I could tell you how Cal became infamous and his mother pleaded guilty to obstruction of justice and filed for bankruptcy. I could tell you about the weeks and weeks it took for my ribs to knit back together. All that did happen, and I was there, but no one looked at me.

I could tell you more about my spell. No one listens to me anymore, which is how it used to feel in the hospital with Mina. I would ask something of a doctor or nurse and it was as if no one had spoken; Mina used to have to repeat my questions. Yes, I could use the bathroom. Yes, food was coming soon. Yes, that's what "carcinogen" meant. It makes you feel like a speck on the wall, an irritating stain, something to frown and sigh heavily at and hope no one else notices. With my side effects, I feel all of those things a hundred times over.

I could tell you how Echo's mom faded fast once Echo died.

She could no longer spell, she was in a great deal of pain, and then she stopped eating. She died before the last of the tourists left in September.

I could tell you that Diana and Ari were so grateful that I saved their lives that we went back to exactly the way things were before—no, better—but that would be a lie.

I am not alone, though. I have Mina. Mina loves me so she can see me despite the spell. She stayed home from school for a semester and took care of me. "What's another year?" She laughed, and for the first time, I saw what she meant. Some things are more important than schedules and plans. Some things you have to do *now*.

Ari tries, too. She calls me; we talk. We're honest with each other. It's real. She gives me what she can afford to give, and I don't expect or demand any more.

It's okay. All I ever wanted was two good friends.

The good thing about my side effects is that it's not just the bad emotions that are amplified. When I'm happy—which is not infrequently—I can feel it clearer and sharper than ever before. When good things happen I can squeeze every last drop from them. And good things happen all the time. Even to me.

Still, some nights I dream I'm stuck in the hardware store, but instead of a locked-up Diana and knocked-out Markos, there's everyone I've ever loved, even a little bit, behind a chain link fence in the woodshop. Mom and Dad and Mina and Echo and Markos and Ari and Diana. I'm the only one there to save them, and I keep running into traps that break my legs and sting my lungs and turn me around in circles. I never see any sign of Cal, only the traps. I get more and more frantic until I'm ripping the chain link with my bare hands, and my loved ones stare at me, horrified, speechless, desperate, and I realize I *am* Cal—I am the bad guy—and they are scared and imprisoned because of me. The horror chokes me as bad as the smoke filling the room—and there's no hekamist there to save us—and then I wake up, gasping.

Glad to be invisible.

64

ARI

A week after Waters Hardware burned down, I went to Echo's funeral with Echo's mom, Diana, Markos, Kay, Mina, and Jess. None of us knew what a hekamist funeral should be, and Echo's mom couldn't tell us, so Kay's parents paid for something simple at the local Unitarian church.

As I sat there in silence—except for Echo's mom's weeping—I thought about how blind and bewildered I'd been at Win's funeral, stuck on my own pain. Rows and rows of people behind me, grieving Win, staring at me as I tried to make up some words to say. And I thought of my parents' funeral. Jess had been a stranger, I hadn't yet befriended Diana, and I'd taken a spell that had plucked out a terrible memory and made my wrist sore. Like at Win's funeral, people had filled the church. I may have felt alone, but my parents hadn't been lonely in their lives.

But we were the only ones there for Echo, and most of us had met her in the past few months, if we'd known her at all. She'd spent nearly her whole life in hiding.

I found myself wishing Win was there. Not for myself, obviously, but for Echo. Someone who she'd cared about, someone who'd probably cared about her, paying his respects. Someone who'd made her life less alone.

Diana held my hand and a bandaged-up Markos held her other one. Diana had cut her burned hair into an asymmetrical bob, and it was redder than ever. Markos's scars made him look even more like a handsome villain. Markos had moved in to Diana's basement after leaving the hospital. Diana told me things were strained with his brothers, and his mother might have to go to jail. Jess had found out that I could sue Cal in civil court for damages, but the Waterses had no money; it had all gone to Echo and her mom over the past nine years. And I didn't want to sue. I believed it was an accident back then and that the shock of remembering it all at once and all of a sudden had pushed Cal into what he did at the hardware store. He seemed to be suffering enough, living with his messed-up mind. After the hospital, he'd moved to the psych ward, where he was likely to spend many years. I didn't forgive him—not yet—but I wanted to, one day.

Word was that the Waterses would move as soon as they could, but that Markos wanted to stay. Markos and I weren't talking too much—again, not yet—and the only thing he said to me at Echo's funeral was out of the corner of his mouth, while Diana was in the bathroom.

"I get it," he said, and then looked away, as if there was anyone there who cared whether or not he spoke to me.

At first I thought he meant he got why I took the spell to

erase Win, but we'd already covered that—my general weakness, not caring enough about Win to remember. When I thought about it more I figured he was talking about Diana, trying to say he got why she was my best friend. And then I started thinking maybe it went even deeper than that. Maybe he understood me and Win, why Win wanted to be with me, why we belonged together. I would've liked to know that myself, but I knew I couldn't ask. It was a secret I'd never know.

I could see why Diana loved him, though. Around her, he showed all the good parts I remembered about being friends with him: he was funny and loyal and quick to defend his friends. All that—plus he listened to her and took her seriously, believed in her completely. It made me think I'd underestimated them both.

After the funeral, he went to Diana's to rest and she and I sat in my room, like we had so often before. Diana was making me laugh about something Markos had said to her when I stopped and blurted out, "I don't think I'm ever going to dance again."

Diana tilted her head, doubtful. "You could get another spell, like the one Echo made for you."

"Knee surgery, too."

"Sure. But a spell and knee surgery aren't that big a deal. You've been training for years. And the Manhattan Ballet . . ."

"If Win hadn't died, I don't think I would've gone to New York. I would've stayed here to be with him."

Diana shook her head. "You've always wanted to dance."

"That doesn't mean I'll never want anything else."

She hugged her arms over her chest. "Echo wanted you to dance."

"Echo wanted to get out of here." That sounded cruel, so I shook my head. "She wanted to save her mother. And I think she wanted . . . people. Other people. She helped us. She gave me what I told her would make me happy. I think . . ." I thought she was in love with Win, actually. But she kept Win's secrets, so I kept hers. "I think she felt guilty about Cal, too."

"You shouldn't feel guilty. If you took another spell, everyone would understand."

"Yeah, maybe."

I pressed my aching wrist to my heart.

I didn't need more spells. It was enough work getting used to the ones I had. The blank of my parents' last moments on earth. The year I'd lost being in love with Win. The different kind of pain I had instead.

"Are you going to be okay?" she asked.

I fought the urge to nod and laugh and say "of course," and instead thought carefully about what I really felt. "I feel like everything's changing and it's totally out of my control," I said.

She nodded. "And you can't dance."

"I can't dance," I said, and ignored the lump that rose in my throat. "But Jess and I are going to New York anyway."

Diana froze, waiting for the joke. "But—why?"

"People who don't dance move to New York all the time."

"You'll leave me here?"

"You won't be alone."

"Don't throw Markos in my face. I never did that to you when you were with Win."

"Not just Markos," I said, and that damn lump kept rising. I tried breathing through my nose. "You have—your parents. You remember the kids at school, the teachers. My memories are fuzzy."

"You remember me," she said fiercely. "You want to forget me, too?"

The nose-breathing didn't work. I was crying, and so was Diana. Ugly, gulping crying. I thought, *You don't deserve to cry*, which only made me cry harder. "I was always going to go. I should've been gone already. What's the difference if it's for the Manhattan Ballet or not?"

She opened and closed her mouth, then wiped her eyes and put her hands on her hips. "Give me some time to think of a reason."

I hugged her. It was a kind of lurchy hug because my bad knee froze up halfway across the room, but it worked—I latched on and wouldn't let go. I was not a hug person, so I didn't know the secret of hugs until that moment: They're not only one person's effort. You hold each other up.

Maybe it was stupid to leave Diana now that I was finally being honest with her. Part of me thought that would be enough, to lean on Diana and let her get me through this. But a bigger part of me knew that what I needed more than anything was a blank slate—and not from hekame this time.

"I'm afraid," I said.

Diana let go and took half a step back. "Of Cal?"

"No. I mean in the future—when I lose someone else, like I lost Win. I'm worried it'll be more than I can handle."

She nodded but didn't say anything.

What else was there to say?

I didn't think I'd choose to forget someone again. Not now, knowing what I did about the costs: to the hekamist to make the spell, with her food, blood, and will; to everyone else, who had to carry their pain alone; and to me—not only the loss of dance but losing the connection between what I was and what I will be.

Until I walked into Waters Hardware for the last time, I'd thought that my parents' death was safely stored away in the past. But the past isn't past—it's who we are every second of the day.

Cal and I both forgot things and became different people than we would've been otherwise. So here's the big question: What would I have been like if I'd kept the memory of my parents' death? I used to think I'd be broken, damaged goods forever. But maybe I'd have been a better person. I didn't mean "good" or "perfect." Better. More whole.

"What are you going to do now?" Diana whispered.

I told her the truth. "I don't know."

But not knowing didn't make me feel trapped or out of control. It made me free.

Jess found us a place on the Lower East Side. It's tiny and practically windowless and funny smells drift up from the sinks. But the stairs outside our apartment door go up to the roof, where someone left a rusted lawn chair.

I climb, legs wobbling, and settle in the chair. The East River's right in front of me; across it, Brooklyn. To my left I can see the top of the Chrysler Building; to my right, more river. We're surrounded by water again.

Tomorrow I start senior year at a new school. A normal high school, no dance, where no one knows me and I know no one. It's dark out and hot and humid and smells like exhaust and garbage. I've been reading a lot—it makes me forget my uncooperative body—and writing to Diana and Kay, but at night I come up here to think. I can't change the choices I've made, or try to piece together the million alternate Aris that might have been. Instead I sit on the roof and try to answer Diana's question for myself.

What am I going to do?

Who am I going to be?

Would I be Markos, an asshole with a heart of gold—or at least silver?

Would I be desperate but bold like Kay?

Open and sincere like Diana?

Would I give myself away to do one good thing?

I only have the rest of my life to find out. It's time to get started.

ACKNOWLEDGMENTS

Thank you to my family, who hopefully will accept this book as my apology for the many years of leaping in front of the computer to block them from reading what I was writing; to my friends, who are smart, funny, and honestly let's just say it: the best people in the world; to my agent, Tina Wexler, and my editor, Donna Bray, whose insights were smart and thoughtful and often simply *right* every step of the way; to everyone else at Balzer + Bray/HarperCollins, including Alessandra Balzer, Kate Jackson, Jordan Brown, Viana Siniscalchi, Bethany Reis, Jenna Stempel, and Maya Packard; to all my colleagues and mentors at Abrams Books, including Susan Van Metre, Howard Reeves, and Tamar Brazis; to all the authors I've been lucky enough to work with over the years, who are generous and brilliant and inspiring; to my amazing classmates at Vermont College of Fine Arts, the Keepers of the Dancing Stars, and the incredible VCFA faculty, including my advisors A. M. Jenkins, Rita Williams-Garcia, Franny Billingsley, and Tim Wynne-Jones; to Jen Jude, who didn't flinch when I asked her about arson and obstructing justice and statutes of limitations (and, I must add, all legal mistakes in the story are mine and mine alone); to Skila Brown, Amy Rose Capetta, Lindsay Eyre, Erin Hagar, Stefanie Lyons, Kristin

Sandoval, and Amy Zinn, who read early drafts and gave invaluable advice and encouragement; and finally, to my husband, Kyle Gilman, who, in addition to providing the daily love and support that helped me to write this book, also solved many plot problems before he even read a word. Who needs a hekamist when you have a Kyle?